Five Golden Rings And A Diamond

Part 1

Ireland:
Romance and pain:
the curse of Cain

1968 - 1971

E. Marie Seltenrych

Copyright page:

©Marie Seltenrych:

Five Golden Rings and a Diamond,

[Part 1] Ireland: Romance and pain; the curse of Cain, 2010

I have an idea that some men are born out of their due place. Accident has cast them amid strangers in their birthplace, and the leafy lanes they may have known from childhood remain but a place of passage. They may spend their whole lives aliens among their kindred and remain aloof among the only scenes they have ever known. Perhaps it is this sense of strangeness that sends men far and wide in the search for something permanent to which they may attach themselves.

The Moon and Sixpence, W. Somerset Maugham, 1919

The 'curse of Cain' idea was glibly accepted by Irish folk for the Tinker tribes because of their moving from town to town for hundreds of years; never putting down roots. Can this curse be broken by our heroine…?

"You shall be a fugitive and a wanderer on the earth."

Gen 4:12 [ESV] http://www.esvstudybible.org/ search?q=wanderer 01/06/2010

Niamh's portrait, 1968: ©Marie Seltenrych, 2010

Niamh hiding behind the pig, 1968. ©Marie Seltenrych, 2010

Chapter one

12th September, 1968, A.M.

I'm looking up from behind the fat bottom of Squealer. He's pink, hairy and obese, shamelessly wriggling his obnoxious rear end in my face, as though he's saying he's proud of being porky. He squeals in fright as a face peers into his. He steps back, bowling me over. I let out a yelp! The face peering at me is pink, with rough grey stubble draped around brown-spotted lips, which open to reveal a dark mouthful of broken, greenish-yellow and occasionally black teeth. Grey whiskers curl from flailing nostrils. The deepest eyes, shaded by black and white peppered thick bushy brows, rise to allow round dark beady lenses to penetrate the recesses of my eyes. My mouth opens and the words jump out,

'Jack Sullivan!'

'Begorrah, ala!' Jack's neck stretches like a turkey's as his face comes even closer. 'A pig that knows my name?' His mouth hangs open. I can see red zigzagged maps in the whites of his eyeballs.

'I thought it was me own sow!' He chuckles as he ogles me, reveling in his peculiar sense of humour. 'The wife!' he says, by way of explanation. I'm sitting on my bottom with Squealer in my lap.

'Shush Jack,' I'm pleading, as I try to heave a thousand pounds of bacon off me.

'Begorrah! You can't fool old Jack. You're not a sow! You're Niamh Murphy.' He's beckoning my father, who's close by. Suddenly he bursts into excitable shouting, mixing his Shelta language with English. 'Aga di'lsa, over here, Sean!'

Squealer rolls off me with a final shove, ripping my skirt in the process. I leap up, vault over the pigsty wall, and make a run for it. I know I'm a good runner. I'm a good dancer and a good runner! I'm glancing back to see if they're on me heels? 'Oh God, they are...' I'm falling over in the high grass. 'Oh, Mammy, Mammy,' I'm shouting. My leg is aching, but I'm up as quick as a flash, ignoring the pain. Oh; God, I'm stumbling all over the place; my leg's bunjaxed. 'No...' I scream as the thunder of heavy breathing encompasses me and I'm tackled to the ground. I close my eyes. 'Just let them kill me,' I pray. I'd rather die than go back to the tinceard's camp! Voices clamber for fame.

'She's down. Come on lads. Get her arms, quick!'

'I've got a leg.'

'Me too!' Two lads have taken hold of my left leg.

'Not this one; ye egit. I've got it. Get the other one, Dan, be quick now.' 'This one?'

'She's only got two, ye Moron!'

'Get her arms someone; the two of them!' My arms are squeezed. I'm kicking and wriggling with every ounce of energy, but 'tis no good, they've got me cornered. The pain in my leg is excruciating, but easier to bear than the burning humiliation I'm suffering as they haul me away like a rabbit, legs first. I can see Jack Sullivan and Dan O'Brien holding my legs, romping along at the front. Seamus Creen and Dennis Buckley have me by the arms. They're like a pack of dogs when they gang up. Every step is a jabbing, searing pain in my leg.

'Gits' I yell. 'Let me go. Jesu Criosta. Oh Mother of God!' My skirt blows above my knees, but I can't move my arms to push it back down again. They're probably hoping it blows right up over my head! They'd love that! I'm glad I've got knickers on me. Thank God for that! I can just see that ugly Jack with his red eyes, stubbly chin and cheesy grin trying to have a good look. 'Stop gawking at me...' I'm yelling at a couple of other fellas with scarves over half their faces. I don't know who they are. 'Cowards! Yellow livers!' I sneer.

'She's a whore!'

'Like her mother!'

I shout 'Leave my dead mother out of this.'

They keep making indecorous comments as they run alongside me. I'm spitting in their faces and cursing and swearing at them. Now I hear different noises, which flood my mind with old memories. I can just see the campfires in the distance. I can hear the shouts of people coming closer to inspect their prize, me!

'We're here thank God! She's like a ton of spuds! Throw her over there lads!'

'Don't call me a sack of potatoes!' I shout, as I land, bottom first, in the dirt.

'What can we call you then, whore?' Aunty Maura's voice bellows out before I can see her face. I turn my angry countenance away from her face. I pull my skirt down over my knees.

'You know my name!'

'Stand up when I'm talking to you!' she orders. She pulls me by the arms.

'Gerroff!' I scream. My arms are all red and nearly blue, and soon will be black. My right leg is throbbing and looks bigger than my other one, the left leg, that is! I'm not even trying to stand up, but just sit as cool as a cucumber in the damp grass, staring straight ahead, resisting the tears pressing on the back of my eyes. Aunty Maura lets go and stands above me, frowning.

'She's become a real little trollop altogether! *Nid'es*

axiver!' she roars as she hits me across the head.

'I never was one! *Dil 'Isa axiver glori* the truth Maura...' She scowls at me.

'Don't worry, I know the whole truth.'

'Nobody asked me what happened...'

'You always were a bloody liar.' I stare at her.

'I must have learned it from you...' She stares back at me, dagger for dagger as her right hand rises to clobber me. 'You'll be the death of me!' She grits her teeth as her arm stiffens in mid air. Her bright blue eyes in her white face are cold and unfeeling. 'Thank God I'm not your mother.' She flips her hand hurriedly to her forehead, chest and shoulders as her own blessing falls on herself. Her eyes soar into their sockets skyward for an instant, then back to focus on my face. I stare at her in disgust. Her dark hair is uncombed and blowing across her face in the wind. Her mouth is a thin rust-coloured scowl with a few bits of egg yolk around the edges. She is hugging her old brown and red tartan rug close to her chest. She's wearing a long grey skirt and dark brown brogues on her feet. They look like two left shoes to me from this angle. She has no stockings on. I can see her dark varicose veins winding up her legs like the branches of a tree.

'Thank God. Amen!' I reply. 'You've got egg on your face,' I add maliciously.

'Shut your gob,' she sputters in reply, pushing my head with a fist filled with hatred.

'Is this how you welcome your own flesh and blood?' I say, covering my head with my fists.

'You belong here, under my care, God help us all! You think you can come and go as you please, without leave or reason? You're very much mistaken, you little trollop!'

'And what have ye all been doing all your life? Going from place to place?' Her wild eyes come close.

'Don't back answer me! You've disgraced your father and me,

running away like that! You're not Irish *ar burt'*

'I'm as Irish as you are. I'm not *agetul* of you!'

'You should be afraid, you faggot!' Maura screams. 'Give us a bit of hand, Betty, Alice, Mary!' Three wiry women, who are standing in a huddle, leap into action, taking an arm or a leg. Now I'm being dragged to an old van nearby. Somehow they squeeze me through the narrow doorway, and hurl me onto the floor. Heavy breathing is the only sound I hear for a moment.

Betty stands in the doorway.

'That'll sober her up!' I'm curling my fingers like claws.

'Yerra, gerroff,' I scream and shake my head, so that my mop of wavy golden hair flies all around my face. I snarl for added effect. Alice pushes Betty out the door, almost knocking Maura over on top of me.

'She's a bloody witch, that's what!' Betty and Alice run off, screaming,

'I think she might be a Banshee! Oh God help us!' Maura steadies herself and scurries out the door after the other two.

'She's mad! She's insane!' 'Lock her up *axonsk*,' Mary screams, leaping out the door on top of Maura. I make a growling sound.

'I'll put a curse on you!'

'Mary's right. Lock her up tonight; quick! For God's sake lock her up. Hurry up!' Someone screams hysterically. The door bangs shut and a bolt is secured. I can hear their voices mingling in high-pitched animation.

'At least I bring a bit of excitement into your miserable lives,' I shout after them. I lie down for a few minutes,

'How in God's name have I come to this?' I wonder. My leg is aching so much I'm feeling faint. Alice and Mary are back again, peering through the foot square, dirty window. I prop myself up. 'Stop gawking at me, you pair of witches!' I yell. Their eyes grow large for an instant, and then with a yelp they disappear. That suits me fine! I lie back cautiously on the splintered ridden floor and stare around me. The van has been stripped bare. All the cupboards have been pulled out, leaving broken walls behind. There's a piece of snapped wood nailed to the floor where a bench used to be. My right foot rests in a space where the floorboard has been removed. I can see the dark green grass below in parts where boards have disappeared, probably for firewood, I muse. The wind is blowing through the holes, making goosebumps rise on my skin. I tug at some of the broken boards, but soon my hand is filled with splinters. I suddenly feel exhausted and the pain in my leg seems worse, and a pain lands on my head like a brick. I try to pluck the splinters out of my fingers, and realize I've got my wedding ring on. I pull it off, pull up my dress at the back and tuck the ring inside my elasticised knickers. I can feel the cold ring safely inside my drawers. That gives me some satisfaction. I'm closing my eyes and the tears are accumulating around my eyelashes. I'm allowing them to find their course down my cheeks and over the tip of my nose and into my hair. I'm falling into a restless slumber, comforting darkness. I escape my pains for a time. You see, everything changed in my life on the day my step-sister Maeve, got married. I want to bring you back to that time: so that you can understand why I'm lying here, locked in a caravan by the witches in my tribe, the Murphys. I'm dreaming of all the exciting things that happened in the past six months... 3:00 PM 12th September, 1968.

Maeve shows her bracelet to Niamh at McCarthy's barn:
McCarthy's barn inspired by "Wonderful Barn [1743]; http://www.irishtourist.com/kildare/towns /

6 months earlier:
Scriob, Ireland, March, 1968

The time is just before Maeve's wedding day! It's a cold March morning when she comes running up to me as I am walking over to McCarthy's barn. Maeve is my step-sister. Her mother, Aunty Maura, married my daddy after my mother died. Maura's husband had died a few years before that, from alcoholic poisoning, they said in whispers!

'Niamh, guess what?' Maeve asks me with her face all red and glowing, like she's found some great treasure; I'm wondering if she'll share it with me.

'What?'

'Paid's asked me to marry him. He gave me this.' She shows me a copper bangle on her arm. It's engraved with shamrocks. She smiles. 'D'you like the shamrocks? That's our secret name for each other. Sham and Rock!'

'Who's Rock and who's Sham then?'

Maeve goes all coy. 'That's for us to know and you to find out!' she says, giggling.

I giggle with her.

'Soon, I'll be Missus Flynn, Missus Paid Flynn, to be exact. So they were wrong, weren't they?'

'Who was wrong, Maeve?' I ask, mystified.

'They always said you were the pretty one. They said 'She'll be snapped up first, that one, with those curls and those bright eyes,' didn't they?'

'Who said that Maeve?' I ask, wondering what she's getting at.

'All the women and the men, that's who! I even heard the rent-man say it once, when we were small!'

'Is that so Maeve? Well, I always thought you were the most beautiful sister I could have.'

'Yerra, go on! Well, the fact of the matter is that I'm getting married first, and Paid thinks I'm the most beautiful woman in the whole world!'

'Sure that's grand Maeve, as long as you're happy, that's the main thing. If you're happy, sure I'm happy too!

'I am very happy. The happiest woman in the world! You'll find out one day!'

'What?'

'About love!'

'Sure I don't want to get married for ages! I can't imagine being with one person for ever. It would be very boring!'

'You're just too immature to understand,' Maeve says, as she tosses her head, and then abruptly looks at me. 'You will be my bridesmaid?'

It's what we talked about, dreamed of. 'I will, of course I will!'

'I'll be the most beautiful bride you've ever seen,' she exclaims happily, waltzing around on the grass as though Paid is with her.

I'm thinking of the two dresses I have, this old green one with the ripped belt at the back and the fraying hem, and another navy blue dress, which is getting too small for me.

'But Maeve, what'll I wear?'

'Don't worry, we'll find something! Be happy for me, that's all I ask.' She's hugging me to pieces and crying.

'Oh, God! Don't cry Maeve. What's up?'

'I'm just happy, so happy,' she says, bawling her eyes out. In the end I join in and we both bawl our eyes out.

...

Paid and Maeve's big day finally arrives! It's Thursday, the thirtieth day of May, nineteen hundred and sixty eight. I remember that date because Maeve kept saying it over and over, in case we all forgot. I'm standing on a bit of a hill, on the west coast of Ireland, in County Galway, watching strangers arriving on foot, by horse and cart and some driving black

'It's a grand sight, wouldn't you say?' It's him with the black teeth, Rhonan, Paid's brother.

I have to agree. "Tis!' I reply. We're both admiring McCarthy's Barn, an amazing structure that seems to have wound its way out of the earth into a barren landscape. Our eyes are tracing its form upwards. The steps go around and around right up to the sky, as if it's a giant ice cream cone standing upside down. Right at the top there are turrets so it looks like a bit of a castle gone wrong. Someone built it just to give the men work around these parts in the early eighteen hundreds. That's a long time ago, before we were even thought of.

'My daddy says his great-great-great-grandfather, Pat Murphy, build this barn,' I say proudly. 'God rest his soul.'

'I heard it was my family that built it, the mighty Flynns!' Rhonan argues. I remember my father's words.

'My daddy says it was his father's father's father's father, so there!' He's eyeing me inquisitively.

'How do you know?'

'He knows!' My father knows everything, I'm thinking. 'My father knows more than your father.'

'My father is bigger than your father.' He knows that's true. His father, Billy Flynn, is a weenie scrawny low sized man who reminds me of chicken with his long face and bony fingers, which are always working with bits of wire and stuff. He makes carrying baskets, which the women love. We're staring defiantly at each other.

'Does it matter at all, at all?' Rhonan asks me, knowing I've got the upper hand now.

'No, I suppose not,' I reply.

'It's ours now.'

"Tis.' I agree with him. I feel like a great rich landowner looking at his private property.

'Do you want to go up?' he asks.

It would be something to do while we wait for Maeve to get here; to get away from the milling onlookers. 'Come on then? Let's have a look at America.' I head up, holding my long frock off the dusty steps and making my way to the top.

'God, what a wonderful sight,' Rhonan mutters, from below me.

'Tis,' I reply. 'I think I can just about see America on a clear day.' Rhonan looks straight up from below me. He's got a smirk on his face.

'I think I saw Canada as well, one day!'

'You did not,' I reply

'I did so!'

'You did not!' I reply, breathing deeply as I reach the top. 'I'd like to go axim a Skai-grut!' I use our Shelta language almost without thinking. 'They say the streets are made of gold!' I say, in awe. The grey blue waters of the Atlantic Ocean stretch as far as the eye can see, leading straight to America. Rhonan puffs for breath as he joins me at the apex.

'Swurt a mun iath!'

'Tis. It does feel like its heaven,' I remark to his comment. 'Heaven and America must be the same?'

'They both have streets of gold. I can see them!' He's

squinting into the distance. I squint into the distance.

'You cannot!'

'Can so!'

We laugh together.

'Ah, maybe we could swim there?' I suggest, immediately imagining myself flying through the water like a mermaid.

'I probably could, but you couldn't!'

'Why not?' I reply, placing my hands on my hips.

'Because, you can't swim.'

'There's nothing to it. You just flap your arms around and that's all!' I retort. That's what it always looks like to me.

'Not at all! You don't know the meaning of the word. I swim every summer in the river. It's very technical. I think you'd end up tur an skai, being a girl.'

'I would not end up at the bottom of the river, just because I'm a girl!' I retort.

'No, it's because you're not interested; if you're not interested, you can't learn,' he explains.

'Are you calling me thick?'

'If you like..., but you're not as thick as my brother Noel. God, but he's as thick as a double ditch,' he adds, shaking his head. Then he looks at me under his eyelids. 'I could teach you to swim... I can just see you in the nip... gorgeous!'

'Awast!' I say, pushing him with my two hands. He hardly moves. His hand feels like a rock on my shoulder. '

You are..., gorgeous. I'd love to...' I push him away again.

'I said get away...'

'I know what you said! I wonder what you mean?' He smiles gleefully at me.

'Niamh, Rhonan, come on down. They're coming. They're coming.' It's my stepmother, Aunty Maura, yelling excitedly.

'She's seen us now?' I say.

'Ax! One day I'll have my own horse and caravan..., sure we can travel anywhere together...'

'Indeed!' I reply haughtily. 'We're coming,' I yell downwards. A sudden gust of wind whirls over the turrets. I shiver. Rhonan's long arm drapes itself around my shoulder, landing between my small breasts.

'Axónšk, I'll warm the cockles of your heart!'

'No you won't! Not tonight; or any other night!' I reply. Whenever he comes to our place my aunty Maura says, 'Here comes Rhonan, with one arm longer than the other.' I think I know what she means now! I stick my tongue out at Rhonan as I dive nimbly under his armpit. 'I'm going down, before Aunty Maura comes up...'

'I was just enjoying the beauty of the place,' he says, grasping my arm, stepping in front of me, blocking my path. My face is getting hot.

'I told you, I'm going down!' I wrench my arm away and manage to get past him. I yank up my dress and nearly fall down the uneven steps to the bottom. The shoe on my left foot slips off, but I hurry on down. I'm at the bottom now and Rhonan leaps down the last five steps, holding my shiny black patent shoe in his right hand.

'I think it's a bit too big for your dainty foot!' he says bending on his knee with the shoe in one hand. I grab the shoe out of his hand and poke my foot into it.

'I'll grow into them.' I clip clop off, scrunching my toes to keep the shoes on. I'm wearing two pairs of socks, one white and the other pink. I put the pink ones on first and then the white ones, so that the white ones are seen. A bit of the pink ones is peeping out the top at the ankle as they're a bit longer than the white ones, but I'm sure nobody will notice; it's not as if they're black or brown or red or any dark colour like that, so I'm safe. Rhonan's suddenly behind me.

'Would you look at that?'

I turn to face him, startled. 'What?'

'You've got pink socks on under the white ones. Why so?' Rhonan asks.

'To keep the shoes on; egit!'

Rhonan smiles, showing his black teeth. 'I'm not an egit, except in love!'

'Gerroff with you!' I march off.

'I hope there're no holes in them?' he calls after me. I stop.

'Holes?'

He catches up with me. 'In your socks; remember the story of the pigs?' I can feel my face turning pink.

'No?' I lie. I wince as I remember that story. There are holes in the toes of my pink socks, and they keep strangling my two big toes.

'Your toes might fall off then!' he says, as though he's reading my thoughts.

...

I'm remembering the story my da tells, of someone who had a hole in their sock that was so big it strangled all the toes; one day the unfortunate man woke up and all the toes were on the ground and they had grown their own legs. That was how the story of the piggies going to market got started. The poor man had to walk on his hands after that, whilst all the toes trotted off to the market without him.

Rhonan speaks just as the story comes into my mind.

'Do you remember what happened to that poor man?' My face gets hotter.

'No!' I trot off, leaving Rhonan behind.

'Are you trying to catch a bus?' The voice of Nell, our local fortune-teller and midwife, stops me. She comes right up to me, smelling like lavender; pinches my cheek. 'Ooh.' I squirm away from her, and nearly collide with Nora, my seven year old cousin, who had moved silently by me; she leaps away and giggles.

'Is Maeve getting married to Paid Flynn then?' Nora asks.
'She is.'
'Will he be her daddy then?'
'No.'
'Why not?' She's so thick, I'm thinking!
'Because she's still got her daddy. My daddy.'

'Oh!' She glances at me for a moment and grins happily, displaying teeth as yellow as her frock. She runs off after a butterfly. She's tripping over her long frock, which has a few extra decorations stuck on the hem, bits of muck and sticks and the odd fly! She's got yellow feathers in her hair, mixed with daisies, which seem to be quite dead. She reminds me of a baby chicken after coming through a hedge, all fluffy and yellow and ruffled.

I feel someone's presence behind me.

'Niamh?' It's Rhonan again, always turning up like the bad penny. I'm wondering what he's after.

'What?'

'You're wearing a new frock,' he says, grinning. I stare at him.

'Am I now? So; what about it, then?' He chews his fingernails, and then spits one out.

'You look like a statue of the virgin Mary.'

'Well I'm not a statue, I'm real, and you're..., a dirty boy for biting your nails like that!' He smiles back.

'I am! And you're a real virgin.'

'Go away!' I run further down the slope, and then stop. I was really enjoying my dress until now. I sit down on the grass, so Rhonan won't notice me, and think I'm a statue of the Virgin Mary. A figure looms above me. I look up.

'What are you doing sitting down in your lovely dress; get up!' My Aunty Maura pulls me up by the arms and starts brushing my skirt down. 'It's all creased now..., look at the green blobs!'

'It was only for a minute!' She admonishes me with a glare. 'Just stop where you are. Maeve is just around the corner.'

I can just see Maeve and Da jogging along the bumpy road. They've got McCarthy's billygoat pulling an open cart, as me da's piebald pony died a while ago. The women have decorated the cart with red, white, sky blue and gold fabric. The deep red and the sky blue fabric have been draped along the sides of the cart, held in scooped fashion by copper bows. The front of the cart is draped with bright white flowing fabric, held in place with painted red flowers. The seat is draped with shiny gold satin and strewn with flower petals. Da is steering *Billygoat* all the way to the makeshift chapel at the back of McCarthy's Barn, where a white canopy, decorated with colourful flowers, has been draped over the wide doorway. The foreboding figure of the priest, Father Seamus O'Reilly can be seen standing stiffly in his vestments: starched long white frock, white collar, and gold coloured scarf, as he waits with his arms folded. There's a wooden table next to him with a big book on it. There are two candles, which the altar boy has to keep lighting when the wind blows them out. There are special communion goblets for the Bride and Groom on the table. The white cloths cover the thin strings attached to them, secretly connected to Father O'Reilly's wrist.

'Come on Maeve,' someone shouts. The crowd begins to chant,

'Get me to the Church on a goat. I'm coming in the royal float.' The goat trots up towards the crowd, going faster and faster for some reason. Then I see he's heading for the bunch of carrots that Rhonan has in his hands. That stops him from eating the floral wreath hanging around his neck! The goat stops abruptly and the cart nearly lands on top of him, with

Maeve and me da flying forward.

'Steady now,' my da shouts. He holds onto the reins and to Maeve and they fall backwards in their wooden seats. Daddy stands up and throws his legs over the side of the cart; then climbs down. He lifts Maeve over the side with a whoosh. Her white linen dress, embroidered on the hem, cuffs and neck with beautiful colours, flies in the air, revealing a blue silk petticoat. The men whistle and shout at this action. There are quite a few folk milling around Maeve and Da as many of our relatives have come here from the other side of Ireland, near Dublin, and others have come up from Cork.

'Go arak! Help your sister now.' Maura pushes me forward, forcing me to run down the slope. I nearly end up on top of Maeve, who's looking quite flustered after her bumpy ride.

'Yerra, what are you doing? Walk in front, and don't trip me up. Where in God's name, is Nora? She's supposed to be here!'

'Nora!' I yell. Like a wild horse, Nora comes galloping from somewhere; she's clinging her long dress, bunch of flowers, and a basket of daisy petals. Half the petals fly out as she leaps down the slope. She lands on her bottom. Maeve yanks her up.

'Walk!' she shouts at Nora and me. We rush off towards the priest. Maeve then rushes after us at a brisk pace, with me da struggling to keep up with her.

Maeve's wedding day 13th May, 1968. ©marieseltenrych2010

'Whoa; not so fast!' I can hear me da saying as he puffs and pants barely holding on to Maeve.

We climb up the last bit of a hill. 'Stand over there,' Maeve directs Nora and me. Me da stands next to Maeve, breathing heavily.

'Who gives this woman to be wedded now?' the priest says,

peering over his black-rimmed glasses. 'Sean?' Maeve nudges me da.

'Right; here she is then,' me da says, as Maeve steps forward and stands next to Paid, who's smile seems to be stuck in a long line on his face. He's wearing a brown suit that's too big for him, a white shirt and bright red tie. His hair is plastered to his head with hair cream.

'Here!' Maeve calls, throwing me her bunch of lavender and mayflowers, which I immediately sniff and then sneeze violently. The priest gives me a nasty stare and then blesses the couple by making the sign of the cross with his hands. He's speaking so fast we wonder what he's saying. Then, more slowly, he says,

'I now pronounce you husband and wife.' He stares at Paid with furled brows as he nods his head, mumbling gruffly, 'You may kiss the bride.'

Paid Flynn is grinning from ear to ear and licking his lips. His front teeth are black and he's reaching up, intending to plant his mouth on my beautiful stepsister's lovely sweet rosebud lips and I can't bear it. She's taller than him, by a good bit with those heels on. Someone gave her a lovely pair of white high-heeled shoes, which were a bit too tight, but like the ugly sister in Cinderella, she squeezed into them. To my way of thinking, she is Cinderella herself and Paid Flynn is an ugly prince. Maeve glows like a primus stove in the night and puckers her lips in expectation. I'm closing my eyes. Oh God, please don't let this happen to me! I am shaking like Nora's chicken feathers. It's like someone is walking on me grave. I'm next. I know it!

'The kiss of death,' I whisper to Nora, who giggles.

After that Father O'Reilly glares into the crowd and all is quite. He turns and heads for the table, praying. We kneel down now. I'm wondering if Aunty Maura will get mad at us for getting grass stains on our nice dresses? After a few more prayers he takes a golden goblet, with its string attached, and puts a round host right in their gob.

'What's that?' Nora asks, digging me in the ribs. I whisper in reply,

'It's God!' The priest holds the goblet and gives them a drink each, wiping the goblet after each one. It makes me feel thirsty.

'What are they drinking?' Nora whispers her question.

'God's blood.'

'Is he dead?'

'Yes,' I reply. 'They murdered him!'

'Murderers!' she shouts, jumping up and waving her flowers.

'Murderers!' I shout, waving my two bunches. A searing pain rushes through my left ear.

'Will you two stop it!' I can barely hear her words as I shake from the fright of Aunty Maura's slap.

'Yes, Mam.'

I look at Nora who is holding her right ear. We don't say another word for a full five minutes. Finally the bride and groom sign the book and turn around to greet the crowd. Immediately the place is in an uproar. Things are flying through the air. As if by magic a glass and a cigarette materialise in every man's hand. 'Slainte,' rings out over the hills like a choir of angels, or more likely, a choir of devils and the choruses of 'Let's have a bit of craic!' resound through the surrounding countryside.

...

Someone is banging a bongo. Another is rattling tin spoons. A pipe screeches through the laughter. People are jumping up and dancing. The lads have several fires going and a pot of Irish stew brewing away in one place and the smell of smoked bacon drifts from another. There are also a few chickens running around, one with its head off! There is also the tantalizing aroma of potato and leek soup wafting through the cold air. Some of the men are testing the meat by putting their forks into the boiling pot, taking out large pieces of cooked meat and devouring them. The women have brought plates of sandwiches, which are piled so high, they're toppling over onto the rough wooden tables that some of the men made. The children are lining up for lemonade, which is being poured by several women from jugs into glasses. The occasional sound of breaking glass is accompanied by curses. A bronze keg of poteen glistens from behind a tree surrounded by the men, who wait for its life giving water, uische beatha!

...

I'm sitting on a rock watching as the tempo rises and one by one the guests make egits of themselves. The drink is flowing, followed by inevitable dancing and ultimately by the frolicking... It always happens like this. A leg of chicken, wrapped in a piece of newspaper is warming my hands. A glass of porter sits precariously on the grass beside me. I wonder if the leg belonged to the chicken with no head. Nora waltzes past me just at that moment. She's still grinning brightly, now in the arms of our cousin Liam, who's only six, and can't dance at all. He's just kicking the ground and occasionally Nora lets out a yelp, and then she kicks him back. He lets out another yelp; they waltz on; I can see Rhonan leaning on the shiny keg, his hand tightly grasping a glass. He's staring at me. He sways to his feet and moves forward, and then falls flat on his face. Two lads drag him back to the keg. All I can see now is the soles of his shoes, with two neat holes in them.

I look away, into the distance. The hills around here are so many shades of green and yellow, with low lying grey stone walls all around them, marking boundaries. Some of the hills look like a ton of rocks fell from above and landed here and then the grass grew over them. The sun is still visible in the sky, but I've got goose bumps all over my forearms and legs, and my teeth are occasionally chattering away, having their own conversation. Sure it's always freezing here on the west coast of Ireland. Da says it's because there are not enough trees around these parts. The few here are leaning over to one side, as if trying to hide from the west winds that come howling from the Atlantic Ocean. The wind blows past the trees and right onto the camp; that's where I live. It's not much of a place, just a bit of ground where we can put our vans. We sleep in the grass in summer, which begins on the first of June. Around six families are living here, and it's a close-knit community, especially when it comes to sharing the demon drink poteen!

As I turn around, I see Da looking at me right now under his bushy eyebrows. A dribble of some alcoholic brew is running down his chin, mingling with a few stuck-on lumps of blood, his own, which eventuated when he cut himself with a sharp razor. He doesn't shave very much these days, because his hands are shaky. He says,

'It's time you were wedded too!'

Oh God, no, not that! He is staring at my growing breasts. My nipples are making two small bumps in my dress. They're sticking out because of the fierce cold wind. I hate this dress now. I quickly hold the newspaper-wrapped leg of chicken in front of my breasts, but it's too late! He's probably thinking of Rhonan, God help me! 'Yes Da!' I answer politely, meaning no!

'Yes indeed. There's a good girl now!' He stares at his empty glass. 'I need another drink. Slainte! The first today,' he says, holding his empty glass high and stumbling away, towards the keg.

...

Da's just shattered all my dreams of going to school and learning things that the swanky people learn - the people who live in lovely houses with biscuits and milk; and gardens and fences and gorgeous children. I want to travel and see what's in the big world out there. At nearly sixteen years of age my life may as well be over! I know he'll not stop now until he gets me wedded to Rhonan! I wish my mammy was here, she'd be on my side, but she died when I was about four. I don't know what happened. When I ask people they just stare into the distance and tell me to shush! I sometimes think I remember her, but I'm not sure about that. All I know is that her name was Niamh, the same as mine, which means 'Queen of the Land'. I had a brother, Rory, but he died a while before Mammy died. He was a tiny babby. Da ends up marrying my aunty Maura, as I told ye. After they were married, Aunty Maura told me that my job was begging. I felt very important, but I didn't like it very much once I found out what I had to do in my new begging job. She would put dirt on my face and run her hands through my hair, making my golden coloured curls all brown and sticky. She would put a ripped dress on me, which wasn't hard really, as most of my dresses were torn in a few places. She would give them another quick rip or two, and then send me to a house, to say 'Please Missus,' to the woman who answered. I remember my first job. It is as clear as day to me still: I just stood outside the door and bawled my eyes out. The woman of the house brought me inside and closed the door. That gave me a shiver of fear. I stopped in the dark hallway, staring at dark maroon wallpaper with gold squiggles. I eyed a stairs leading up to a dark looking landing. The stairs had dark brown carpet down the middle, with wooden bits each side. I stood there, shivering with the wonder of what was about to happen to me. That fearful thought only lasted a minute.

'It's too cold out there. Come on in here to the kitchen; the fire's burning,' the woman called out.

I followed her into a bright kitchen. There was a big window on one side, with a sink below. The table had a vivid tablecloth. There were wooden chairs around the table and a little glass vase with flowers. The fire was in a dark grey box, with a door on one side. 'Come over here near the oven,' she said, smiling at me.

I gasped for fear. I had heard that some people cooked children in those ovens, and I shivered, even though it was warm in the kitchen. Stiffly I moved towards the oven and thankfully she moved away. I relaxed and looked around and could see a small light coloured dresser with two doors, the drawers above them had shiny knobs, and above the drawers were shelves where lovely cups of various colours hung proudly. Behind them the matching plates stood boldly, ready to be of service to 'Missus'. There was a picture of the 'Sacred Heart of Jesus' over the table. It was a lovely kitchen altogether. Perfect! She went to her cupboard and brought out a bottle of milk and a glass. I soon decided that I liked this woman and every ounce of fear flew away as she handed me a glass of creamy milk and then put a big tin on the table. She lifted me onto a chair and I sat there, like a queen, with my legs dangling, eating off her beautiful table. She handed me the open tin. For a moment I thought she was giving me the lot, but then she said, 'Have a biscuit: just one. I don't want to spoil your dinner!'

Spoil my dinner? I'd be lucky to get dinner at all most days; just one. Oh; God, what a choice. I trembled with excitement, wondering which biscuit to choose. I had never seen so many biscuits all lined up and ready to eat, in one place. My mouth watered as I tried to make up my mind. I finally decided on a chocolate coloured one with pink cream. I could just see the pink colour peeping at me.

'What do you say?' she said, staring at me. I answered promptly,

'Please Missus.' She smiled and said,

'That'll do.'

I remember how creamy the milk was, probably straight from the cow now that I think of it. I never tasted anything like that feast in my whole life before. There and then I made up my mind that one day I would have a house with creamy milk and stuck-together biscuits in it, and I would give them to girls like me. Well, that was nearly eleven years ago and I have seen inside some lovely houses since, but I have never had such a heavenly experience again. I sometimes wonder if it was just a dream, but when I remember what happened after that, I know it was real!

Aunty Maura was hopping mad with me when I came out the door. She scowled and said,

'There're white whiskers on your face. You've had something to drink.' She slapped me on the face.

'Next time bring the milk to me. I'll decide who needs it.' My lips trembled as I replied,

'Yes Mam.'

Since then I always ask to take the food, or whatever I get, back for my younger half-sister, Pauline, who died from pneumonia about six years ago, when she was eight, or my half-brother, who is called Kam a K'ena, which is 'Son of the house'. That's Diarmud, who was just a wee baby then. He's twelve now. Maeve is older than me, by a few years. Maeve and Diarmud had to go to school when they were seven, but I had a good job, so I couldn't go very often.

One time a man answered the door and I said, 'Please Missus'. I thought that was the right thing to say. He just stared at me and handed me two bob from his fob pocket and said, 'Off with ye now, I'm skint!' Aunty Maura heard the whole thing. She was hiding behind a bush.

'What in God's name did you say?' she screamed as I came out the front gate, pulling her hair out with madness. I just stared at her, wondering what I had done to make her so wild. She took me by the ear and dragged me away from the house.

'If it's a man, say 'Please Sir'. Say it!'

'Ppl...' I began to cry.

'Say it, or I'll kill you!' I just blubbered.

'Get home,' she yelled, as she opened my tight fist and took the two bob from my hand. I ran home, feeling very confused.

I remember another day when a kindly, tall woman with curly brown hair gave me a book with three pigs on the front cover and a big dog with fangs for teeth. I did a very bad thing, I didn't tell Aunty Maura about it. I told myself that if I couldn't eat it I didn't have to tell her about it. I hid it in my knickers. I used to take it out and look at the pictures and pretend to read the words. One day Aunty Maura saw me reading it.

'Where did you get that?' I was dumb struck! I couldn't tell her. All my words were stuck inside my mouth.

'You probably stole it. Give it here!' She snatched it from me and gave it to Maeve, who was sick with the measles. I never got it back, even when I had the measles two weeks later. I still miss that book. Aunty Maura says I'm a 'strong willed little brat'.

...

I'm sitting here, thinking about my childhood days, hugging my knees to keep myself warm and trying to keep my breasts covered. Maybe that kind woman lives in a house around here? I could work for her. Maybe then I can meet a nice man who has a job in a factory perhaps, who would marry me and take care of me, when I'm a good bit older that is. Anyone but Rhonan!

I watch a lovely yellow butterfly flitting away until it's a small dot in the distance. I wish I were a butterfly, and then I could fly away to wherever I wanted. I see Rhonan out of the corner of my eye. He's falling over again! Down he goes, now with a glass of porter in his hand. He lies there with not a drop missing. He's getting up. He's coming to get me! My heart is starting to belt and bump so rapidly I wonder if it will fall out of my mouth soon. I'm chewing my nails until I'm eating my fingertips. From the corner of my eye I can see Aunty Maura leaping and dancing with Paid, her new son in law. Before I can think about anything else, I'm clutching my newspaper with the leg of chicken and making a run for it.

...

The shadow is running ahead of me and the hills are calling me towards them. I'm leaping and running as fast as I can, feeling like a butterfly as I flit through the hills, until I can't hear the noise of the drumming, singing and intoxicated laughter. When I look back all I see are hills and a bit of smoke in the distance. Nobody is on me tail! My chest feels tight as though it's longing for air. I breathe deeply of the air of freedom. I can hear my heart thumping in my ears. I'm sitting down beside the stream to have a bit of a rest, and to think about crossing over.

Chapter two

The water is a good bit higher than it usually is, because of all the rain we had lately. I can barely see the slippery rocks I sometimes use to cross over when I want to get to the mushrooms growing on the other side. The water is making a gurgling, rushing sound, as if it's in a big hurry to get on down the track, over the rocks, and into the vast sea. Me da's words, *It's time you were wedded* echo in the rushing water. Rhonan's face crashes into my mind, 'You can't swim,' he says. I don't need to swim to cross the stream. I'll jump as far as I can. Before I can think of anything else, in one leap I'm in the middle of the stream. I'm steadying myself trying to keep standing up. The waters are roaring past my ankles, sloshing against my legs, saying, 'go on, go on', and nearly knocking me over with the force. The wind is howling by me. One more leap and I'll be on the other side. I leap. Oh God, the rocks are slippery. I'm being hurled forward and I can feel the water pouring over me. I wave my arms about in an effort to swim. I see a branch dangling near me. I try to grasp it with my fingers. I hold on to it for a second, and then it breaks away, and I'm flying backwards through the icy cold water.

Something's smacked against my head and now my head feels as if it's detached from my body. Everything's going black. Pain is shooting through my temple like millions of arrows. My eyes burst open and my feet touch the bottom of the river simultaneously. Rhonan's words come flooding into my mind, *'Tur an skai'*. Little minnow scurry over my face. I can hear myself screaming inside my head. My whole body is filling with water. I'm struggling to breathe. I know I'm calling 'Rhonan, help!' but my voice seems to be right inside my head. My neck feels like it's being squeezed, as though I'm being strangled. My legs find something and I feel steadier. My head is immediately above the water. I take a deep gulp of air, but my feet are slipping and I slither off the rock. I'm back in the deep water. I'm under the water now. Different colours flash by me, black, purple and yellow. I can see my mother. I'm calling her, 'Mammy'. She's so beautiful, just like I imagined. Her long red hair swirls through the water. Her ruby red lips smile at me, exposing white teeth. She's holding her long graceful hand out towards me but I can't reach her. She vaporises before my eyes. I see a city, a bright golden city, in the distance. I move forward into its light. A dark shadow confronts me, blocking my path. I stare upwards into the face of the bogeyman with a giant shillelagh. His head is merely bones with eyes that are black holes. He throws his head back and laughs. I scream. I see the shillelagh towering above me. It's hitting me on the head, crushing me.

I look up and there's a big black hole above me! Now I'm inside the black hole, which feels like a slippery slide. I've no control over where I'm going any more. Now the whole place is black, like an ash pit where the fire has been and gone. Fear twists me into a tight ball, like knotted wool. It's grasping my arm and dragging me down, down so deep through another black tunnel with the sound of bats in my ears. Now my arm feels like it's stretching. I try to fight but I can't. I long for sleep, deep sleep. My lips are pulled apart. My eyes open. I see a face, the face of some stranger. My eyelids are as heavy as copper. A river gushes out of my mouth. Stars sparkle all around my head, pretty blinking stars. I'm coughing and spluttering. My eyelids are prized open. Now a face comes towards mine and my eyes close. I can feel lips firmly on my mouth. I suck up oxygen. A voice sounds in my ears,

'Hello there, are you all right then?' It seems so far away. Balls of bright colour come towards me as I open my eyes. Three pairs of eyes are staring down at me. I gasp! It's the Trinity? I can't face God.

Niamh being rescued by Niall, dusk, 13th May, 1968.
'Oh God,' I hear myself speaking inside my head.

'Hey there, don't go back to sleep now. Come on; come on now, wakey, wakey.' My head and shoulders are being raised onto clouds; Heaven? I force my eyes open again. This time I see just one face in front of me.

'Peter?' My voice sounds squeaky, like a small child's voice. It doesn't say the words correctly.

'Niall's the name. What's yours?'

'Name;' the words seem like little balls rolling out of my mouth.

'Try to drink this then.' Niall gently helps me sit up. I sip a big mug of warm liquid. It leaves a bittersweet taste in my mouth. My stomach wants to throw it back up. I'm trying not to vomit! A basin is stuck in front of my mouth. I'm retching. My mouth is being wiped. My head is lying on a firm shoulder and there's an arm around me. I shiver with the cold running through me. A pain hurries through my head like a sharp needle. I hear a voice saying,

'I found you in the stream; you were nearly drowned. You're very lucky you know. That bush saved your life. The hem of your frock was caught on it. I don't usually go by that way, but thank God I did this day. You'll be all right now.' I'm sobbing hysterically, but I don't know why.

'There, there, don't cry now. You're safe here.' The person called Niall holds me close to him. I feel comforted.

'Is the girleen back with us then?' The voice emerges softly from the doorway of the room.

'She is, Missus Connor, and I think she'll be fine,' Niall replies.

'Tom is gone to get the doctor. I expect they'll be a little while yet. Has she had a drink of tea?' She scurries towards the fireplace.

'She has,' Niall says back to her.

'I'll put a bit more turf on the fire.' She turns around and looks at Niall. 'You had better get that soiled shirt off. Put it in the bucket on the verandah.'

'I'm sorry about that, Missus Connor. I didn't mean to get blood on the lovely shirt you gave me.'

'Yerra, don't worry about it. We'll get it looking great again with a bit of bleach. Thank God it was the white one! I'm just happy that the girleen didn't lose much more blood, or she might not be with us now. Can you give this fire a poke Niall? I'll go and get a bit of bread to toast for the girleen. What's her name?'

'I don't know. Do you know what your name is, girl?' I'd love to yell out my name but it won't come. I can't think what it is! My head feels like a big ball of wool. I start to cry again. 'It doesn't matter,' he assures me. 'She doesn't know, Missus Connor.'

'She's a gift from God,' Missus Connor whispers, smiling down at me. 'I know it! God's gift to me! God knows what I've been praying for these last twenty years or more!' I stare at her. She's not Mammy!

'It'll come to you. You had a big bang on the head.' Niall's eyes stare softly at me. 'We've bandaged your head. Can you feel it?' He's holding my hand to my head. I feel a bandage wrapped around it. 'Good. She's got beautiful eyes Missus Connor, all those lovely colours sparkling like diamonds,' Niall tells the woman. 'She knows we're looking after her.'

'We are. We'll knit you back together again.' Her face draws close to mine. Her pale watery eyes crinkle with her smile. She rises up. 'We'll call her *Kathleen* for now. Kathleen Connor, that's your name.' Her face brightens as it comes close to mine again.

I can feel her love for me. *Kathleen Connor.* I must be smiling.

'You like that name. I can tell. Sure you'll be fine Kathleen.' She's squeezing my cold hand in her warm rough grasp.

'I'll give the fire a poke Missus Connor...' My eyes close. The next thing I know I hear a different voice. I open my eyes try to orientate myself to the situation. It's a deep, masculine voice.

'She's suffering from temporal amnesia. The most important thing is, when she wakes up, is that she converses with you. Try to communicate with her. Different things trigger the memory, so ask her what she remembers from before her accident. If the amnesia is retrograde she may not have remote memory. Do you understand what I mean?'

'We understand,' Missus Connor replies, staring into his eyes.

'The only danger is that she may fall into a coma. If she does, give me a call. We'll have to put her in the hospital.' Missus Connor stares at the doctor as she asks curtly,

'So what can they do for her up there?' The doctor takes a breath, coughs and stares for a moment.

'They can do a lot! The stitches...'

'Sure I can do that myself...' Missus Connor offers. 'I used to work with the Red Cross in my younger days.' 'Is that so?'

'Tis!'

'Right; whatever you think is best for the child Missus Connor!'

'That's what I think is best here!' They walk a few paces towards the door, and then stop. 'Doctor, if she wakes, we're to try and help her to remember! If she *is* in a coma, how will we know 'tis a coma?'

'I thought you said you nursed people?' The doctor confronts Missus Connor now, whose face remains expressionless.

'I did indeed, but they were always awake,' she answers smartly.

The doctor gives a gentlemanly cough at this. 'It's hard to tell, but basically she'll be in a very deep sleep. You won't be able to wake her up.'

'If we can't wake her up we can't get to talk to her.'

'No, because she'll be in a coma, as I explained.'

'So all we can do is to pray that she wakes up?'

'Well, yes, that's correct! We do have a visiting neurological surgeon at the hospital one day every month'

'Which day is that?' Missus Connor steps to the 'under the stairs' wall where there's a huge calendar.

'Let me see.' He rubs his chin. 'The last Wednesday of the month, I believe.'

'And today is the last Thursday.'

'That's right.' The doctor looks a bit frustrated. He coughs again. 'We just missed that golden opportunity. But there's always next month.' He seems satisfied with his remark, for he looks up and smiles. 'If there are any complications, Tom, come and get me.' He looks at Tom who's standing behind his wife. Mister Connor nods his head.

'We most certainly will,' Missus Connor declares as she leads the Doctor into the hallway, and passes him his hat and umbrella.

'I'll come around tomorrow evening and see how she is. The bleeding has stopped, so that's the main thing. Her colour is good.'

'Sure she's a real beauty with those bronze curls and those eyes, just like...' Missus Connor suddenly seems lost for words.

'Like whom?' the doctor asks.

'Just like, my sister Monica...' His eyes narrow,

'I'm sure she is; but I didn't mean her colouring; I meant her colour!'

'I don't see any difference!' Missus Connor replies, her brows crinkling together.

'Never mind; it doesn't matter.' Doctor Cassidy steps outside, and then steps back inside again. 'I hope you'll excuse my ignorance, but where has that lovely daughter of yours been stopping? I haven't seen her around these parts before. In fact, I didn't realize you had a daughter at all!'

I can see Missus Connor's face puckering up and the frown appearing on her forehead. Mister Connor shifts back from the doctor and pushes his hands so deep into the pockets of his trousers I think they might come out at his feet. He coughs and goes a bright red. Missus Connor stares straight into the doctor's face.

'Oh, I nearly forgot! Tom, go and bring that gift we had put aside for the good doctor,' Missus Connor says, giving Tom a shove.

'The gift?'

'You know! Yerra go on; in the sugar bag!'

'The sugar bag? Oh; yes, exactly!' he says, marching off down the hallway.

'Now doctor, I'll get back to your question about our lovely little girl. You see Kathleen was such a special girl, and our only child, so we gave her the best education we could afford, at a very expensive boarding school near Dublin. She sometimes stays with my sister Monica in Bray. She loves her little cousins; the two of them are nearly her age, Dymphna and Doreen. Remember I told you she was the spitting image of my sister Monica...?'

'Yes, I remember. You've not called me on her account before though!' he states softly.

'We have had no need to call you, thank God; that's why you haven't seen her.' I can just see her side profile, and she is smiling very sweetly.

'Of course! She must be eating an apple a day?' He laughs for a moment. 'Just one more question, if I may?'

'Well, like yourself, I was going to do the devil and all today; but certainly you may! Go ahead! Ask anything at all, at all.' Missus

Connor's face is set firm as she outstares the doctor.

'How did she obtain the injury?' Just at that moment Tom comes running in, holding a big brown paper bag. He hands it to the doctor.

'Really, there was no need...' the doctor protests as he takes the gift. He appears to know what is in the bag without looking inside.

'Yerra! It's nothing. You've done us a great service. 'Tis small thanks. And there's plenty more where that came from!' Missus Connor says happily, giving the doctor such a nudge in the ribs that he almost loses his balance. There is a silent pause after that. Missus Connor is urging the doctor towards the front door. The doctor turns towards the door then back again.

'So, how did she injure herself?' Missus Connor takes a deep breath.

'I thought you already asked that question?'

'I did, but we were..., interrupted,' the doctor replies, holding his hat to his heart. Missus Connor takes a deep breath and then replies:

'She was horse riding; you know what young people are like, fearless! They rush into places where angels fear to tread.'

'Horse riding?' Tom Connor exclaims. Missus Connor stares at him.

'Kathleen's fall!' she says. He moves back a pace.

'Oh..., right!' Mister Connor replies as though he's forgotten what happened already. He folds his arms and goes into deep thought, then suddenly speaks. 'She was racing over the hills and jumping walls, and I think she overdid it somehow, and fell off...; there, there you, you, have it!' His speech is suddenly stuttered and his face is coloured bright red. He pauses to catch his breath.

'She hasn't got a psychotic problem at all?' Mister Connor stares at the doctor with his mouth open. Missus Connor butts in at this point.

'I wouldn't be surprised at what's going on in that pretty head of hers. She's psychotic all right.'

'Is there anything specific bothering her that you know of: such as problems at school?' Missus Connor interjects with an answer:

'There's nothing that won't work itself right with time! It's her age. She's a bit wild at the moment, with all those hormones working day and night! You know, like the birds and the bees? Can you remember when you were that young and carefree, or careless as the case may be; sowing wild oats and all that?' The doctor quickly steps away as Missus Connor raises her elbow for a big nudge again. Mister Connor is just standing with his mouth open. The doctor steps a few paces away from the Connors.

'Well now, you might be right there!' Doctor Cassidy reflects for a moment. He is smiling. 'Sure, she'll probably grow out of that wild stage, that's what'll happen.'

'I'm sure you've hit the nail on the head Doctor Cassidy, as always,' Missus Connor says most agreeably.

'I'll bid you good evening then.' He tips his hat. 'Call me, if there're any further repercussions before tomorrow evening.' Doctor Cassidy steps through the front door once more and heads off into the wind, the door following on his heels.

'That was close,' Missus Connor says softly, leaning on the closed door.

'You made me feel like an egit!' Mister Connor says curtly.

'Well, I thought you did right well. That was a great idea about Kathleen jumping over walls!'

'Lies, all lies. Why did you have to bring your sister Monica into this? You haven't spoken to her for years.'

'Well, I'm not telling her about Kathleen until I'm good and ready. I don't want her going to the garda, nosey parker that she is.'

'That's a good subject Kathleen. Tell me what's going to happen if someone comes looking for a missing girleen? What are we going to do if the garda come here?' His voice is low and harsh.

'We'll cross our bridges when we come to them.'

'I hope you know what you're doing woman! And what about you telling the good doctor that there's plenty more from where that's come from?' he says, mimicking Missus Connor. 'That was my last drop!'

'Don't be like that now, Tom. There, there now!' she says comfortingly, kissing his cheek. 'You can go and see your man about some more. You were always able to do that until this minute.'

'But woman, this is serious business. We don't know who the girleen is. What if she's escaped from some mad house? What if she's psy..., whatever he said?'

'Psychotic! Not at all! You're a worrywart man. Can't you see she's been sent as a gift because we can't have our own children? Are we going to fly in the face of God?'

'You're raving mad, woman,' Mister Connor says to this remark.

'I'm not mad. I've come to my senses, more like it!'

'You don't make any sense to me Woman,' he shouts at her.

'Keep your drawers on. I don't give a tinkers' curse what you say. She's mine, and that's that!' She rises to her full height and places her hands on her hips.

'Don't vex me, Woman,' he snarls. Missus Connor ignores his snarl.

'I won't vex you at all if you just co-operate.' She stares at him and smiles sweetly. 'I'm off to make a cup of tea, would you like one?' she says, changing the topic.

'And what are we supposed to do with a sick girleen? I didn't understand one word the doctor said.'

'Don't worry about that. I understand, perfectly.' Her chin

lifts as she continues, 'Remember I was in the Red Cross.'

'As a cleaner!'

'There's nothing wrong with being a cleaner. I'm proud of the job I did for them; the place was always spick and span! I learned a lot of education there.'

'All right! I'm sorry Kathleen; I know you did a grand job there! I'm totally bamboozled by all this. I don't know why you didn't want her to go to the hospital. That's where she should be.'

'You go to the hospital to die!'

'You're a stubborn woman!' Mister Connor marches through the hallway into the kitchen and out the back door. I can hear his footsteps as he stomps away.

It's my fault they're having all this trouble. Missus Connor seems to really care about me. I wish she were my real mother! I know my mother was someone with red hair! I remember that! My memory must be coming back. Missus Connor has curly brown hair, so it can't be her. She's a lovely woman. I know she loves me. Maybe she's my God Mother! I heard her say something about God! That's grand. I love being with my Godparents.   Kathleen Connor, that's who I am now, and I don't want to know who I was before! Oh, God, I'm praying, don't let me come between Mister and Missus Connor. I like the warm fireplace and the smell of toasted bread.

...

My head is throbbing. I'm turning over on my pillow and facing the fire. From my sitting room sofa bed I'm staring into the flickering flames. I'm watching the funny flame shapes form and leap up, changing colour from red to orange then yellow. Then they turn into a plume of smoke....; twirling upwards into the black chimney cavity. I must have fallen asleep after that, because the next thing I know, it's morning. Missus Connor is holding a nice hot cup of tea under my nose.

'My, you look better already, Kathleen; the fire's dead! I'll just give this peat a bit of a poke. It'll warm the cockles of your heart in no time.'

'Thank you...; Missus.'

'Call me, 'Mam! Niall,' she says, turning to Niall who is suddenly nearby. 'She sounds like a little child; my own baby that I've prayed for.' She sniffs and wipes her eyes. 'The smoke's in me eyes; can you have a little chat with her? I'll go and feed the chickens..., you can check Finn McCool later.'

'I gave him his nose bag already Missus Connor. And I'd love to talk to..., Kathleen. What will I say to her?'

'Ask her what she remembers from before her fall, but,' she pauses, 'we'll keep it to ourselves for now!'

'Right, I'll do that.'

...

Niall spends an hour every morning and afternoon with me from then. He's been asking what I remember. I find it very tiring, and can't seem to remember hardly anything from before my accident. My speech is returning quickly though. The doctor says I am making good progress. I want to cheer Niall up by remembering something important. I squeeze my mind with all my might, but nothing comes to mind, except Missus Connor poking the peat.

After two weeks of intensive care, the doctor says I'm now well enough to visit him if I need to, at Missus Connor's discretion. Around this time, Niall sits down next to me as usual.

'So, how are you feeling today, Kathleen?' I open my eyes. 'I think I'm getting... better,' I lie.

'You're looking grand. I think you could do a jig for me!'

'Jig?'

'That's a dance! You're a dancer! Remember I told you that you had one lovely hornpipe shoe on when I found you?' I stare at Niall.

'Dance.' Somehow that word seemed to tumble through my mind like a huge drum. Niall takes my hands in his. I can feel his warmth. It's like an electric charge, giving me strength. I'm closing my eyes.

'Niall... I remember playing... with other children in a... circle. We are dancing. Someone is saying, 'let's... dance... all the day.' I say slowly, and then open my eyes. Niall's face is bright with expectation.

'That's great. Can you see the people you're dancing with?'
I'm closing my eyes. 'There's a girl with long... light brown hair...; tied back. There's another girl with short dark hair. She's..., smaller.' I open my eyes. 'They're gone.'

'It's coming back. You're doing great. Are you tired now?' Niall seems to sense my frailty so well.

'I am... a bit.'

'Well, I'll tell you a story. It's about three pigs...'

'Three pigs! I remember three pigs.'

'Oh God, but you're a marvel. Your memory is working again!' I giggle. I'm really enjoying Niall's story telling. He sometimes tells me jokes that I don't understand, but he makes me laugh anyway. Seeing those children dancing in a circle has started something happening in my mind. The following day I am really feeling much better, so I tell Niall that. I don't have to lie any more. My memory is coming back.

'You know, Kathleen,' he whispers, 'it won't be long before you'll know exactly who you are.' Maybe I was beginning to do just that.

'Niall, I can remember... being in a white dress... and a veil,' I tell him excitedly.

'Oh; God, you're married! No, you can't be. You didn't have a wedding ring on when I found you!'

'There are lots of other girls; in white; all have veils on their heads,' I whisper.

'I know,' he says excitedly. 'Your first communion! All the

girls wear veils and white dresses. You're probably a Catholic.'

'A Catholic; is that bad?'

'No; unless I was a Protestant!'

'What's a Protestant?'

'It's a name for a religion. Never mind that now. Can you remember a big building? A church?'

'I'm not sure.'

'What about someone, saying your name?'

'No. But I remember calling someone: May; no, *Maeve*. She's my age, or maybe a bit older. She could be my friend, or my sister?'

'What about her last name?' I shake my head.

I can't imagine any other place on earth where I want to be. Niall is one of the reasons why I'm happy here! He is so handsome he makes my heart flip over every time I catch a glimpse of him. He's a lot taller than me, with dark wavy hair, with a strand falling forward like a small boy. His deep-set brown eyes pierce into my soul and make me feel weak at the knees. It's an exciting feeling and I'm enjoying it as much as I can. He is the farmhand around here. He has come from Dublin, and he tells me he lived in Kildare as well, so he calls himself a bit of a wanderer.

I often re-live the first time I saw him when he was kissing my lips and giving me his breath. It makes me feel tingly all over to think about that. I wish I'd taken more advantage of the opportunity and said something nice to him. It makes me blush like a beetroot when I think of him kissing me, and I'm not exactly sure why! I notice he's always looking at me. Now that I'm recovering, and the bandage is off my head, I've been allowed to join the family for meals. When we're at the dinner table Niall keeps staring at me, then looking down and burying his face in his dinner; I think I saw him looking like a beetroot too, a few times!

One evening about six weeks after I've been living here, I'm busy with a stiff brush in my hands, shining up Finn Mc Cool's coat until it glistens. He's a beautiful chestnut coloured horse with a white stripe down his slender face. I was a bit afraid of him at first but Niall makes me feel completely at ease with the Connor's favourite horse. I think I'm just happy to be near Niall. As I'm stepping back to admire my work, I trip over Niall's big feet. I'm falling over. He's catching me by the elbows and somehow I'm falling into his arms. His arms are around me. His hand holds my left breast for a moment. My heart pounds in response. He quickly moves his hand away and holds me by the shoulders.

'Steady there. Are you all right?'

'I'm fine,' I'm saying, weakly. I feel my face turning into a beetroot so I'm spinning away to pick up the stiff brush; grabbing it and then dashing off to the house; rushing up the stairs, holding the stiff brush tightly. I don't even realize I'm holding it until I sit down on my bed and gasp for air. 'What's happening to me?' I push the brush under the bed with my foot, and then I hear Missus Connor calling,

'Kathleen, dinner's ready. Wash your hands and come on down before it's cold.' I'm coming slowly down the stairs and now I'm standing in the doorway to the kitchen.

'What's up with you Kathleen? You look like you've been struck by lightning.'

'I'm not feeling very hungry. Do you mind if I just go to my room and rest?'

'Niall, help her to her room. I don't want her falling down the stairs.'

'No... It's fine. I can go by myself. I just need a rest.'

'All right! Go and have a lie down, Kathleen! I'll take you up a bit of tea later. Would you like that Alanna?' I smile weakly.

'I would.'

'Right. I'll do that then; off with you now and rest your weary head.'

Missus Connor's best cup with golden brown tea sits on the little table in my room. Thinly sliced butter toast sits up in triangles on her best fine porcelain plate. I can't bring myself to drink or eat. My hand is resting on my left breast. All night long I feel the imprint of his hand like I've been branded with a hot iron. 'Niall!' I whisper.

That fateful night brings with it a sword that cuts my soul into two people. One is a little girl playing with a happy boy, whose face looks like Niall's. The other is a tormented woman who screams as monsters come to destroy her with giant shillelaghs and pitchforks. Every night now I'm waking up with horrific nightmares. Faces from my past life are beginning to materialise. They are the faces of killer monsters that seem determined to destroy me. I don't know who they are, and I don't want to know.

I'm trying to forget the nightmares and think about Niall as much as I can. I wouldn't even dare tell anyone what is happening to me at night. The Connors might really think I'm 'psychotic' and lock me up if they knew how I'm now spending many hours at night staring out the window into the dark night, with its weird shadows and shapes. My mind seems like the shadowy dark night, with its terrifying shapes banging on the door of my memory, trying to get back into me. I can shut the window and draw the curtains on the dark shapes of the night, but not on the dark shapes in my dreams. The windows of my mind are getting harder to close. The monstrous shapes and faces are beating my doors and windows down. I know that. I'm feeling weaker as they return every night, slithering through little cracks in the windows of my nightmares, plastering their selves to my mind like wallpaper to a wall.

...

One evening at the beginning of August, about two weeks after my nightmares begun, I'm sitting on a chair gathering the last of the heat of the sun. My eyes are half closed as I'm enjoying the laziness of the feeling. The soft summer sun is warm and friendly. I'm thinking of Niall and me playing games together, like two children.

'Lovely evening;' Niall's voice startles me. 'Sorry, I didn't mean to frighten you.'

'That's all right. I'm fine. I was cat napping. It's such a beautiful evening.'

''Tis; beautiful,' he says. I know he's staring at me as he says the words. I know I'm blushing like a red rose now.

'Kathleen,' he says, after a pause, bending on his knee and taking my hands in his.

'What is it?' I sit bolt upright. My hand feels like a wet chicken after being plucked.

'I..., I wanted to tell you something.' He stops.

'Tell me,' I whisper. I think I've got instant laryngitis. I can hardly speak. His look takes my breath away. I'm trying to think what else to say. He's as shy as me. He's got his mouth open. I know I want to hear what he's wanting to say, even though I don't have any idea what that is! I wish I could squeeze the words out of him; beautiful words. I look into his eyes; begging with my eyes. He's looking away; weakening; his knee is shaking like there's an earthquake.

'I think the dinner is ready; have to go.' He's getting off his wobbly knee and releasing my hand.

'Niall!' I'm leaping off the chair and holding my hand out to him, and he's taking it again. I'm staring at him; lowering my eyelids. I can't let this opportunity go; holding his hand tightly. Maybe if he holds me the nightmares will go away; the key to my happiness; I know it!

'Sure is that all you want to say to me now?' My words feel like creamy butter, smooth and rich. I'm surprised at myself. May God forgive me!

'No; look, Katheen, you're too good for me. I know that. I'm just a farmhand with very little to offer. You're probably from a very rich family. You know what I think?'

'No,' I reply, my eyes fixated on his.

'I think you were locked in a tower, like Rapunzzel, and you got out, so they tried to drown you, and now you're here, with us! I don't want them to come and take you away, because...' He suddenly stops.

'Niall, please don't stop! I'll be what you want me to be!' We're standing close together now. I want him to fill my mind, night and day. I can feel the heat from his body radiating to me. 'You're the most..., kindest man I ever met, if I ever knew another man, but I can't remember; I can only remember: monsters!' There, I've said it. I stare into his face.

'Kathleen. You've been through so much. But I'm here for you now!' Somehow he's holding me in his arms and I'm weeping into his clean shirt.

'You saved my life.' Liquid from my nose is mingling with my tears onto his shirt. 'Sorry!' I whisper. He doesn't even notice.

'Oh, Kathleen, I can't stop thinking of you, night and day. I love you to distraction. I want to marry you. Please marry me. Everything I have is yours. Please say yes.' His eyes stare down into mine. The desire to kiss his soft round lips is coming upon me. I can barely say the next small word.

'Yes?' I whisper.

'Is that yes with a question, or just plain yes?'

'Yes, plain yes! A thousand times! Yes, I'll marry you.' 'Oh; Kathleen, I adore you. I'll give you: the whole world.' He's grasping me in his strong arms and lifting me into his strong chest. His lips are bending to mine and we are pressed together. I cannot remember having felt such a belonging kiss before. I want our kisses to last forever. I feel like a little bird being whisked away from the monsters by its mother and flying through the sky. His cheeks are wet, his shirt is wet, my face is wet, but I feel like I'm being washed of my fears. They're all being washed away with our love.

...

That night, as I'm climbing softly to my room upstairs, I overhear Mister and Missus Connor,

'So, now they want to get married, what are we going to do?' Mister Connor poses this question to Missus Connor, who is sitting, knitting away at a huge green jumper for Mister Connor.

'Let them get married. They're in love.'

'In love,' Mister Connor sneers. Missus Connor pauses and stares at her husband. 'They love each other.'

'But she's only a girleen.'

'She's at least seventeen or eighteen years old. I was married at seventeen, if you can remember back that far.'

'You were so young! I was a young strapping lad myself then. God be with those days.' He fills his pipe and stares into the fireplace at the smouldering embers. 'I still think of her the day Niall found her. She was wearing children's socks, like a little girleen.'

'But, you may or may not have noticed that the girleen has become a young woman since she arrived here.'

'You know, Kate, you're a very observant woman. You're right. She is looking more: how would you say it?' He's scratching his balding temple trying to locate the right word here.

'Womanly?' Missus Connor finishes his thoughts.

'That's the word. Yes, womanly.'

'Right; she should be married if she's a woman. The time is right.'

I'm shocked to think they've noticed such personal changes in me. But Missus Connor is right. Since I arrived my breasts have become rounder. In fact I'm rounder all over. I have become a real woman in just a few months! I thought it was just the good cooking Missus Connor does. I'm blushing when I think of my big breasts. Missus Connor kindly left two brassieres on my bed a few weeks ago, which I'm wearing all the time. Now my breasts don't bounce when I run.

'So, are you ready to give her away in marriage?' He bangs his pipe on the fire grate before he replies.

'I hardly know her. She doesn't even know who she is. How can I do that?'

'You're her father. It's your job.'

'Her kidnapper; we could end up in gaol for this.' Missus Connor stares at him.

'Don't say such a thing! Think of yourself as her Stepfather. To the outside world you're her real father. Put that in your pipe and smoke it!'

'All right: have it your way! But if the priest asks for her birth certificate, what are we going to do?' She smiles with her eyes, above her knitting.

'Don't worry your head about a thing. I'll fix it! Everything will be all right, you'll see.' She pauses from her knitting and stares at Mister Connor until she catches his eye. 'Tom, all you have to do is walk down the aisle with herself on your arm, and when the priest asks who gives her to Niall, you say, 'I do'.'

'I do?'

'Yes; 'I do'.'

'Is that all?'

'No.'

'What else?'

'Get in the spirits for the wedding. You know what I mean?'

'I do.'

'Right: do you want a cup of tea?'

'I do. No, I mean, I don't want a cup of tea. I want a bit of peace. I want sanity in this house.'

'Are you sure you don't want a cup of tea. You'll feel better then; 'tis no bother...' Missus Connor acts as if a cup of tea will bring peace and sanity to the house, even to the whole world if necessary. She's rolling the wool into a big ball, and then plunging the knitting needles right through the centre of the wound ball. 'Right you are; I'll go and make us a cup of tea, anyway.'

Chapter three

I'm quietly racing up to my bedroom, two stairs at a time, and plonking myself on the side of the bed. I'm in love! I know it now! It's a wonderful feeling! I know Mister Connor will be a lovely father for me on my wedding day. Missus Connor will see to that! I'm gazing around my room. It's a lovely room with beige wallpaper with tiny pink roses splashed all over it, a little wooden dresser with a mirror, and a tall wardrobe with a long mirror inside. That's also where I hang all the nice clothes the Connors have given me. This room has been my haven of refuge and my battleground for the past two months. My eye is wandering to the window on one side with soft pink curtains. They blow in the breeze when the window is open. Like it is now! I see Niall walking across the yard, his shadow long and firm in the evening light. My heart is leaping. I can't stop staring at his attractive stature as he strides along. He looks happy, like me! I'm staring until he disappears through the barn and into his own room at the back. That is the picture I want to keep in my mind forever, and not those awful monsters that are coming to get me at night!

I'm having a quick wash with my little jug of water and a washbowl that sits on a small table in the corner of the room. All the time I'm thinking of Niall. He fills my whole mind. Missus Connor says I should brush my hair a hundred times to get the hair growing faster and make it shine. I pull my flannelette nightie over my head, drag the soft brush through my hair, counting quickly, 'One, twenty, forty, fifty, ninety, one hundred?' They're all the numbers I seem to be able to remember, so that's how I do it! 'Ouch!' I've hit the sore bit. I'm rubbing the spot with my fingers. A pain is shooting through my head for a moment.

I'm climbing slowly into my little bed. I'm pulling the crisp white sheets over me, and then the warm fluffy blanket. 'Thank you God,' I'm mumbling as the pain dies down. I'm drifting into sleep, the first pleasant sleep I've had for ages.

...

I wake up feeling like a new person; all bright and happy like the sparkling sun coming out from behind a black cloud.

Missus Connor goes into action straight away. She has Tom Connor running off to find an old friend who is a priest. Two weeks later, a woman called Missus Brady is bustling into the sitting room carrying a big tissue wrapped package.

'So, you're the lucky bride to be, Kathleen?'

'I am!' She stares at me. 'I don't know why they've kept you hidden for so long, you're a real beauty!' She unveils the parcel on the wooden table at the side of the room.

'We'll see how this fits.'

'What is it?'

'It's your wedding dress! Step into it and pull it up over your hips. That's the best way to get it on. I'll squeeze you in!' I'm wondering if she expects me to take my clothes off, here. I blush, just thinking about that.

'I won't need help putting a dress on. Do I have to do it here?'

'God but you're shy. You can go up to your room; go on; come straight back down here.' She places the dress in my outstretched arms, and then folds the end over, so it doesn't trail on the floor. I'm carrying the gown with the fear that I'm going to fall over or, even worse, step on it. I'm thinking, maybe I should just bare all and try it on right here. No, I said I didn't need help, so I'm heading up to my bedroom. Climbing the stairs is a new nightmare. I trip up and fall into the bundle of fabric. Missus Brady shouts, 'Don't ruin it! Turn yourself around, it's easier that way.'

'I'll try that!' I reply, moving my feet in a semi-circle, ever so slowly.

'Stop there,' Missus Brady yells when I am facing the way I usually come down the stairs.

'Now move backwards up the stairs,' she instructs. 'I'll take the end for you.'

'It works!' I call out. We eventually enter my room without tripping up again.

'Well, I'll leave you for a minute,' she says, leaving the door slightly ajar.

I never saw such a dress! It's got bones all down the front and back bodice, and no matter how I twist my arms I can't get the back done up. I'm not even sure I'm putting it on the right way round. I'm having a private dressing nightmare for a few minutes. I'm puzzled about this big lump around the back. It's all twisted up. Maybe it comes off and goes on me head!

'Missus Brady,' I'm calling. Immediately she's beside me in the room.

'Sure, you're all twisted up.' She yanks the sides of the bodice and pulls my brassier strap up a little higher. 'Brings up the bust line, that's what it does; flattering!' My breasts are staring me in the eyes as I'm looking down. They're just under my chin. The neckline is a 'v' shape and reveals my cleavage. I can feel the blood pouring into my face. I don't know if it's from embarrassment, or the tight dress.

'It's a bit…, on the low side,' I venture to whisper.

'Voluptuous you mean. Sure, you've got a great shape. You won't always have that; flaunt it while you've got it, that's what I always say!' After an arduous ten minutes of Missus Brady's bustling around me, tucking bits in here and there, she says: 'Hold your breath now. I'm going to lace you up.' I hold my breath and she pulls at the hooks in the bodice. I feel like I'm being squeezed to death, and wonder why my ribs don't break? I'm gasping for air. 'Take small breaths, or else the hooks will burst asunder!' I'm trying to breathe quietly.

'Now, hold your breath again. I'm going to zip you up.' I'm holding my breath.

'Pull your shoulders back. Stand straight, bottom tight, stomach in.' She's roaring at me, while the zip slowly inches its way up my back, going up higher and higher, like a train winding its way along a track uphill. She is holding her breath during the last six inches of zipping. She's letting out a gasp. 'Done; wait a minute; now turn around and see yourself.' I'm turning towards the mirror that hangs in the inside door of the wardrobe. It's almost a full body length mirror. Is it really me? I'm staring at this lovely 'antique' white dress with pearls all over the front.

'It's a beautiful frock,' I say after staring a while.

'Frock; it's a gown; a gorgeous gown,' Missus Brady says tugging at the waist.

'It is…' The bust is a bit high for my liking and the neckline too low; the overall picture is of someone I don't really know.

'You're a real picture, that's what you are! What a figure; film star in the making,' Missus Brady says, completely flattering me, or that person in the mirror. I'm placing my hand at the neckline, trying to cover a bit of skin. She notices my activity and comments.

'It is a bit bare at the neck; don't worry about that because Missus Connor says you can wear these pearls.' I am dumbstruck with awe as she opens a box with layered strings of beautiful creamy-white pearls. She's standing close to me, being careful not to tread on the hem of the dress. She's hanging them around my neck. Four rows of glistening pearls extend just to the apex of my bust-line.

'That should draw attention away from your cleavage, without detracting from your feminine beauty.' I cannot get my eyes off those shiny, shimmering pearls.

'They're lovely.'

'Lovely; they're glorious!' Missus Brady insists. 'There you are now!' she exclaims, standing back and admiring me as though she had just carved me from ivory. I'm staring into the mirror again. The bodice glistens even in the dimly lit bedroom. A ray of sunshine bursts into the room and I light up like a crystal. I turn slowly, viewing the cut of the dress from every angle. The bodice is very tight, sloping towards my waist into a 'v' shape just above my hipbones. The sleeves fit tightly on the edges of my shoulders, and cling like skin to my arms, making them look sleek and long; with a 'v' shaped piece hanging down near my wrist, and a tiny pearl on the tip at the end. The twisted up lump at the back miraculously turns into a 'bustle', as Missus Brady calls it. It makes my bottom look like a duck's, sticking out behind me as I walk. The fabric is tucked into rolled layers and leads the eye to a long train of soft silky material. There's so much material trailing behind me you could've made three dresses with it. 'It's our own fabric. Made right here in Ireland,' Missus Brady declares, as if she wove it all herself. 'I'll just tidy this a bit.' She is fingering the bustle. *How do you tidy a bustle!* I wonder?

'It's a bit..., duckish!' I stammer.

'The more duckish the better; that's what I say; they have to be like that; bustles are all the rage around here again!'

'Did you make the dress?' I ask timorously, hoping it is the right question.

'I did indeed; 'tis a long story!'

I stare at my reflection. I'm not sure I want to hear the long story.

'Is that right?' Missus Brady stares at my face in the mirror.

'You remind me a bit of my Angel.'

'You saw your angel?'

'Angela. I made the dress for her. She was only nineteen, around your size. She never got to wear it. I hope it brings you luck.'

'Luck..., so, what happened to your daughter?'

'We adopted her when she was five,' she begins.

'I'm sorry,' I say haltingly.

'Don't be. It's not a secret; such a beautiful, angelic child; we called her Angela. Her real name was Veronica.' She pauses and takes a deep breath, as though recalling a precious moment with Angela. She's shaking her head. I can see tears in her eyes. 'She met this pilot; young fellow, Raphael Gilmore was his name; Raphael and Angela, two lovely angels; madly in love.'

'So did they get married?'

'They flew away and never came back; like angels in the sky.'

'Where did they fly to?' I question. I mean you had to fly somewhere, to another place.

'Their 'plane was found two days later, all smashed up, nothing was left. Their bodies were found, wrapped around each other, like two little black babes.'

'They died?'

'Two days before the wedding.' I shiver. 'Tis two days before my wedding! Missus Connor appears in the doorway.

'Oh, she looks just like Queen Mary!'

'Begorrah, you're quick off the mark Kathleen! The gown is a copy of her wedding gown!'

'Sure I know all about the royal family... I have a bit of royalty in me. I believe we're the descendants of King Rory O'Connor!' She wanders forward as she speaks. 'Alice, you've done a great job.' She has a handkerchief in her hand. 'My little princess Kathleen is all grown up now..., nearly eighteen. The dress fits like a glove.'

'It does. Maybe it was meant for your Kathleen?' Missus Brady discretely brushes a tear away and stands a couple of steps away. 'You'd better put your high heels on too. It's a bit trailing. You might trip up.'

'I happened to see these perfect white satin shoes the other day. They were just staring at me from Lynch's shop window, so I bought them. I'll get them.' Missus Connor hurries to her own bedroom and triumphantly arrives with a box filled with tissues and pearly-white satin court-style shoes with a huge pearl at the 'v' shaped front.

'Try these on for size.' I hold on to Missus Brady as Missus Connor huddles down at my feet and places the shoes on my bare feet. 'God but your feet are as rough as sandpaper; push!' I feel myself rising up like the sun on a winter's morning.

'You'll have to get those feet softened up, and then you can wear silk stockings! They fit like a glove, Kathleen, child,' Missus Connor says, clambering to her feet. She glances at Missus Brady. 'A mother's instinct!' She sighs, and then hugs me. 'Alanna. You remind me of my sister; the image of her!' I respond like a true daughter,

'Thanks; Mammy,' I whisper.

She stands a little away from me, smiling smugly and holding my shoulders; then running her eyes down my form from head to toe where her gaze rests.

'We'll use the pumice stone and get those feet as smooth as a baby's bottom!' I wonder what a pumice stone is, but instinctively can almost feel the pain I am about to endure.

Missus Brady heads downstairs and brings up her large bag filled with bits and pieces. She extracts a pincushion with pins.

'Breathe in.' I gasp in fright and hold my breath.

'Don't worry, I'm just sticking pins in the dress, not in you!' she mumbles through a mouthful of pins. 'Out!' Relieved, I relax.

'No; not that much.' She glares at me and I breathe in a bit and hold it in.

'For the next two days, just stay away from apple pie and custard! You can't afford to put even one ounce on. Do you understand me?'

'I do,' I whisper.

I have hardly eaten at all for the last two days, for fear of 'bursting asunder' in my tight wedding gown. It's been hard to resist Missus Connor's hot apple pies with lashings of custard made from fresh milk and eggs, which has become one of my favourite foods these past months.

Missus Connor asked Noleen, a young hairdresser, and beautician, to come and do my face and hair.

'Sit in front of the mirror, Kathleen,' she instructs. Here I am, sitting down in front of the mirror and she's working on me as though I'm a masterpiece. She places a white elastic band around my head, holding the hair back from my face.

'First, you need to cleanse tone and moisturise, that's the latest technique.' She begins to rub my face with a cream. Next she uses a soft cotton ball and cleans my face again and then she rubs cream all over my face and neck. 'I'm just going to put a first foundation layer on now.' I watch as she rubs some skin coloured stuff all over my face.

'Do you think I look a bit pale?' I ask. Her eyebrows frown. 'Hold your horses, I'm not half finished,' she snaps.

'Sorry,' I whisper.

'Never mind.' She removes the white band and tugs at my hair as she pushes a thick brush through it. Next she divides my hair and some falls in front of my eyes. I don't move in case I upset her. But I can hardly see a thing.

'Did you want curls towards the back?' I nod. After some time she begins to work on the front pieces. I look into the mirror. She has some of the hair piled high and curls hanging down the back of my head to the nape of my neck. She's rolling some of the hair from the front under, so it looks like a sleek sausage shape on top of my head.

'Your hair seems a bit thin on this side, where there's a nasty scar.' She looks at me in the mirror and I catch her eye. 'What happened?'

'I fell off the horse,' I lie.

'When?'

'A while ago now...,' I reply.

'It still looks sore,' she adds as I squirm when she brushes the spot.

'Just a bit.'

'Well, I'll cover it with makeup and then let the hair come softly over it.' She cocks her head from side to side, moving a piece of hair as she works out her plan. 'There! Nobody will notice anything,' she says, dabbing something on the scar and gently easing the hair over the mark.

'Magic!' I exclaim, peering into the mirror to try and see the scar. 'It's gone!' I can see the big smile on her face.

'Yerra, it's not gone. It's not gone at all. It's just hidden.'

'I can't see it at all. You've done great,' I say amazed.

'It is my profession. I am happy with that though!' She sighs and admires her work in the mirror. 'Now keep still. I want this to look straight,' she says, placing a gold crown that she places right behind the rolled piece of hair on my forehead.

'I look like a real princess,' I say exuberantly.

'It's not real gold; just plastic coated!' She smiles in amusement and delight at my astonishment. 'I'm glad you like it. I didn't think a floral wreath would suit that gorgeous gown you're wearing. You have a real royal look, that's why I suggested the crown.'

I just smile. She opens a shiny black box to reveal a row of colours. 'But, the magic transformation is not quite finished,' she announces. 'This is my secret to success in my business. I'm going to put another layer of foundation on.

'Do you use this every day?' I ask inquisitively.

'I do. It doesn't take me very long now!'

'How long does it take?'

'Fifteen minutes; that doesn't include my hair...'

'That's quick,' I remark.

'I know, but it gets easier with practice. I've been doing this for a few years now.' She stops plucking at my hair and looks intently at my face. 'You should be doing something with your skin now. The climate in the West is not the best for our fair skins. You can get wind burn very easily.' I smile in silent reply.

'I sell beauty products at the shop. Come on down and have a look. Your skin could really do with a good beauty routine. Now that you're getting married you need to keep yourself looking great. I don't believe in letting yourself go, just because you're married. You need to keep your husband interested.'

'Right,' I reply, wondering how on earth I ever got Niall interested without any of this stuff in the first place. She selects a box with face powder and dunks a big fluffy powder puff into the contents.

'So, what school did you go to?' She dabs the powder all over my face as she speaks.

'School?'

'You did go to school? I breathe deeply.

'Mm' I mumble.

'I never saw you there.'

'Where?'

'At the local school!'

'I didn't go there... much.'

'Did you go to Dublin?'

'Mmm,' I say behind the makeup.

'I suppose you have the money, that's the thing!' She finishes her dabbing process, and takes a big brush from her box. 'Close your eyes.' I close them.

'So what were the lads like there?' She gently flicks the brush over my face. I wait until she stops to reply.

'I think it was an all-girls school.'

'How do you mean, you think it was an all-girls school? Don't you know?'

'Well, it was, except for some of the teachers!'

'I see. What were they like?'

'Who?'

'The male teachers?'

'Oh, they were very old. Really old, like, my daddy, Mister Connor!' She pauses for a moment.

'You don't have to tell me who your father is. He is a bit of an old goat! Sorry, I didn't mean to insult you...'

'He is.' I laugh to hide my nervousness, the fear that I'll let the Connors down and she'll discover they're just my step parents, my God parents really. 'But he's a wonderful father. He's always giving me things...'

'Not like my father! Never mind about that! Tell me about the rest of the time in the all girl boarding school? Did you go to any of the Dublin clubs or that?'

'Clubs?'
'Surely you weren't locked in the school all the time?'
'I was…'
'That's awful. Then where did you meet Niall?'
'Here!'
'I see! Now keep your eyelids down. Did you want eyeliner?'
'Whatever you think…' I reply immediately.

'It's highly fashionable now, and mascara,' she adds. 'I'll use the dark brown to give a softer touch. Don't blink. Hold it there.' She moves along my lashes with a tiny brush. 'Now for the lipstick;' she holds up a bright lipstick.

'It looks a bit bright,' I mumble.

'You can wear it, with those lips,' she states emphatically. 'Say 'aw'. Great!' 'Now, we'll just attach the veil; there now; finished!' She lifts the veil over my face. 'Have a gander!' I open my eyes and stare. I make a face in the mirror to make sure it's not a picture of another person. It's really me!

'Don't you like it?'

'I do. It's grand. I just wondered if it was meself.'

'Now, smile.' I smile widely.

'Less.' I move my lips closer.

'More.' I move my lips out a bit.

'Great! Hold that smile there.' I try to retain the smile as she speaks.

'Now that's the one you want when you walk down the aisle. Get the feel of it. Keep that smile, even when the veil is over your face. You can relax now. But remember not to cry! You'll ruin all my good work! I'll just do your nails. Spread your fingers and keep them stiff.' Noleen sits down on a chair beside me and places her nail kit on the dressing table. 'Good God!'

'What?'

'Your nails!'

'What's wrong with them?' I ask, staring at them.

'I've never seen such neglected nails. Do you bite them?'
'Sometimes.'

'I can only do my best. Do not bite these again until after your wedding, or I'll come and haunt you when I die.'

'I won't,' I reply, suddenly feeling terrified at the thought of Noleen coming to terrorise me at night with all the other monsters.

'Promise now!'
'Promise!'
'Good.'

'That's today! Oh God! What are you doing now?'

'I'm going to give you some long nails. These are fakes.' I stare at the row of nails. I never saw such a thing before, but I say nothing. I decide to ask her a few questions before she asks me too many questions I can't answer.

'Is this what you do every day?'

'It is. I've been working at it since I was fourteen. That was when I bought my first lipstick.'

'Now you have so many lipsticks!'

'I've earned them, I can tell you that. But it costs me a bit of money. Everything costs money these days.' I smile. She glances up at my face. 'You don't have to worry about things like that!'

'What do you mean?' I ask, wondering what she's getting at.
'Money.'

'Me? No, I never worry about money,' I say lightly.

'I never stop worrying about money, ever since I've been married.'

'So, you're married already are you?'

'I am married.' She holds up her left hand. 'See!'

'It's lovely,' I comment, admiring her wedding ring. 'You probably thought I'm too young. Is that right?' I never thought of that!

'I did! You look very young.'

'Everyone says that! But I'm very mature for my years!' She probably is, I'm thinking.

'You are!' I exclaim.

'You look young yourself,' she says, moving her eyes from my fingernails to my blushing face in the mirror, just for a moment. I smile.

'Thanks.' There's a pause and then I think of another question. 'So, how long have you been married?'

'Over a year now.' Suddenly her face becomes bright pink, which I can detect even under the double makeup. 'Expecting our first; did you notice?'

'What?'

'My bulge?'

'No!' I answer truthfully. I'm not sure what she is talking about, but she pats her stomach as she says it, so I know it's got something to do with the stomach.

'Vincent says I hide it well.'

'Vincent?'

'My husband.'

'He's right, you hide it well,' I say, not sure what she's keen on hiding. That seems to please her.

'Well, what do you think?'

'About your bulge?'

'No, your nails?' I stare at my spread out fingers. My mouth drops open.

'How did you do that?'

'Trade secret! If you want refills you'll need to visit the salon. They're half price until December twentieth.'

'They're so..., pearly and..., long; like cat's claws!'

'The longer..., the lovelier, that's what I say. Just don't move them for fifteen minutes, 'till everything sets. I'm finished Missus Brady,' Noleen yells as she starts to pack up her beauty products into their special places in her black box. 'I'll give you a hand with the dress.'

'What a beauty queen,' Missus Brady says, bustling into the room carrying a small flat box. Together they pull my dress over my slip and into its strangulating position.

'She's got a great shape,' Noleen says, lacing the dress at the back.

'She won't always have this. Not after a few buns in the oven,' Missus Brady remarks. They both laugh as though I'm not here.

After an allocated fifteen minutes on Noleen's instructions, wrist-high satin gloves, with the fingers chopped off, are taken from their flat box and pulled over my hands. A bouquet of fresh apricot coloured roses and forget-me-nots, trimmed with sweet-smelling lavender, created by Missus Connor, is placed in my hands, the smell of which keeps wafting to my nose and making me sneeze.

'You're not allowed to sneeze. Look at the light if you feel one coming on,' Noleen instructs at the last minute. 'God bless you now!' She leans forward and kisses my cheek and then rubs it. 'Lipstick. I wish they'd invent one that doesn't leave a mark!' She smiles and rushes off. She has to be at her work by nine o'clock, so she leaves before the ceremony begins. I noticed Missus Connor giving her a fat envelope as she leaves the house. I just catch a glimpse of her from my bedroom window. She's opening the envelope and glancing back as she walks towards her bright pink car, a huge smile on her face. She jumps inside and away she goes like the wind. I wish I could be so modern and confident.

...

The wedding is in the rose garden next to the house. Mister Connor has been keeping all the open buds for the last two days.
I've seen some of the guests arrive in the last few minutes. There's Mister and Missus Connor, all dressed up to the nines; the priest, Father Patrick Buckley, a sombre looking man who used

a walking stick to walk up the footpath to the house. He takes a full ten minutes to go ten yards. As soon as he arrives he's lighting his pipe. Then there's Missus Brady who brought the dress. Missus Kearney is here to help with the food preparation. With Missus Brady's help I travel safely to the bottom of the stairs and enter the sitting room. There's a young woman standing, staring out into the garden. She turns around as I enter.

'Now, have you got something old, something new, something borrowed and something blue?' Missus Brady asks. 'I don't know?' I reply.

'The dress is borrowed, the shoes are new, the pearls are very old..., Oh; God, this is a disaster.' She looks as though she might faint. She cups her hands over her face; 'nothing blue!'

'I have!' I suddenly remember as I extract a blue handkerchief from between my bosoms. 'Mammy gave me this. And I have these,' I point to my forget-me-nots.

'God bless her, thank God!' she says, almost swooning with delight; 'got your horse-shoe?'

'I have,' I reply, raising my left hand to show her the newly crafted silvery shoe dangling on my arm.

'You'll have great blessings and good luck then,' she says, completely satisfied. She's all yours now,' she says to the girl, and then she turns to address me. 'This is Bridget. She's your brides-maid,' Missus Brady announces. We smile at one another. Bridget is about my age, a little shorter than me, and with short brown hair. She's wearing an ankle length pink frilly frock and a wide brimmed bonnet trimmed with pink roses. She's wearing white gloves and holds a small bouquet of pink roses and lavender. 'She's Missus Kearney's daughter,' Missus Brady explains. 'You probably know one another?'

'Probably,' I say, feeling hot under my makeup. I can't remember her at all. Bridget stares at me and smiles, exposing her giant teeth and pink gums. She shrugs her shoulders.

'Where is Tom?' Missus Connor rushes through the double doors, and stops when she sees Bridget and me. She cups her face in her hands and shakes her head. 'You're beautiful. You too, Bridget!' With that she dashes outside, looking for Mister Connor.

The window next to the double doors is wide open, so the guests can see me if they turn around. Through the nylon lace curtain I can just see them waiting nervously in the garden, sipping drinks. There's Nancy Crowe standing near the rose bushes, looking like a rose bush herself. She's dressed in a large-print floral suit in pink tones, with a huge pink, brimmed hat, which keeps bobbing as she talks. A brighter pink ribbon is wound around the crown of it and there's a bunch of plastic looking snowdrops stuck on one side. She is wearing high-heeled black shoes and stockings that glitter when she moves. She is checking them now for snags. I think she should move away from the rose bushes! Pink gloves and a black patent handbag complete her outfit. Bright pink lipstick enhances her lips and her cheeks are very rosy. She keeps blowing kisses to Ned, who's standing near a table with decanters filled to the brim with varying coloured liquids. Ned keeps raising his eyebrows in response. He is dressed in his best black suit complimented by a bright red cravat with flowers on it. Ned is our part time stable hand, and is Niall's Best man today. He has been courting Nancy for over twenty years, so Missus Connor reports. Missus Connor rushes in through the front door, and gasps for breath. 'He's on me heels,' she calls to me. She seats herself at the ivory keys. The high backed piano shines like brand new from polishing. We can hear Mister Connor's cough as he comes through the sitting room door. I turn around and his mouth drops open.

'Get over there and take her arm. Hurry on now. Remember, she's your only daughter!'

'Right you are.' He staggers towards me, his mouth still open. I place my arm in his. He just keeps staring at me. I beam at him.

'Doesn't she look a picture?' Missus Connor says, swiveling on her piano stool, squeaking and beaming at once.

'A real picture,' Mister Connor agrees, 'a film star.'

'Open the double doors,' Missus Connor instructs Missus Brady, waving her arms out and back again. 'We're ready!' A note is sounded on the piano. I step through the double doors. The sounds of 'Beautiful,' reach my ears. I'm suddenly feeling nervous and shake for a moment. I stare straight ahead at the priest.

Father Patrick Buckley grunts like a pig. He's wearing his long white surplus and scapula. He's got his arms folded and if we didn't start moving I think he might have fallen asleep. He's placed his pipe on a little table. It's still emitting whirls of smoke. It's a fine sunny day, with a little breeze, which makes my veil flutter like a little dove. Where's Niall? For a split second I feel panicky as I'm thinking 'he's not here'. Suddenly my hero appears from behind the bushes at the side of the house. I breathe a sigh of relief. I walk towards Niall, who is now standing at the end of the garden near the spot where he proposed to me. I'm treading cautiously along the little stepping-stones. With the long gown and the high heels to maneuver I feel like a giant on stilts. I suddenly feel a bit giddy. I'm slipping on the smooth stones. For an instant I can feel water running over me, all icy and cold. I shiver. Mister Connor steadies me and we keep walking. Missus Connor is playing: 'da, da, da da, da, da da da', something like that; hammering the old piano. The music flows into the garden. As we get closer, Niall's eyes bulge out of their sockets as he stares at me. He looks ten feet tall with his hair black and shiny, slicked down with hair tonic and his fine black suit and apricot coloured cravat. His white straight teeth sparkle from scrubbing. They match his brilliant white shirt, freshly pressed by Missus

Connor and starched so that it could stand all by itself. My mouth is automatically smiling in return, hidden under my veil. My heart throbs. This is the pinnacle of my life. Nothing will ever compare to this splendid moment. I am a queen for a day! Niall's queen!

The priest moans in prayer.

'Join hands' he instructs us. He then asks Niall if he takes me as his wife.

'I do,' Niall replies, his eyes shining; the priest turns to me.

'Do you, Kathleen Mary Connor, take this man, Niall Finbar Dempsey, as your lawfully wedded husband...?' His voice moans on. The priest is staring at me, mouthing *I do*. I say,

'I do.' That wasn't too hard. I feel more relaxed now, and then we have to repeat everything Father Buckley says, which all seems like a dream to me. Then Niall gives me a lovely *Claddagh* ring; just the right size for my finger; the priest says,

'You are now husband and wife.' There's a slight pause and then gruffly, he says, 'You may kiss the bride.' Niall raises my veil and our faces meet for the first time as man and wife. His face is glowing with happiness and I can feel mine reflecting his joy.

The kiss, Niall and Niamh: 21st August, 1968
©marieseltenrych2010

'Wait on there!' Just as our lips merge, Ned Smith has the camera out. 'Just hold it there for a tick.' We hold our mouths together for several minutes whilst he adjusts his settings. We start to laugh. 'Ready steady, hold on; hold on! Can the priest move in a little bit closer, just between the two?' Father Buckley grumbles as he shuffles a few feet to the left behind us. 'Great, that's great. Now keep those lips puckered together. Right, that's great. ' He finally clicks his camera. After a few more snaps with Mister and Missus Connor, and one with the guests, we head to a table in the hallway where an open book lies atop a clean white tablecloth sticking out like a ballerina's dress. A pen with a quill attached awaits our capture. I have been practicing my writing for the last few days. I seem to have forgotten how to write! Niall has been helping me form the letters again, but it seems so hard that I don't know if I'll ever be able to write properly again, or read for that matter. Niall places his hand over mine to stop me shaking as I write. He guides the pen over the parchment.

'That's grand.' He then signs his name and I lovingly follow every move of his fingers with my eyes. He has beautiful, strong, manly hands, I note. Father Buckley has just gone outside to light his pipe that must have gone out. He returns and peers at our signatures.

'Right, sure that's lovely.' He signs his wobbly signature and the date of our marriage as Wednesday, 21st August nineteen hundred and sixty eight. After the signing ordeal, I am determined to enjoy myself. We walk through the sitting room doors together, as husband and wife. A loud cheer greets our ears. Bridget is following behind us, holding up the train of my dress. Missus Connor goes into loud mode on the piano, and she's belting the thing and hopping off her chair with the force of her hands and arms. Her whole body is rocking with the rhythm all the time. Now we're all kissing each other and being really friendly. Nancy Crowe is sniffing into her pink lace handkerchief, and Missus Brady is wiping her tears with a white handkerchief. Why do people cry when they are so happy? It makes me want to cry, but I'm afraid to cry with all the makeup on my face, like Noleen warned me about. There's a mountain of food spread on Missus Connor's table, plates of neatly cut triangular sandwiches, a bowl of sausages, sausage rolls, meatballs. There's a beautiful iced wedding cake, with a little figurine of a man and a woman getting married on the top. Her best tablecloth is stiff and starched, but you can barely see it for the food. There's a silver pot with tea in it and cream in the jug. On another side table there are jugs of orange juice and bottles of porter. There are also unidentified bottles of a clear liquid that I thought was water, but after taking a mouthful realized it has a burning action in my throat that takes my breath away. I believe it's the poteen. There are also a few bottles of whiskey and brandy with little glasses by them. From the kitchen we can smell the aromas of boiled corned meat, roast beef, roast ham and roast chicken, and roasting potatoes. Missus Kearney is busy preparing the food, with a couple of helpers. Missus Connor has her best china and polished silverware on display on the grand dining table. We all sit at the table and Missus Kearney and the two young lasses pass the food around. The wedding cake is taken away after Niall and I cut it together. I'm told that the top tier is reserved for our first child. We finish our meal with a small sample of the wedding cake, which is a whiskey fruitcake. After that Mister Connor rises up and says,

'God brought us our little girl, Kathleen. We love her and hereby give every blessing in her new life with Niall.'

Ned then gives a talk, complimenting the bridesmaid and those who helped to make this day possible. He tells us all about Niall's excellent character traits, which I know already. Next the table is cleared and made smaller, then pushed into a corner. Niall puts on the record player and we all jump around dancing. It's a grand day altogether. I end up dancing with all the men at the wedding, including Father Buckley, who is very lively after a wee drop. I'm nearly 'bunched' by the time evening comes.

...

The Connor's have given us the 'guest room', a room outside the kitchen and to the left. It's got its own entry, like a little house in itself, but it's just one big room. It has a little table and a jug and bowl for us to wash in. Mister Connor has also placed an old enamel bathtub in the middle of the floor, which we can fill up and have a bath together! Everything is heavenly. The bed has a soft mattress bursting with feathers. Niall and I just feel like staying here forever, our skin touching each other, being 'one flesh' in obedience to what the priest said at the marriage, and then he glared at us with his red eyes. I go red meself when I think of it, but when I'm with Niall it feels like it was meant to be and we don't feel like beetroots at all. I'm thinking this is what heaven must be like.

...

Two days after the wedding, Mister and Missus Connor look really downcast as they sit in front of their laid out bacon, eggs, black pudding, sausages, tomatoes and fried bread. The food is on the kitchen table, next to the radio. They turn the volume down as Niall and I arrive. Niall gives me a quick kiss just before we walk in the door. He squeezes my hand in his. I give him a special smile. My heart is overjoyed with love for this wonderful man. Nothing will ever change that.

'What's the matter?' Niall asks Mister and Missus Connor. 'You look as though someone's died.'

Missus Connor stares at Niall. 'How did you know?'

'Know what?'

'Someone's died.'

'So, who's died then?' Niall picks up his fork and plunges it into a plump sausage.

'Not Finn McCool?' I ask stopping my bread buttering action.

'Not Finn McCool! It's Father Buckley!'

'Thank God,' I say spontaneously. 'Sorry, I mean...'

'Good God! What happened?' Niall asks.

'He's dead!' Mister Connor advises sombrely.

'But, he was dancing with me a couple of days ago. He was a good dancer and all!' I exclaim. I notice I have dropped my butter knife.

'He's dancing with the angels now,' Missus Connor says, shaking salt vigorously over her eggs. 'He was a grand old priest.'

'So, when did this happen?'

'Some time through the night! He was found in his bed this morning. He was supposed to take the morning Mass and the new young curate; what's his name? Father Oglvie I think. Well, he found him still in his bed. Stone cold dead! We heard it just a few minutes ago on the radio. Well, may God rest his soul. Would you like a cup of tea?' Missus Connor picks up the teapot, which is covered in a colourful blue and red tea cosy with black eyes each side of the spout.

'Thank you, that'd be grand.'

'We'll have to go the wake, then the funeral Mass at Lisdoonvarna on Friday. So, we'll leave the both of you to look after the place for a few days. Did you ask Ned to come over on Friday, Tom?'

'Yesterday he said he might see me on Friday, and then he said he mightn't.'

'Right: well, if he does come, make him a bit of lunch, Kathleen Mary. Will you do that for me Alanna?'

'I will,' I reply, wondering how many more names I have. Niall and I eat our breakfast in silence after that. We just don't know what else to say.

Chapter four

Two weeks after our wedding, I am being persuaded by Niall to climb on Finn McCool, and have a ride. I feel excited but fearful at the same time. Anyway, I'm finally sitting upright in the saddle and my fear is gone. Sure Niall can persuade me to do anything!

'It feels grand. I love it!'

'I knew you would.' Niall is smiling and his eyes are like stars.

Niamh on Finn McCool for the first time©marieseltenrych, 2010

Suddenly, Toby the dog comes running after the ginger cat and they come right up to Finn Mc Cool's front legs. He makes a neighing sound and leaps into the air. I fly through the sky and land in the mud.

'Kathleen.' Niall shouts my name. The sound is far away for a minute, and then I can hear him all right again.

'I'm all right.' He's lifting me up, very gently, cursing the dog and the cat at the same time, and apologizing profusely to me. He's taking me inside and laying me on the bed. My head aches. That night I wake up, screaming. I can see monsters coming to take me away again. One face belongs to someone I remember! I know who the monsters are! I remember who I am. I scream. Niall wakes up.

'I'm not a famous pampered dancer living in a tower. I'm a..., they call us..., Tinceard...! Oh, Niall, why would you want to be married to me?'

'Sure, I'm totally in love with you, Kathleen. I don't care about all that class distinction stuff. You're the most wonderful girl I've ever met, and the most gorgeous! The important thing is: can you remember your name then?'

'Niamh: that's my name: Niamh Murphy.' He is holding me tightly and I'm pouring out the things I remember and relating my dream to him. 'What would the Connors say if they knew I was a tinceard?'

'Don't worry; I won't say one word to them! This is between you and me and God! Whether you're Kathleen or Niamh, you'll always be a famous dancer, and my queen. Begorrah, we'll get away from this place. Listen to me now Kathleen Niamh!' Somehow he makes me look into his face. He kisses my forehead and continues, 'I have a bit of money in the bank. Just let me sort out a few things, and then we'll go far away from here. We'll just ride off into the sunset.' My crying and trembling stop as I lie in Niall's comforting arms the rest of the night.

'Niamh Kathleen,' I hear my name and struggle to open my eyes. Niall's face is close to mine. 'My one true love, do you mind if I move my arm.'

'I'm sorry!' I raise my head.

'It's as stiff as a dead cat,' he moans.

'Oh Niall, I'm sorry. Are you all right?'

'It's going all pins and needles, so it must be still alive.' He turns to me, rubbing his strong, hairy, arm. 'But you're worth having pins and needles for any time.' He kisses me softly on the forehead again. I throw my arms around his neck and we indulge in a very passionate kiss. For a long moment we lose ourselves in each other. After a while we both need to breathe again. I can't help smiling.

'I feel better, much better..; after that terrible dream; Niall, don't ever stop kissing me like that!'

'Don't worry, if I live to be a hundred I'll always kiss you like that. Niamh Kathleen, I think everything is going to be grand.' His lips find mine once more.

...

Later that day, I'm busy in the kitchen, rolling pastry for Missus Connor. She's just gone outside to sharpen a knife on a stone. We're making apple pies. Niall comes in and speaks quietly in case Missus Connor hurries in unexpectedly.

'Listen, Niamh, Tom wants me to go up to Dublin with him. He's got a good tip on a fine racing horse. He wants my advice. While I'm up that way, I'll get the money.' He gently squeezes my shoulders.

'Oh Niall, please don't leave me.' I grab his arm. He holds me tightly and flour is going all over his shirt. He's kissing my forehead and hair.

'We'll be back in less than a week; I'll make some arrangements while I'm in Dublin.'

'Take me to Dublin with you.'

'I will. We'll go there and be happy ever after. Right now, you have to stay here. Missus Connor will be good company for you. I'll be back in no time at all.'

'Take me now, please!'

'I wish I could, but I can't! I promise I will take you there in a week or two!'

'All right then. Remember, you promised!' A thought flies through my mind right then. *'What must be must be.* My Aunty Maura used to say that! I can remember so much. Oh, Niall.'

'Your Aunty is right. I'll come back to you. I will, cross my heart and hope to die. We'll dance all night in Dublin, that's a promise!'

'Oh, Niall, I keep getting horrible visions, even during the daytime now! I can see my drunken father, falling over me in a shed. Then my Aunty Maura is having a stand up fight with him, banging him with a brass pot or a stick to stop him doing something bad...' I gulp for air between my words and tears.

'Now, now; 'tis going to be all right; these thoughts will go away; they're only in your mind.'

'I can't bear them. I can see Maeve and me huddled together. We're frightened to death by the cursing and swearing of my da...'

'It must have been terrible for you. But you're safe with me now. I'm your very own man; your husband.'

'Hold me Niall.'

'It's all right.' I keep talking as I lean into his breast.

'I am always shivering and hungry in my visions. I can see myself going from door to door asking for a bit of bread and my stomach turning itself into knots with the growling and groaning. I hate the life I had and now I want to keep the life I've found. You know something, Niall?' I look up into his concerned face.

'What?'

'I wish I never got my memory back. But then, I'm glad because now we'll get away from this place forever.'

'We will, we will. I promise: if it's the last thing I do, I'll take you away from here.' He bends his mouth to mine and we indulge ourselves in a long passionate kiss...

'A hem..., well now, I think Tom is getting anxious to be off...' Missus Connor tries to be discrete as she comes in the door. We pull our lips apart from each other. My mouth tingles from the passion of Niall's kiss.

'Sorry Missus Connor. I'll be off.' I smile at my beloved Niall as he shyly lowers his red face and hurries off. He turns and looks into my face once more as he exits, his eyes betraying the deep passion in his heart. In that instance it seems that our hearts leap from our bosoms and fuse together. Suddenly, he's gone, leaving me with only an ache where my heart used to be!

...

Niall and Tom Connor have been away for two days now and I'm kept right busy with all the extra work around the place. Each night I'm waking up in a sweat, my da's face in front of me; him with a pitch fork in one hand and a bottle of the drink in the other. He always says, 'You need to be wedded now.' His face comes right up to mine. His face is cut and blood drops onto me. His eyes are red as though they've been roasted in the fire. His teeth are clenched and coloured brown. His face is imprinted with blue and red lines, like streaks of lightening zigzagging across his cheeks and nose. His nose is red and huge, like it's a Christmas light. Long whiskers poke out of his nostrils, which move in and out like a bellowing bull. Spittle drools from the sides of his lips. His tongue is green and red and has lumps on it. He holds the huge rusty fork in his rough hands. The long prongs of the fork are held against my neck. I wake up at this point, trying to scream, but I can't because of the prongs on my neck. My forehead is always dripping and my heart is nearly leaping out of my bosom with fear. Through the day I repeat what Niall said, 'Everything is going to be fine!' After that I feel better.

'Kathleen; I need to go into town today.' Missus Connor

announces as we sit down for breakfast at seven on the morning of Wednesday 13th September. Her words bring a strangling fear to my chest.

'Why so?'

'I want to get a bit of wool,' she says slowly, looking away. 'I've got nary a bit left. I think we might be needin' some little garments in the not too distant future, the way you and Niall are, well, carrying on.' She looks sheepishly at me. I stare. What on earth does she mean? I'm thinking. Suddenly my face feels hot. I bury my head and stare at my sausages, black pudding, fried eggs, tomato and bacon. My stomach heaves by just seeing the food.

'You don't mean a babby!'

'Well, you never know. I'm very hopeful. I've never been a grandmother. I think it would suit me fine.'

She's very hopeful! What about me? I never even thought of such a thing happening until this minute. 'Excuse me...' Before I take a mouthful of food I feel so sick I have to run outside.

By nine o'clock she is all spruced up in her best jacket, her light grey; the one she wore at our wedding, with her dark grey pleated skirt and light grey hat with flowers on the brim. She even has stockings on. She's wearing her deep pink, double frill blouse, which gives her an enormous bust. Her lips are bright red. She looks really strange climbing into the old rusty truck. Toby leaps up beside her before we can stop him. She tries to shoo him away, but he is stuck to the seat and won't budge. He whines and looks sad.

'He can come for a spin,' she says. 'You're all right now?'

'I'm fine thanks,' I reply, smiling as brightly as I can. 'I think I just overate.'

'Sure you need to keep your strength up. You take care of the place now, won't you Kathleen, mo vhoirneen? The fowl need feeding and the pigsty needs a bit of a wash down. Keep yourself busy. Idle hands are the devil's work.'*

'Yes, Mam.' I'm keeping very busy cleaning up the kitchen, feeding Ginger the cat, and the chickens; I'm filling a bucket with water and carrying it across to the pig sty. I wish they put the pump a bit nearer the pen. I don't particularly like the pigs, but they remind me of my pig book, so I put up with their honking. I am not sure how to clean their home with them in it. Tom or Niall, and sometimes Ned do this job. Maybe, I'm thinking, I should take the pigs out and put them on the grass, and then put them back in. But what if they run away? My thoughts are interrupted by the sound of voices.

'Thank God,' I say aloud. I look up hopefully, expecting to see Niall and Mister Connor coming back early; but there before my eyes I see a band of men, yelling and howling. I remember my nightmares, and then I'm making a run for it. I can see me da. He's lagging behind the front-runners. I can see his grey jacket flapping in the breeze. He's got some weapon in his hand, a pitchfork! I'm looking for a place to hide. I jump over the pigsty wall in one leap. The pigs are a bit startled and back off as I crouch down behind them. They stink and make noises like sirens and I tell them to *shush*. I'm grabbing one of them and trying to hold it in front of me, but he's making a terrible screaming sound. I'm letting him go; lying as low to the ground as I can. He's burying his snout in the ground and sticking his curly tail in my face. *Niall, Niall,* my heart is crying out. The next thing I know, Jack Sullivan is peering over the pigsty wall.

12th September, 1968, 6:00 P.M.

It's some time later and I'm fully awake! I'm on the cold floor, in the little van where the four women dumped me. There's a horrible cold draught rushing at my face from beneath the van. It's getting dark, so I must have dozed for a number of hours. I curl up to try to stop the shivers going through me. There's a gap of about an inch under the door, and I can see a bit of light under it, but any cockroach can come walking in. I close my eyes, as I'm still feeling too tired to care if a thousand cockroaches come and crawl all over me. I shiver at that thought. I wish this was a nightmare, but I know it's not because the pain in my leg is fierce. I can hear someone banging on the door of the van.

'Oh God, let it be Niall, please.' Then the door bursts open! It's Nell Doran and my step-sister, Maeve.

'Maeve, Nell, thank God you're here. I think my leg's broken.'

'Serves you right, running off like that!' Nell says, tut tutting beside me with her hands on her hips. She's swaying back and forth. She smells like a brewery. I'm holding my nose.

'You stink!'

'Pig! You stink yourself!' She almost falls on top of me.

'You've caused more than enough trouble Niamh. I'll go and get something.' Maeve rushes off, leaving Nell and me. We stare at each other for a time.

'So, are you going to run away again? Going back to your pigs, or your buccal?'

'What do you mean: my buccal?' Maeve rushes back in the door, carrying an elastic half stocking in her hand.

'I found this. It's Mam's, for the varicose veins. She doesn't use it. Here, put it on. It might help a bit.' She pulls the thing over my foot and proceeds to yank it up over my leg. 'Where's it broke?'

'Ouch. Easy on. The pain…, it's everywhere. I think it's near my ankle, maybe about there.' I point to an area, which is sore to touch just above my ankle. I'm on the verge of screaming as she pulls the stocking over the area. I have to hang on to her arm to keep myself sitting up and not to faint.

'You always were such a baby! I'm doing my best for you, and you're just ungrateful!'

'I know. I'm sorry for complaining Maeve,' I reply.

'I can get you something for the pain,' Nell says, swaying and peering at my leg.

'What?'

'My secret recipe; I'll be back.' Off she stumbles through the door, disappearing into the darkness. She returns a few minutes later with something wrapped in newspaper. When she unfolds the layers of newspaper, there's a tiny amount of green powder sitting in the middle of the large page.

'Try some.' She pinches a little with her finger and puts it on her tongue.

'I don't know Nell. It might kill me!'

'It didn't kill me; herbal remedy.' She pops her eyes wide open at this remark.

'All right.' I pinch a little between my thumb and forefinger and place it on my tongue. It tastes bitter, but bearable, like a piece of lemon skin.

'Have a bit more,' Nell coaxes. I take another pinch. I can still feel the pain in my leg. It has become a throbbing, low, burning sensation.

'Give it a bit of time. Now we want you to come for a bit of craic, mo chaileen ban.'

'What's the occasion?' Nell turns to stare at me, her eyebrows raised.

'We've decided to celebrate your homecoming. You've come back from the dead to us.' Nell explains in her 'mystic' voice.

'From the dead?' I ask.

'That's right, Niamh. We thought you had drowned. Someone found one of the shoes you wore to my wedding,' Maeve informs me in a low voice.

'So, if you thought I had drowned how did you know I was alive?' Maeve moves away a pace.

'It's a long story. Come on; everyone is waiting for us.'

'Give us a hand up, then.' Maeve and Nell come on either side of me and we hobble and wobble as we make our way down the step of the van and move slowly towards the campfire.

I can see the flames flickering in the dark night, and hear the rumble of voices as we come closer. A few people call out to me. 'Y'are back?' 'There you are!' 'You're looking great!' I try to smile, but I just don't feel I belong here any longer. About twenty people are sitting around the fire, roasting chestnuts. They smell good enough to eat! I realise I am very hungry. We sit down and Maeve hands me a stick with a chestnut on it. I lean forward and put it into the bright flame.

'She's back. Our queen is back.' Jack Sullivan's sarcastic voice rises up in the darkness near me.

'Treason!' someone else shouts and throws a chestnut at me, laughing. It hits me on the arm.

'Witch,' another voice shouts and suddenly I am being bombarded with chestnuts and other stuff.

'Deserter,' someone else shouts. A number of voices rise up in reply, 'Deserter, not good enough for you now!' A barrage of stones and chestnuts are hurled at me. Maeve and I cover our heads with our arms.

'Get her, lads!' Suddenly, two lads take my arm and drag me away from Maeve, towards the fire.

'Stop, it's too hot.'

'You'll burn in hell. Get a taste now.' It is Jack again, and his drunken friend, Seamus Creen. I heard some lad shouting from the shadows.

'Burn her, she's a witch!' I can feel the heat of the fire on my feet and face. They push me closer to the fire, and then stop. I recognise Nell's sneering voice, shouting,

'She's a traitor. Queen!' Mixed voices shout,

'Burn her. Burn the Queen!' I turn around and see the group coming closer and closer, shuffling their feet as they draw near. They draw close to one side of me. The fire is on the other side.

'Oh, God, help!' I'm crying. A spark flies out and hits me on my skirt, singing a small black hole. I quickly brush it away.

'Put more wood on the fire,' someone shouts. The flames lick close to my legs. Someone starts pushing me by the shoulders. I fall to the ground, holding on to the grass to stop myself being pushed right into the fire.

'Help me. Somebody, help me,' I scream as a spark strikes my hair and I can smell the burning lock. I can see the feet of the crowd getting closer, and they shuffle a jig in unison and cry out,

'Burn her!' Ara go on, we're only joking. Ara go on, go on, go on, we're pulling your leg.' Someone throws a half burned stick, which ignites my skirt for a second. I stamp it out with my hand.

'You're all mad!' Suddenly I feel a great anger rising up in me. 'Get away. Get away or I'll put a curse on the lot of you,' I hiss. I begin to rise up, kneeling on my right knee, the bad leg, and placing my left foot in front of me. They stop moving.

'She's cursed,' Nell yells, pointing at me. The crowd scurries towards me once more. I pick up the half burned stick and stand up on both legs. I glare at the crowd, waving the burning stick towards them. The backs of my legs and bottom feel like they're being singed.

'She's just like her mother.' The voice is Nell's.

'Stop it, the lot of you!' a voice roars loudly behind the crowd.

It's my father! 'She's my girleen. Leave her alone or you'll get no more drink...' Instantly, the crowd is breaking into two groups, one on either side, leaving him a clear walkway. Maeve rushes to me.

Picture of Niamh being threatened by fire because she betrayed her clan: 12th September, 1968.
© Marie Seltenrych, 2010

'Egit, be quick, here's your chance; get out.'
'Get a new queen,' Maeve shouts: 'Nell!' A voice calls out 'Nell is our queen.'
'I'd be proud to be your queen,' Nell's voice roars. 'I'm very obliged to you all.' The crowd shouts,

'Let's drink to Nell.'

Maeve and I head through the break in the crowd towards me da. He's coming towards us. The crowd closes in as we move through. Father places his hands on my shoulders and the feeling of total relief sweeps over me. I cling onto him as the three of us stumble back to Maeve and Paid's van.

'I'll get something to cover the sofa. I don't want you marking it with all that black stuff,' she says, hurrying into the adjacent room and bringing out a white sheet. She throws this over her bright yellow sofa, with purple dancing flowers, her pride and joy. We sit down.

'Where's Paid?' I ask.

'Why do you want to know that?' I shrug my shoulders, 'Why shouldn't I; sure I like Paid.'

'I know that right well. But I'll warn you now, keep your hands off him!'

'What?' I ask wondering what she's getting at.

'Nothing! Don't worry! He's working hard if you must know! He's in county Mayo, helping with fencing a very big farm property.'

My teeth are suddenly chattering. Maeve immediately seems concerned for me.

'You look like death warmed up. Did you burn yourself?'

'I'm not sure. My foot...' I say, pulling my black left foot up for inspection.

'Ax; it's only soot. Sure I think I got more singes than that.' She gets up. 'I'll put the kettle on and we can have a nice cup of tea.' My da just sits, silently.

'Thanks da. You saved my life then!'

'Don't worry about it...' Now that I have got his attention, I ask him

'Why did you bring me back da?' Da furls his lip under. He looks at Maeve.

'He wants you to be wed,' Maeve says, as she finishes

pouring the tea. The words to explain that I am already married are stuck in me

'Maeve's right. Sure now he's a fine fellow, from a grand family.' Da smacks his lips to show his satisfaction.

'What about my choice?'

'Your mother and I know what's best for you...'

'My mother's dead,' I retort. He stares at me with red eyes.

'I loved your mother too! Your Aunty Maura has been more than a mother to you since she died. God damn it girl, but you're an ungrateful wench.' He suddenly rises and marches out the door.

'What about your tea?' Maeve calls after him. I stare at the door rocking back and forth in the breeze.

'Don't just watch it; shut the bloody door, Niamh!' I feel too numb with fear to move.

'I'll do it myself.' She rushes over and bolts the door. 'Nobody can break in now!' She hands me a cup of tea in her best cup, sitting on a saucer that doesn't quite match.

'It's lovely Maeve; just the way I like it, hot and sweet.'

'Sure I've always spoiled you rotten.' A few moments later, I ask a question.

'Maeve, why did they try to burn me?'

'Take no notice of them at all. They just got carried away. They've been drinking the poteen since this morning! They won't even remember it tomorrow.' She stares at me. 'Do you think I enjoyed it? Look at me arms!' she says, showing me a red patch. 'I got burned too you know.'

'I know,' I reply. We're silent for a minute. 'What's this about me getting married?'

'You're safer being married. At least you'll have a husband to protect you.'

'I am married!'

'Ah, go on, you're pulling my leg. Sure you've only been gone just over three months.'

'I can prove it,' I say. I pull the ring from my drawers. I tell her about Niall and me and our secret marriage. She stares at me as I relate the whole story.

'If you value your life, don't say one word about this to Sean.'

'I have to, Maeve?' She comes close to my face.

'You aren't married at all!' she says viciously. 'You can't get married if you don't know who you bloody well are!' She stares at me. 'Now, you made me swear!'

'I'm sorry Maeve, but Niall loves me. We're going to run away...'

'It's no use running away all your life. Da's made a grand match for you now. You belong with your own kind. Once you've been back with your family Niall won't want you any more, you know that, don't you? The country people are all like that. Sure if Niall and Sean ever met, there'd be fireworks all right. Your da can kill a full-grown sheep with his bare hands. Niall would be like putty in his hands.'

'Niall is very strong too, and he loves me.'

'And your new husband will love you.' She speaks more softly to me now. 'Listen to me Niamh, for I know what's best for you. Just obey your father, that's the fourth commandment; everything will work out just grand. Not another word about this now; all right? Niall is better off with his own kind, someone educated! Get him out of your mutton head.'

I'm shaking all over with fear and confusion. Her words sound right, but I know that I love Niall and he loves me. But reason tells me that I have to get him out of my head, for his sake as well as mine. She's right, Niall is better off with someone educated, not a muttonhead like me! She hands me one of Paid's handkerchiefs.

'Blow your nose. There now. Let the rivers run dry.' I stick my nose in the hanky and blow hard.

'That's settled then. Promise you'll not run away again?'

'I promise.'

'Would you like a biscuit with your cup of tea?' Maeve takes a small tin out of the cupboard. She opens it and hands it to me. 'They're only wheat-meal. Do you want a bit of oid on them?'

'No thanks Maeve. I've been feeling sick at the sight of butter lately.'

'You'll feel better, axaram! Go on, have one biscuit; go on!'

'Tomorrow never comes, Maeve!' I accept one of her biscuits. My love for Niall is pressed deep into my heart, even if my mind forgets him, which doesn't seem possible right now. I bite into the biscuit as I'm thinking of him. I nearly bite my finger. 'Ah!' Maeve is keen to change the topic now.

'This reminds me of when we were small, and I saved that chocolate wheaten biscuit until we went to bed.'

'I remember,' I reply. 'You kept it in your drawers and it melted.' I suck my sore finger for a moment.

'We ate it anyway.'

We sit silently together. In the background we can hear a bit of yelling and laughter at the campfire. I shiver. I never want to sit at a campfire again after tonight. I crunch on the wheat-meal biscuit, and try not to think of Niall.

'You give yourself a bit of analken, and get some rest.' She places a little basin of hot water on the chair in front of me. 'Everything will be all right in the morning, you'll see. Goodnight, sleep tight, don't let the fleas bite,' she says lightly. She pulls a curtain across, behind which lies her and Paid's bedroom. A moment later, she emerges holding a green and brown tartan woolen blanket. 'I'll let you have me best spare blanket. But make sure you wash yourself before you soil it.' She folds it and places it on the sofa.

'Thanks Maeve!'

...

After I turn the clean water into a black mess, I feel too fearful to throw it out the door. I can't stand on me leg, so I hop to the little table and leave the basin with the black water and the now blackened soap there. I lie on her couch until morning, glad to be alive and clean. Even my bad leg doesn't seem so bad now. Even though I said I would forget Niall, I'm thinking of him all night long. He's going to think I ran away again, and Mister and Missus Connor will think the same thing? I can't go back and tell them I was taken from them, because then the Connors will know I'm a tinceard and they won't want me then. Now, I'm wondering what Nell insinuated when she said, 'Just like her mother?' Nobody ever told me why she died. I thought it was the consumption, but now I'm wondering about the truth of that. It's almost dawn when I pull the soft blanket over my head and drift into a restless sleep. I awake shortly after, thinking the bed is on fire.

Every day I long to run back to the Connors, but my head tells me that will only bring more trouble on everyone, including Niall. My leg is too painful to walk on, let alone run anywhere. The women have been visiting me, talking excitedly about my forthcoming marriage. You'd think they were all getting married, not me.

'God has let you have a broken leg so you can't run off this time,' Nell says, laughing as she passes by the van a week after I was brought back.

'It's not broken. It's sprained!' I retort.

'He's dead you know, R.I.P,' she says through the window.

'Who?'

'Buccal deas, fell off a horse. Slean leat!'

Later that evening I question Maeve. 'Nell talked about someone falling off a horse?' I say. 'Do you know anything?'

'Don't take any notice of Nell. She's raving mad, you know that!'

'She might be, but still, where there's smoke, there's fire. Did someone get killed around here?'

'Maybe.'

'Who? When? Where?'

Maeve is fussing over a petticoat she's hand-sewing, and doesn't even look up. 'God, you're full of questions. I don't know who he was. All I know is that a man fell off a horse near Bealanbrack River and they thought he was killed.'

'Maeve, it might have been Niall.'

'Sure I told you to get that name out of your mind. It was probably a stranger in these parts.'

'What if it was Niall?'

'Niamh, I won't tell you again, I don't know! I just heard it from Jack and Sean.'

'Niall is a great rider. He wouldn't fall off Finn McCool. Tell me it wasn't him, please Maeve.'

'God, you get on me goat! I have to go and see Mary.' Maeve folds her petticoat up, stuffs it in a crocheted bag and leaves.

I know it was Niall; otherwise they'd say who it was. I feel suddenly faint. I lie down on Maeve's couch and close my eyes. The hope of ever seeing Niall again fades in my heart.

Jim and Niamh, 26th September 1968

...

On Thursday, 26th September, nineteen hundred and sixty eight, just two weeks after I was brought back to the camp, I find myself standing on my painful leg, wearing the dress Maeve wore on her wedding day, in the same place that Maeve and Paid were wedded, near McCarthy's barn. This is where I'll meet my new husband. Maeve is my matron of honour. She looks great in a lime green coloured dress down to her ankles and a halo of the last of the wild roses on her head. She's got two wild roses tied together with lime green ribbon in her hands. The same wild roses are made into a little bunch and I'm carrying them. The blustering winds of autumn have arrived; blowing our lovely flowers away. Maeve bends over behind her posy, and whispers, 'Would you look at the get-up of him.'

I see Rhonan standing proudly, all spruced up in a suit. He's got a black suit and brown shoes and a red bowtie. His hair is slicked down with pig fat. He's grinning from ear to ear. His teeth are not black; they're not there at all. He's gummy!

'What happened to his teeth?'

'He had a fight. I think it was over you!' Maeve whispers back.

'Oh God,' I moan.

'But he didn't win!' she adds. Just at that moment, from the corner of my eye I see a young man coming out from behind the barn.

'He was having a piddle,' I hear Nora, my bridesmaid, whispering to me from the other side. She giggles. I am so relieved I almost drop my bouquet. I'm viewing him through the misty outlook of this veil.

'It's him!' Maeve says excitedly.

'Who?' I ask.

'Your man!'

I hold the veil still as I take a good look. He's quite tall, with sandy coloured hair and a tanned face, which has a flush of pink on it as he walks towards the wedding party. He's grinning from ear to ear. He seems to have all his teeth in place. It's Jimmy Farrell! I remember him from a few years ago when he did some work in these parts. A shiver suddenly creeps over my neck and arms.

'Are you cold?' Maeve asks.

'A bit,' I whisper back.

'You'll soon be Missus Farrell, and then he'll warm you up.

He's a fiery one that fellow,' she whispers.

My hands suddenly feel clammy. 'You make my blood boil!' I whisper back.

'You're warming up then?' she says cynically. I glare at her through my veil, but she looks straight ahead.

...

I'm now going through the ritual with the same priest officiating as Maeve had, Father Seamus O'Reilly. He talks so fast and low that I don't know what he's saying at all. I catch words like: worse; poorer; sickness; death; and then I'm repeating something after him. My voice seeming to speed up, saying, 'I do,' at one stage, as though we are all in a hurry to catch a bus. I'm nearly saying 'I don't, but he interrupts at I do. Even as I say the words, I look around, wondering if Niall will come back alive from heaven itself and gallop through the throng on Finn McCool. We could fly away to Dublin. That would be grand!

Now I'm getting a lovely bright gold ring on my finger. I never saw such a ring in my life before. It's very wide and made of very shiny dark gold. I can hardly believe that this is my second wedding ring, and my sixteenth birthday is not until the thirty-first of October. Everything is going according to plan and the next thing I know, I'm Missus Farrell. I don't know how to write the name Niamh Farrell, and I realize that I have never learned how to write! Niall did teach me how to write 'Kathleen Connor'.

'Put an X there,' the priest shouts and points to the spot where my name is written as *Niamh Murphy*. I just sign an X there. Jim does the same with his name. So, there we are, mister and missus X.

'It's a grand ring,' I tell Jim a little while later when we get a chance to say a few words to each other.

'I made it myself. I'm pleased you like it. The gold is very soft, so you'll have to take good care of it.' He looks into my eyes. 'I know you will,' he says quietly, giving me a kiss on my lips. I let him kiss me for a moment; I gently ease myself away.

'So', I ask, 'where did you get such grand gold?'

'Niamh, I can't tell you that; it's my own business.' He holds me tightly by the shoulders and stares into my face. I gasp as his hazel coloured eyes meet mine. His eyes are reflecting the fire the lads have lit to cook the meat and to keep us warm. 'I don't ever want you to question what I do. I don't want you to be one of those nosey, stupid women with nothin' in their heads but wild stories. You're my wife and you have to obey me, or else. Do you hear me now?' A cold fear creeps over my skin.

'I do. Whatever you want. Let me go, you're hurting me!'

'Sorry!' He lets his grip go. 'You seem cold. Come over to the fire,' he says more gently. I follow him to the bon fire.

Jim is very devoted to me for the first month or so as I've been feeling sick nearly every day. He brings me lovely flowers, which he picks on his way home from work. Sometimes they look more like flowers from someone's garden, or even, God help us, from the graveyard, but I never say a word about that! I'm trying to respond to him as a wife but my heart is not in it. I feel like I'm just doing my duty as a wife. I think I know more about the bedtime things than he does, but I can't let on, or he'll find out I've been married before! I try to act like an egit, which suits him, as it makes him think he's better at husband and wife things than me. Winter is nigh, and it's freezing cold here in the west.

...

Jim has a job as a labourer with the local county council, mainly doing roadwork. He has a trade of making pots and pans, but there's not enough money in that to keep the clothes on our backs and food on the table. One night he comes home looking happier than usual. After we have eaten our simple stew comprising boiled potatoes, leeks, bacon and parsnips, he sits down beside me.

'You're looking happy!' I say, being careful not to ask him why.

'I am. I've got the most beautiful wife in the world, and a good job. What more could I want?'

'A child?'

'A child of my own.' He bends over and kisses me gently. The next thing I know, he's carrying me into our small bed. I try to enjoy his rough lovemaking by closing my eyes and remembering Niall. Jim seems to be enjoying it anyway, and doesn't even notice my eyes are closed the whole time. Afterwards, we lay there. My eyes are opened now and we're staring at the brown stained ceiling of the van.

'Did I ever tell you about my father?' he asks, turning to me. The light falling on his face gives him a chiseled, almost handsome look. Some would call him a 'fine fellow'. Maybe I'll get to love him one day, when this ache for Niall goes away from my heart.

'I heard he was a great one for the pots and pans. A real artist and all!'

'He was that.'

'He also was a great 'poteen' maker. I think it killed him in the end.' He pauses.

'Go on!' I urge him.

'It's true. Do you know what happened when he died?' 'No, what happened?'

Jim sits up and leans on his elbow. He runs his finger down my cheekbone as he tells me the story of his da's demise. 'The people who touched him after he died had a drunken party on the spot, without drinking a drop.'

'Go on!'

'Tis true! They say the smell off him was so intoxicating that the priest fell into the hole in the ground when they went to bury him.'

'Was it Father Buckley?'

'Don't interrupt me, Niamh. The name of the priest doesn't

matter. The important thing is that it was a priest. Now I don't know where I was.' Those flames of fire suddenly flicker in his eyes again. A fear creeps over me, just like before.

'I'm sorry. They went to bury him ' He relaxes and the fire in his eyes is snuffed out.

'Right, that's so. They went to bury him, and the priest fell in the hole. They tried to haul the priest out. He was laughing so much that the people hauling him fell in too, and were laughing at the bottom of the grave for hours. In the end they had to throw buckets of cold water on top of them to sober 'em up; and then they all nearly drowned.' It sounded like an exaggeration to me.

'Yerra, go on!'

'It's as true as the nose on your face.' Jim smiles and the corners of his mouth make these deep creases in his face. His hair tumbles forward, giving him an impish look, like a leprechaun, I think. I smile at my own thoughts.

'You're full of the Blarney,' I exclaim laughing.

'I'm just like me da, that's what!' he says. He lies on his back and stares at the ceiling. 'He was a good man... C'me here to me.' He pulls me close with his strong right arm. My head lies comfortably in the nook of his armpit, near his almost hairless chest. We lie huddled together all night long. Through the night I wake up in the middle of a dream. Niall is so real in my dream. He's smiling at me.

'Niall,' I'm calling his name when I wake up. I'm still lying on Jim's chest, so I try to move away by gently lifting his arm. Jim suddenly sits up, giving me a shocking fright.

'Who's Niall?' He shouts, shaking me by the shoulders.

'Nobody. It was just a dream.' His voice rises with anger.

'Why did you call him?' I start to tremble with fright.

'I don't know why!'

'Why are you so frightened? You're hiding something!'

'No I'm not!' I reply.

'Niamh, I know you well. You have to tell me who he is.' He suddenly drops his voice and says threateningly, 'or I'll kill you.'

'All right; if you must know.' My mouth feels dry. 'I used to play with him when I was a child.'

'Where is he now?' he asks quietly. I shrug my shoulders. 'He died!' I say quickly. At least that's true, I'm thinking. He sits up and his form looks fearful in the moonlight. 'I can't remember a Niall around these parts...' I feel very cold all over as I try to calm him down.

'You didn't live around here back then. I think it was a nick name.' There's silence for a moment. Jim gets out of bed and stands. I can see his silhouette in the light.

'You wouldn't lie to me, would you?' I swallow before I speak. My breath is shallow.

'No,' I whisper. He leans towards me.

'Niamh; I'm your husband; you can't lie to me.' He takes my wrists and pulls me up to him. I know that he's too strong for me to resist.

'I know that!' I reply. He throws me onto the bed. He looks at me, and then suddenly falls on top of me.

'You're my woman!' He kisses me roughly, and then hits me in the face. 'Don't do the wrong thing by me, or else... Ah!' he says in a controlled voice. I curl up in a ball and hold my hands over my head. There's silence for a minute, then I feel a blast of cold wind as the van door opens. It creaks on its hinges. I breathe a sigh of relief as Jim stomps out the door.

...

It's three days after that incident. Maeve comes over that afternoon with an apple tart she baked in her new gas oven.

'What do you think about that?'

'Maeve, it looks delicious. Can I have a bit?'

'You and Jim can have it all. Happy birthday! And we want to give you this.' She hands me something in a red wrapper with a gold bow.

'What did you get me?' I ask, hurriedly removing the wrapping.

'Don't tear the paper. You can use it again,' she reminds me. I try to be careful not to tear the paper to bits.

'It's lovely. I haven't got one.'

'Paid made it himself,' she says happily.

'I'll go around and thank him later.' I stare at Maeve. 'Honestly, I forgot about my birthday.'

'Well I didn't. You're sixteen now, a real woman. But remember it's also Halloween!' She looks at me, smiling happily. 'Paid brought me this big bag of flour and a bag of crab apples and two pounds of sugar. I learned this great recipe and I wanted to try it out. Every tart was a success. Tell Jim to get an oven like mine, and then you can bake things for him. That'd put a smile on his face.'

'You've noticed then?'

'Noticed what?'

'Jim and me: we haven't been talking.'

'Well, now that you mention it, I have noticed Jim's not himself at the moment. What did you do now?' She sits down.

'Why do you think it's always me?'

'I know you, Niamh. You're a born troublemaker; what happened?'

'We had a falling out. He heard me calling Niall in my sleep.'

'No wonder he's down and out! Niamh, that fellow is well and truly gone by now! Stop bringing up his name and then you won't have trouble.'

'Maeve, I was asleep. I couldn't help it! I know Niall's dead.'

'Here you are, talking about him again.'

'I'm just telling you about my dream!'

'So; go on, what happened after that: after your

dream?'

'Jim won't speak to me now. It's like being a nun in a convent.'

She sniggers. 'Well, you'll never be a nun! Only in Saint Joseph's Order - two heads on one pillow.'

'It's serious Maeve. Ah, I don't know what to do.'

'You're his wife aren't you?'

'I am! So, how does that help?'

'Come on Niamh. You know!'

'No. I don't know!'

'And you think Rhonan is thick!' She shakes her head in despair. 'Be nice to him. Give him love!'

'You mean, sex!'

'Well, whatever vulgar name you want to call it. Matrimony is a sacred state! Just encourage him in your matrimonial duties!'

'So, what'll that do?'

'You'll see. Awast! You're sixteen - and you've been married a month now!'

'Maybe I can try.'

'It's your birthday. Give him the gift of yourself!' She places the tart on the small table and brushes flour from her skirt. 'I'm off now. Paid is coming home today, so I want to prepare myself for him.' She steps out the door.

'Thanks for the tart!'

She turns back. 'Awart; sure that's what sisters are for. Promise me you'll put Niall out of your head and comb your hair before Jim comes home!'

'I promise.' I immediately search for my hairbrush, and drag it through my knotty hair. I run a sticky bright red, broken lipstick over my lips. I found it on the road one day. I stare into the lovely mirror that Maeve has just given me for my birthday. I press my lips together, and decide I look like a bit of a tart! Maybe Jim will like that! I rummage in my clothes box and find a purple coloured blouse, which someone gave me. I pull it over my head. It's loose, with gathers around the neckline. My skin looks so white. The neckline is quite low, so I can see the tops of my breasts. 'I hate it!' I mumble and pull it off, over my head. I stop as I hear the door open.

'Jim.' I quickly pull the top back on.

'You're all dressed up and wearing lipstick. What for? Are you off somewhere?'

I force a smile. 'No! I just wanted to look nice for you. It's my birthday.'

'Niamh, you're beautiful without lipstick. Come here to me.'

He pulls me into his arms and kisses me so hard my lips are stinging.

'I'm trying to be a good wife...'

He's quite for a moment, and then speaks. 'Every man is jealous of me. I'm so worried about someone taking you away from me.'

'Nobody will do that!' I say instantly, remembering that Niall is dead!

'I'd kill them if they did!' he replies emotionally. 'Let me give you something special for your birthday,' he says, lifting me in his arms and taking me into our tiny bedroom to give me his love.

The next day, Maeve comes running over. 'Jim looked happy this morning. He was whistling on his way down the road.'

'I know. We're pals, arirt. Thanks for your good advice Maeve.'

'I told you it would work; 'twill be all right now!'

Chapter five

Tis about three months since Jim and I were wedded; we haven't had a row for a month.

'You're not still in bed, you lazy lump,' Maeve says, peering behind the curtain separating our small bedroom from the rest of the van. 'I made lovely fresh soda bread! What's up with you now?'

'I feel terrible,' I say, pulling myself into a sitting position.

She comes closer. 'You do look a bit pasty. When did this come on?'

'I've been feeling sick on and off for months!' I pause before saying that I think it's because I'm sick with longing for Niall. 'But this morning I collapsed in a heap while making Jim breakfast. He carried me back to bed and left me here.' I suddenly cough. 'I've probably got consumption. It's a slow death they say.'

'It's not an infection from your sore leg, is it?' Maeve asks, pulling down the blanket and lifting my nightie. 'It still looks a bit red and swollen.'

'It feels all right.' She pulls the blanket over me again.

'It's the low tops!' she says, sternly.

'You've probably caught a chill going around half naked.'

'How do you mean?'

'You know what I mean!' she says curtly. My face feels red.

'I only wear them when Jim's coming home!'

'I hope so!' she retorts. 'Will I make you a cup of tea?' she offers in a kinder tone. 'You can have a bit of soda bread as well.'

'I'll try.' She pulls the bedroom curtain over and moves to the kitchen table. I can hear her striking a match and lighting the primus stove. She pours water from a jug into the copper kettle and places it over the flame.

'Jim's asked Nell Doran to come and see what's up with me.' I call from the bedroom. As if she heard me, Nell's voice sounds in the doorway.

'The top of the morning to you!'

'Come in Nell,' Maeve says. 'I was just making a cup of tea. Would you like one?'

'I would, begorrah! It's chilly today!' She pulls the curtain on the bedroom over and stares at me lying on the bed. She walks back and forward in the tiny space, smacks her lips and mumbles something that sounds mysterious. She likes to think she has magical powers. 'I can see a tiny baby in the distance,' she says, with her eyes closed and her hands touching her forehead. She opens her eyes and stares at me, 'You're going to have a child, that's all.'

'I am?' Then she turns to Maeve, who is now standing behind her, holding the copper teapot that Jim made me.

'I'll let this draw for five minutes.' I'm sitting up, staring into the kitchen, happy.

'I'm going to have a babby Maeve!' Maeve nearly drops

the teapot.

'Glory be! I don't believe it!' Nell speaks to Maeve,

'So, Maeve, have you been feeling all right?'

'I have. I'm feeling on top of the world.'

'You're going to have a child too!'

'Is that right? Are you sure now,' Maeve questions, taking a couple of cups off the dresser, and pouring the tea. 'Sugar and milk?'

'That's right. Two lumps, maybe three!' Nell replies, sitting down on a rickety wooden chair that Jim is going to fix.

'Would you like a piece of my freshly made soda bread, Nell?'

'Begorrah I would, with jam. Can I have the teapot too?'

'Niamh, she wants the teapot.' I get out of bed, drape the blanket around me and stand in the doorway.

'Jim made it for me.'

'Have you got money then?' Nell asks. 'Ain punt.'

'No, I haven't. Take the teapot!' I moan. Anything to keep the peace, I'm thinking. After she finishes her tea, Nell hurries off carrying my shiny teapot as if she won a great prize. I sit on the rickety chair. 'What's he going to say, Maeve?'

'He asked her to come. He can make another one!' Maeve stares out the door. 'She took the tea and all! And I didn't even get a cup myself.'

'Here, have mine,' I encourage Maeve. 'I don't want it now,' I say.

'What's wrong with it?'

'Nothing; I feel sick,' I say, pushing the cup and saucer towards her.

'Well, I wouldn't want to catch anything!'

'I'm going to have a babby Maeve, not the mumps!'

'I was married long before you, so I'm the one who should have a babby first,' she says, sipping the tea I gave her.

'But what if God gives me one first?'

'Well, you don't deserve it. I've never seen you saying the rosary. I said and I say the rosary every night hoping for a child. You are a bit of a lazy lump, too,' Maeve assures me. 'It just wouldn't be fair, that's all.' She sits on our wooden stool reflecting.

'So you don't think she's right?' I ask.

Maeve gets up and puts the cup in the little basin and drains the tea dregs out. 'Ax; I hope you're not going to have one before me, that's all.' She stares out the tiny window. I know she's going to ask something very personal. People here don't usually talk about personal things easily. 'When did you last have your granny?' I feel my face turning red as I reply,

'Not since I was at the Connors.'

'Not a spot?' she inquires, turning towards me.

'No. I only got me granny once before that anyway, remember I told ye, just before your wedding, and then once before I got married,' I add. 'I didn't like having it, anyway.'

'Niamh, you're a terrible egit when it comes to these sorts of things.'

'I am!' I reply. 'I remember now. Missus Connor told me it would come every month, but it hasn't...'

'It stops when you're going to have a babby. For nine months! You're so thick, Niamh.' She stares into the cup. 'I think I see a babby in here!' she exclaims. 'Look!' she holds the cup with tealeaves stuck to the sides. 'There, it looks like a child's hand.'

'Maybe that's the sign?' I say, thinking I might be having a child after all and that's why I've been so sick every day for months. Maeve smiles brightly.

'It could be. I drank the tea, so it must be my child. Oh, God, I hope so! Me granny's not due for another week. I'll know for sure then.' I just stare at her. It was my cup of tea, so I don't know what to say. I try to look happy. She gives me a more compassionate look. 'I hope you do have a child one day, but not before me!'

'I think Jim would love a child,' I say.

'It's Paid's dream, to be a daddy!' she replies brightly. 'Do you mind if I take this cup home and show it to Paid?'

'No, go on, take it!' I reply.

'I'll wash it after that,' she says. 'Now I'm off to scrub the draining board, and the floor.' She marches out the door of the van, humming to herself.

...

Before I see Jim Nell has spread the news that Maeve and I are having babies. Jim promptly goes off with the lads for a drink after work. He comes home in the early hours of the morning, singing at the top of his voice, 'Oh, Father dear, now do not fear, for your babby is nearly here...' and then he falls down on top of me and begins to snore. I shove him off me and he rolls over onto the floor with a bang. He sleeps soundly on the floor, until half-eleven the next day!

Since the news has gone around that I'm going to have a child, Jim has been staying away every evening, drinking. I wait up for him, to make sure he does come back home. I usually pretend to be sleeping. I'm getting a bit worried about him as he's been sleeping in the daytime and not going off to work regularly like he did before. He seems to be drinking through the day as well lately. I know that, because whenever I've gone over to Maeve's place for a while and then come back, I can smell the sour smell of alcohol in the place, and fried sausages. Jim always has fried sausages and black pudding fried in lard when he's had too much to drink. The smell is enough to turn my stomach.

Maeve is definitely having a child too, just like Nell said. The snow arrives, just after Christmas, and I'm not feeling sick any more, which makes me feel happier. Jim found an old kerosene heater on the dump and got his pal Kieran to fix it. It's nice and warm in the van now. The world outside the van is white and frozen, even the washing on the line that Jim set up for me freezes in half an hour after hanging it up. Jim finished with the council job and has been spending his time hammering bits of tin and copper. He's making a shiny copper teapot that is even nicer than the one Nell took. He is also making little cups and plates for the baby. At least it's keeping him occupied during the cold weather. Food is scarce, and we have used up all our tins of food long before spring comes. All we can afford to buy is an old frozen rabbit or a bit of mutton or tripe for dinner. Sometimes my da comes over with a bag of bread or a cake. He has a knack of finding food when times are hard. Jim isn't like that. He expects everything to suddenly appear as if by magic. I've been knitting with some wool and needles Maeve gave me. She showed me how to follow a pattern for a baby's dress and cardigan, so I'm working on that with this soft blue and pink wool. I've decided to put both colours together, so then it can be for a girl or a boy.

The first day of spring, March first, is finally here and I've finished knitting the baby's dress, cardigan, bootees and a bonnet, so I'm well pleased with myself. When I gaze out the half-frosted window the sun is finally reappearing from its wintry hibernation and melting the crisp snow. Small puddles of melted ice dot the land like saucers of water to give the birds a cool drink. Other melting ponds are turned into brown slush by human footprints. In other places fresh green tufts of grass are appearing; beautiful snowdrops, buttercups and cowslips are popping their heads up, as though they have been in a deep sleep, and now they are stretching upwards as they awake. The most delicate of flowers, the velvety violets push their way through the hard ground and suddenly spruce up the dull corners of the bush undergrowth, like beautiful royal jewels.

The lambs are arriving too. Yesterday I saw a couple hopping around on their four legs as though they had springs in them. My baby seems to know that spring is here and it's time to leap and jump for joy. Little angular shaped bulges suddenly appear and are gone again. I can hardly get around the van without bumping into things. I can see Maeve coming along the track to the van.

'Come in Maeve.'

'It's hard to believe that it's spring,' she comments, taking her shawl off and hanging it on a nail at the back of the door.

'It's a bit warmer,' I say, turning up the heater a bit.

'Turn that thing down a bit Niamh! What I meant was, Spring comes quickly when you're happy, expecting.'

'I suppose so,' I reply. 'Maeve, I finished these yesterday,' I say, proudly displaying my baby garments.

'Is that all?'

'I thought it was tucks,' I reply.

'You'd better get a move on; your stitches are very baggy; I've got ten times that much done already.'

'But Paid has been getting the wool for you,' I say lamely.

'That's no excuse. I said I'd give you as much as you want. You're like Lady Muck, hardly moving a finger.' 'I did me best Maeve,' I reply.

'Well, anyway, I came to tell you that Paid said there's work at the glass factory if Jim wants it.'

'He's gone off with Kieran,' I reply.

'If he's ready at six in the morning he can go with Paid.'

'I'll tell him.'

'Niamh, your job is to make breakfast for your husband, and get him ready. Can you do that tomorrow?'

'I'll try, although I have been sleeping in a bit lately.'

'I know. I've knocked on your door at ten o'clock and you've still been in bed. You'll have to get out of that lazy habit if Jim has to get up for work.'

'I'll try, but we don't have a clock, so it's hard Maeve.' 'Well, just for once, I'll come over at five and give you three knocks on the door.'

'Five? But it's freezing then, and dark.'

'That's when Paid and I get up every day. If we can do it, you can.'

For a whole month I have been getting Jim up at five in the morning. Maeve gave the knocks on the first morning, but after that I have been staying awake most of the night, waiting to see the little lamp going on in her van. It lights up at five every morning. I go back to bed after Jim and Paid leave around six.

...

April turns into beautiful May, followed by a dazzling June, and the onset of summer. It's a year since Maeve got married and I ran off. On the breezy sunny Wednesday morning, the 4th June, nineteen hundred and sixty nine, after a few days of rain, at around eleven, Maeve turns up at the door, wearing her warm shawl and holding a copper bucket that Paid made. 'Are you up yet?'

'Of course I am,' I reply. I've only just got out of bed. I smother a yawn. She comes inside.

'Do you want to pick mushrooms? There're loads down the fields, so Paid said.'

'Surely, I'd love to Maeve. I feel great these last few months. I'll just take a warm shawl with me.' I feel excited at the thought of getting out of the stuffy van.

'I can't wait to get a bit of exercise,' Maeve remarks as we step out of the van and stroll off with our empty buckets and our rubber boots. 'I've been feeling on top of the world. Ma says having a confinement suits me, and I think she's right!' We head off in the bright sun, which gives a nice warm feeling on our faces.

'I can hardly believe we're both 'expecting' at the same time.

I hope mine comes first.' I catch my breath at the sudden pain across my bulge.

'Are you all right?'

'It's a cramp.'

'God, I haven't seen you standing for a month. Begorrah you're as fat as a pig that's ready for market,' she says, staring at my monstrous sized bulge, comparing it with hers.

'I know!' I reply. Maeve stares at me.

'It's all that porridge you've been eating.'

'It's supposed to be good for me,' I reply.

'Not if you eat too much! I've seen you gobbling up a whole pot full!'

'I think I've been making up for all those months when I could hardly eat at all. I feel so hungry in the mornings!' I say lamely.

'You still have to be careful. I only eat cornflakes now, with tinned fruit!' she says smugly, as she moves swiftly through the fresh dewy green grass. I try to keep up with her. We soon run into a whole field of mushrooms. We start picking them by the stalks.

'Would you look at the size of them,' she says, holding one in the palm of her hand.

'It's like mushroom heaven,' I comment. We spend the next three or four hours together, laughing and talking, and picking buckets of mushrooms. Whenever we feel tired or hungry we sit down and eat a few mushrooms and drink fresh water from a stream.

'There's nothing like the spring fresh water running in the west,' I say as the cool water dribbles down my chin. 'It's really sweet today.'

'Tis,' Maeve says, scooping up a handful of fresh water.

'Maybe we should bottle it and sell it?' I suggest.

'Now that's a grand idea. If anyone would consider buying bottled water; we could get Paid and Jim to blow bottles and we could fill them.' We're laughing about everything. I am bulging so much I can hardly lean into the stream to get a drink.

'Oh; it's the cramps again.' I'm holding my breath.

'All this water is making me want to do a wee, wee,' Maeve says, running off behind a bush a few yards away. I can hear the faint rustling of Maeve as she relieves herself. That makes me feel the need to go too! I head in the other direction by a few yards. It is then I notice that I am very wet. I dry myself off with one of Jim's big hankies.

Maeve and I decide to have a bit of a rest then. We're sitting with our backs against a rock and our faces towards the sun. After a while my cramps are coming again. I'm breathing heavily. Then I feel myself relaxing. Then I feel the cramps again. They seem to be coming every five minutes or so.

Maeve has her eyes shut. I close my eyes too, trying to ignore the pains. I open my eyes and then I see a most wondrous vision. I rub my eyes and stand up to take a good look. 'Maeve, I know that place!'

'Too well, I should think!' she mumbles, with her eyes still half-closed.

'You knew I lived there?'

'Where?' She's awake now; her face turns pink.

'Connor's farm; Maeve, did you know where I was?'

'Of course I did!' she replies harshly. 'We all knew.'

'Did you tell me Da?'

'For God's sake Niamh, I had to tell Sean. We were out of our wits with worry. What would these people do with you if they found out you were a common tinceard? You know how these gentry feel about us?' She stands by me and places her hand on my shoulder.

'I was very happy there.'

'Because they didn't know who you were. If they knew they would have sent you back to where you belong; surely you're happy now?'

'No!' I reply curtly.

'You don't know what's good for you. Here you are with a loving husband, a place to live and a bouncing baby on the way. You should be over the moon!'

'Maeve, I'm not over the moon as much as I was then.'

'You always want more. Greed should be your middle name. Well, there's no more!' she says, pulling me around to face her. I push her away. She stumbles and nearly falls over.

'I'm sorry Maeve.' She steadies herself and brushes her skirt.

'Are you trying to kill me now?' she asks curtly.

'No, but I do have a crow to pluck with you.'

'What?' She sits down. I stay standing.

'Did he give you something?'

'Who; what?'

'Da: did he give you something for snitching on me?'

'I told him the truth. I didn't snitch.'

'So, he did give you something. You, and Paid?'

'We didn't take any of the drink from him. Paid doesn't drink anymore.' I sit in the grass beside her feet. 'So, he gave you all drink?'

'No. It was for the wedding. The lads were given some for bringing you back.' She looks at her feet for a moment, thinking.

'All right, I'll tell you the truth. Sean had an offer.'

'What kind of offer?' She plucks a piece of grass.

'If you married Jim Farrell, he could have a keg of poteen from Jim's uncle on the Aran Islands. He gave them a hundred pounds dowry for you. That was the night of our wedding. He was drunk. When you went missing it nearly broke Sean. He was devastated when he thought you were drowned. When I saw you at the Connors' he was so happy he did a jig on the spot!'

'So; he had to get me back to get the poteen!'

'They're very cunning, the Farrells. They wouldn't give him the drink unless he could guarantee the wedding was going ahead. He had to get you back.'

'Or he'd lose the money.'

'I don't know what would have happened because we found you and the wedding went ahead as planned.'

'So, if you didn't get poteen, what did you get?' I grab her shoulders, tightly. She lifts her head.

'It was only money!'

'Money; how much?'

'Niamh, it doesn't matter now. We wanted to have you back with us...'

'How much?' I squeeze her shoulders. Her face turns white.

'Fifty.'

'Shillings?'

'No, they're not shillings any more now, egit! It was fifty pounds.'

My rubber boots feel heavy as I move, so I pull them off and leave them with my bucket of mushrooms. I can move more quickly now. They only wanted the money and the drink. I can't see for the tears in my eyes. Maeve bought me with fifty pounds! Da never gave me even five shillings! I always had to beg for everything. My heart suddenly burns with fierce hatred for my father, and Maeve...

'Stop running away. I'm telling you: stop!' Maeve screams at me. I keep going until the pains in my stomach make me stop. I double up in agony. 'Niamh, come back,' I can hear Maeve's voice coming closer, shouting my name. Suddenly she's kneeling beside me, breathing heavily. 'Honest Niamh. I didn't really do it for the money.' I stare at her. I can't speak.

'What's the matter?' She crouches down beside me. Tears are streaming down my cheeks.

'My stomach hurts. It must be the mushrooms. Maeve; I feel so awful.'

'Lie down for a minute.' I lie down and stare at the blue sky with wispy clouds scurrying towards the east. I close my eyes as pain sweeps over me. Everything is going quiet and blank. I can hear Maeve's concerned tones. 'Try to get up now. You're just upset.' The pain stops as suddenly as it started. I feel really calm. I sit up.

'I think they're gone.'

'Thank God,' Maeve says. 'Come on, we'd better get on home.' I get up on my hands and knees, and then crumple into a ball, breathless. I look up at Maeve's worried expression.

'I know what it is. You're having the baby; but it's too soon! You're supposed to be due after me!'

'They've stopped again,' I say, relaxing again.

'You just lie here. We need boiling water. I'll go to the house! Maybe they'll help...'

'Please don't go, not now! Remember you said the country folk hate the tinceards? I don't want them to know where I came from.' The pains come back. 'Mother of God!' I'm grasping Maeve's arm.

'I'll not leave you, then. Come on, I'll help you home.' Maeve tries to lift me under the arms and help me to get up.

'It's too late! I can feel it. It's coming. Oh; God...;' I gasp. Maeve gently lowers me to the ground. She pulls my skirt up.

'I'll have a look. I helped deliver Sheamus, remember? I know what to do. It's dark up there,' she says, pulling my skirt down again.

'Maeve...,' I gasp again. She looks again.

'I still can't see anything, except your navy drawers.' The pains stop again.

'I'll help you get them off,' Maeve says, catching hold of the elasticised legs of my drawers and pulling them down. She kneels up.

'Mother of God, blood! You're bleeding! It's a sign!' She lifts her own skirt and pulls her white half-slip off and places it under my bottom. She looks at me.

'Jesus, Mary and Joseph...,' she says, as though she's seen an apparition; her voice trembles: 'Niamh, it's a baby!'

'A baby!' I exclaim; what else could it be?

'It's nearly here. Bear down. Push, come on, one more,' she urges me. I lean forward, and suddenly I hear a loud cry as the pushing stops. I gasp for air and look at Maeve. Almost magically, she's holding a little black haired, pink coloured baby. Its arms are waving and it's crying boldly. Maeve gently wraps it in the white petticoat and takes it into her arms.

'A little girleen,' she says. 'She's perfect. Then she stares at me. 'So, it hasn't turned out the way we wanted. You had to have your baby first to spite me!'

'No Maeve.' I feel cramps again.

'Well, you're lucky to have me with you today. Here hold on to her, while I go and get a sharp stone to get rid of that cord thing. Nell said you have to do that! I remember now!' She's placing the warm baby across my body. I hold her with one hand and prop myself up with the other.

'Hello there?' I say. She's looking at me and twisting her mouth. 'You're beautiful. Look at your lovely dark hair. You're a picture!' I stare into her small pink face and another face comes to mind. 'You remind me of... dearest Niall.'

'Niall?' Maeve suddenly says, looking up from her kneeling position between my legs. She has pulled my skirt just over my knees, so I can't quite see her. She is busy cutting the cord thing.

'You have to wait until it stops beating, so Nell says,' she explains, chopping steadily. 'Then you clamp it. I'll use a strip of this.' She tears a strip off the petticoat.

'Your good petticoat is ruined.'

'I've made another. Remember I'm a diligent person.'

'I'm glad you're with me Maeve.'

'Finished!' Maeve says, her face appearing above my knees.

'Here, let me wrap her properly,' she states, taking the baby from me and rearranging the white petticoat.

'You need something to lie on.' She pulls off her jumper, folds it and puts that under my head. She shivers in her thin blouse but her gaze is set on my face. 'Now I understand.'

'What?' I ask.

'Niall's her father, isn't he? But you said you got your granny before you were married...' I nod my head.

'To Niall!'

'You lied to me. I thought it was your marriage to Jim. That was a real marriage.'

'Yes, Maeve, but what will Jim say if he finds out that it's Niall's child?'

'Well, I'd say you're in for trouble. She's not a bit like him. And she's early by about a month!'

'Jim won't know that! Sure he doesn't even remember which day is what! He got up to go to work one Sunday, thinking it was Monday.'

'He'll find out.' Suddenly I scream. Maeve turns back and kneels next to me.

'What's up now?'

'Pain...' I gasp. She takes the baby from me as I lean forward with my head almost touching my knees, hardly able to breathe.

'...Something's wrong.' I gasp the words out. 'I think my guts are coming out...' She takes the little girl and places her on the grass. She lifts my blood soaked dress.

'Jesus, Mary and Joseph! I'll have to get a doctor...'

'Maeve, I'm a-dying. 'Suddenly her voice changes.
'Wait on a minute! Ala! It's another one!'
'Another baby?' I say in amazement
'Ala! That's why you're so fat!'
'Maeve...'

'Push; one good push; don't stop.' I've got such a shock I'm sitting up straight away, pushing the little flat blue slimy package out into the wide world. It comes out like a fish in a waterfall. Maeve catches the tiny living creature in her arms.

'Mother of God!' I stare at the flat blue-grey infant. I hardly notice my first baby screaming beside me.

'It's a boy.' Maeve quickly removes something from his mouth and turns him over in her hands like turning a pancake. The little flat blue-grey bundle suddenly makes a loud cry, and miraculously becomes a round pink wiggling baby in an instant. The pair of babies are crying loudly now. I smile at Maeve. She scowls back.

'I don't believe it. You've had a boy and girl on purpose. You had to be better than me.'

'No Maeve. I thought I was only having one, honestly.'

'What am I supposed to wrap him in? I've given my petticoat.'

'Here, use my shawl.' I throw my warm shawl towards her. She grabs it and places it under the baby's tiny form.

'Maybe there's more?' I say as Maeve wraps the little baby boy.

'There're too many already, so stop raving Niamh! Just hold him while I cut the cord thing again.' I gaze at the tiny pink bundle lying on my thigh. He looks like me with his pink face and hair so light he looks bald. He has little reddish coloured eyebrows! He cries loud and sharp. I stare down at my babies.

'So, what do we do now?'

'You'd better feed them, egit!' She picks up the baby girl and places her on my right side. I pull my jumper up; my baby girl turns her head and makes cute shapes with her mouth. I don't have a brassier to fit anymore, so I just haven't been wearing anything these last few weeks. She sucks hungrily.

'Oh, that hurts,' I say as I feel pinpricks around my breast. Maeve picks up the baby boy and places it on my left side.

'You'd better get used to it. Here comes alamax!'

'I lie back on Maeve's woolen jumper and try to relax. I can't believe I've suddenly got two babies, one on each breast, feeding hungrily. I wonder if the milk tastes like mushrooms. I stare up at the sky. Maeve's face appears in the picture, framed by the misty sky.

'You still have a big bulge down there.'

'Do you think there might be a third?'

'I think it's fat!'

'You're probably right. Remember all the porridge?' I say lightly. After a short few minutes, Maeve looks restlessly towards the Connor's house.

'I still think I should go to that house and just ask for some clean water to analk in. I can go back to the stream; but it's a fair walk; I'm very tired.'

'Maeve,' I say quietly.

'What?'

'Would you do something really special for me?' She replied instantly. 'I've given you my petticoat, what else can I do?'

'I have an idea. If I give this child to Missus Connor, she'll have a grand life. She's been praying for a child for years.'

[Niamh with her twins, Kaitlin and James, 4th June, 1969 ©Marie Seltenrych, 2010]

'Well, you take the cake, Niamh. You can just give your own child away like that?'

'I can, because it's the best thing for Kathleen. Jim won't see her, and he'll be happy with a boy who looks like me. He won't ask questions. I wanted a life for myself there, but I can't have that now. Kathleen can have a good life instead.'

'I never heard of such deception in all my life! But you have a good point there; at least Jim won't be suspicious; I think one child is enough work for a lazy mother such as you.'

'That's right Maeve. If I have two babies I'll be asking you for help every day.'

'You're right. Missus Connor will probably make a better mother for her than you.'

'She will indeed, Maeve. I know that!'

'I'll do it! But on one condition: 'if ever you tell anyone about this I'll tell Jim it was your idea: that you gave the child away.'

'That suits me fine. Can you take her now?'

'Give her to me.' She snatches the little bundle in her arms. 'She's not one of us anyway! What'll I say?'

'Leave her in the big fuel bucket at the back door. It'll have peat in it. Yell out her name... Kathleen, then make a run for it. Make sure she doesn't see you, or she'll know it's a Tinceard's child!'

'Kathleen?'

'Yes. That's her name. Please hurry Maeve, it's getting cool.'

Maeve gives me one last look and then races off like a greyhound, (a fat one).

I can hardly believe I've just given Kathleen away, but I believe it's for the best. I'm staring at my little baby boy, 'One day I'll tell you about your lovely sister.' I watch the horizon for Maeve, counting every minute, willing her success! Suddenly she's coming thought the high grass over the hill, just as the sun starts to dip its rays beyond it.

'Thank God!' She pants for air as she flops down in the grass.

'Mother of God that was no joke. I'm exhausted now. Someone was coming as I ran off; I don't think they saw me.'

'Maeve, you've done really well. A thousand thanks Maeve.' I pause and stare at my little boy. 'He's getting cold.'

'I'm hot!' she replies. 'Here, have this;' she places her shawl around my shoulders. 'I'll go and get the lads.' She heads off again. 'I'll be back in the twinkling of an eye.'

'Thanks!' I follow her with my eyes as she disappears in the other direction now. Then I look towards the Connors' house and find myself praying that they'll find Kathleen. What would happen if they didn't find her until morning? No, I assure myself as I notice a whiff of smoke spiraling upwards from their chimney. They'll be bringing in extra peat now. In my mind I can see the lovely sitting room with the warm fire burning and the room all neat and tidy, with the soft carpet on the floor. Mister and Missus Connor would be sitting down now, wondering how God sent them this beautiful girl, delighting in having their very own baby at last!

...

It seems like a long time passes before I hear voices coming over the hills. I see a figure hurrying towards me.

'Niamh!' he calls.

'Jim!' I call back as loudly as possible. He sees me and runs towards me.

'Our son,' I say to him as he nears me.

'You shouldn't be going walking so far.' His face is bright with happiness, even thought he is scolding me. He kneels on the grass beside us and places his large finger into the little boy's hand, which grasps his finger tightly. 'James, our little James, after me da,' he adds. Maeve comes running from behind Jim. Behind her is Nell, carrying a bucket of water and some towels. Jim puts his arms around us both for a moment; he holds the baby as Nell and Maeve try to clean me up as discretely as possible. Nell's eyes grow large as she notices the bloody mess on the ground.

'Such a lot of blood.' she exclaims. Maeve looks at me and then at Nell.

'Tis!' Maeve agrees, and then tries to divert her attention from the messy scene. 'Nell, do you know that lovely brass vase you like; on the shelf near the window of the van?'

'I do; what of it?'

'You can have it, if we get Niamh cleaned up quickly, before nightfall.' Nell's eyes bulge with delight.

'Right so!' Nell briskly wipes my legs and places a towel around my bottom under my skirt. She is very discrete and suddenly speeds up her actions.

'I knew it was a lad?' Nell exclaims happily.

'You're always right' Maeve remarks, glancing at me.

'And you're a really great nurse,' I add.

'Yerra, go on now. I'm just doing what any woman would do,' she replies humbly. Her face beams with pleasure.

'I'll take James,' Maeve says, lifting the child from my arms, and hugging him tightly.

'I'll carry you Niamh,' Jim says, gently lifting me into his arms. I feel as though I'm as light as a feather. For a moment my head rests on his shoulder. I wish I could be more open with him, but I can't share the truth about Niall's children, or he'd surely get so wild he'd throw James and me in the river. This time there's no Niall to rescue us! I keep my eyes closed as he marches through the high grass. He carries me all the way back to the camp. Maeve follows close behind with little James in her arms, crooning away to him. Nell follows behind her, with the bucket and towels over her arms, singing happily,

'I can cook and I can sew. I can keep a house right tidy...'

...

We arrive at the campsite: Maeve and Jim boil up some hot water on the stove, to make a nice hot bath for James and me. Soon I am sitting in our copper bath, made by Jim. Maeve bathes James in a large copper pot, which is just the right size for his tiny wiggling body. She finds some clean things to put on his fine silken skin, a muslin nappy and a flannelette nightie with a little blue ribbon at the neck. She puts some little socks on his red feet.

'It's a good thing that I had some spare clothes Niamh. You ought to be ashamed of yourself, not being prepared for this.'

'I did try Maeve,' I reply; 'I made some things.'

'That will fit when he's three months old; 'I don't know what you'd do without people to help you. You're a hopeless case.'

'I'm sorry if I am a hopeless case Maeve, but isn't he a lovely baby,' I say, gazing at my beautiful son.

'He's a fine fellow,' she agrees.

'Maeve, you look exhausted, you should have a rest now,' I say, noticing the dark circles under her eyes.

'You're right! I'm very tired now; I think I'll be off.' She hurries out the door. 'And we'll have to go looking for your boots and bucket in the morning, before some codger nicks them; the mushrooms in the bucket will be rotten by then.'

'I'm sorry about that, Maeve.' A few minutes later there's a knock on the door. It's Nell.

'I made a nice pot of tea.' She's clutching the teapot she demanded when she announced that I was expecting. She beams with happiness as she pours me a cup of strong tea and puts four lumps of sugar into it.

'Thanks Nell,' I say, sipping the sweet golden drop. She makes sure she doesn't forget to take the teapot back with her when she leaves.

...

James is three months old now and he can wear the things I made, just like Maeve predicted. Maeve comes over to see James and me, just before lunch. She's moaning.

'I've been awake half the night!' She holds her back. 'I've got pains all over, in me back, and terrible stomach cramps for the past six hours.'

'Have you been eating too many blackberries?'

'Yerra no! I think the baby's arriving, egit!'

'Oh Maeve, that's wonderful! What can I do, pick mushrooms, boil the kettle?' Maeve laughs.

'At least I'm ready, not like someone I know. I'd love a cup of tea.'

'I'll put the kettle on,' I say, reaching for the jug of water and pouring some into the kettle. I strike a match and touch its sizzling flame to the methylated spirits in the primus stove. Instantly the bright blue flame leaps around the element. I place the copper kettle on top. Maeve sits on the chair that Jim has fixed.

'I'm hoping for a little girl. That's what Paid wants anyway.'

'What if it's a boy?'

'I'd rather have a girl, seeing you were the first to have a boy. That way we can both have a first!'

'But I had a girl...'

'Yerra, stop that now; I don't want to hear it! So, how are you and Jim getting along?'

'All right since James arrived. He's a great little lad, always sleeping his head off.'

'You're very lucky to have such a wonderful baby.' She suddenly gasps for breath, bends over and holds her stomach for a few minutes. 'I'd better call Nell,' Maeve says, as she stands up. 'The baby's due the first week in September, which is this week!'

'You're such a clever person Maeve, working all that out.'

'I know! I was always good at counting!' She smiles smugly. 'And, organizing things: I've even made Paid's tea for today, a few extra apple tarts and a blackberry tart yesterday!' She suddenly holds her breath again. 'I'm off then.'

'I'll come with you,' I say. 'I'll call Nora and ask her to keep an eye on James.'

Moiré arrives four hours later, on Monday the $_1$st September. Maeve skillfully delivers a perfect little girl, around six pounds weight, helped by Nell, Mary, and Maeve's mother, Maura, who came back from praying at the chapel in the nick of time to see the birth.

'Do you hear that?' Maura asks as she gazes at her grandchild.

'What, Mam?' Maeve asks.

'The bell is ringing. We should say the Angelus!' She bursts into rapid prayer for a few moments. 'God must want you to call her Mary,' Maura says.

'You mean because the Angelus reminds us about Mary's visit from the angel, when Jesus was conceived?'

'That's right. I think it's a grand name for our very first grand-daughter!'

'Tis, Mam!' Maeve agrees, casting a glance at me that says, *'Don't ever mention your daughter!'* Paid and I wanted to call her Moiré.'

'Would you believe that, now; that's the Gaelic for Mary. That's my name in Gaelic too,' Maura says happily. 'She is the most beautiful child I have ever laid eyes on,' she adds.

'She is a very beautiful child, your grand-daughter! We thought Ellen would be a good middle name, after Nell!' Maeve replies.

'That's a grand name altogether,' Nell says, picking up the bucket with soiled lined and taking it outside.

'Sure, here's Paid, now,' Maura says, meeting Paid outside on his way home from work; 'you've got a lovely girleen, Mary Ellen, God bless ye, and may there be many more little toes to count.'

Chapter six

Winter comes suddenly in October, with snow, sleet and rain arriving together on my birthday, the 31st. After that I hardly go out at all because of the pelting rain and cold wind. I try to stay in the van with James, so that he doesn't catch a cold. I do take him to Mass at Christmas and show him the little stable with Jesus and Mary, Joseph and shepherd statues there, with some animals. I'm taking a bit of the straw to keep. It's supposed to bring good luck. The Saint Vincent de Paul people have come around, bringing gifts for all the children. James loves his little ball and bag of sweets. They also give each family a box of lovely food. We have a lovely dinner together, the whole lot of us, with roast turkey, ham, Christmas pudding and even custard. Da, Jim and Kieran manage to get a bottle of poteen and the three of them are drunk by the afternoon. After the Christmas celebrations I'm feeling sick in the mornings. I am expecting Jim's child, that's a certainty!

Two months later Jim comes home late. James is sleeping and I have been dozing, waiting for him.

'I want you, Niamh,' he says, pulling me towards him. 'Not now, Jim. I'm sick.'

'I need you Niamh; now!'

'No, Jim, you're drunk!'

'You're my wife, damn you!' He violently tries to force me to have sex with him, but in the end he collapses in a heap on top of me. I climb out from under him and sleep in the chair the rest of the night.

The next morning I feel sick again. I got up and cut a piece of dry bread. That helps. I feed James.

Jim is sleeping his head off. 'Get up. Aren't you going to work today?'

'Go away!' He rolls over and closes his eyes.

Maeve comes over a few minutes later with some fresh bread. 'Moiré is sleeping, so I thought you could use this!'

'Can I come over to your place,' I whisper. 'Jim's not well.'

'As long as you're very quiet, come on!'

We walk to her and Paid's van. 'We're sorry to hear about Jim,' she says kindly.

'He's just had too much to drink. He'll be at work tomorrow,' I explain.

She turns her head sharply towards me as we enter her van. 'So, he hasn't told ye then?' she asks.

'What?'

'He got the sack!'

'No, he hasn't said a word about that. Do you know why, Maeve?' I ask.

'He was drunk on the job, so Paid said!'

'No wonder he's been in a raging mood again.'

'So; what have you done to him now, Niamh?'

'I've done nothing!'

'As usual; you lazy faggot! You've got to fight, Niamh.'

'I did. I fought him last night. He gave up in the end.'

'No. You egit! Fight to keep him! You're going to lose him, that's on the cards!'

'What can I do?' I ask helplessly.

'I told you before. Give him lots of love!'

'I'm expecting again; I've been sick.'

'How come you're always the one who gets sick?'
'I can't help it!'
'Well, I think it's all in your mind.'
'You're probably right!'
'Try to think of other things, then you'll forget about being sick,' Maeve suggests. I'm feeling better already.
'I'm going to give it a try.'
'That's better!' Maeve says, happily. 'I'll cut you a big slice of bread and jam Niamh!'
'Thanks Maeve. I'm going to enjoy it too!' I say, accepting Maeve's offer.
A couple of minutes later I'm biting into a neatly cut slice of bread and jam. 'Lovely!'
'Do you want a piece of fresh bread and strawberry jam, James,' Maeve asks James, who's wiggling on my knees.
James' eyes light up as she breaks off a piece of bread and piles jam on top.
'Maeve,' I say hurriedly, 'can you hold on to James, I'm going to be sick.' I rush outside and throw up all over the grass.

...

Jim has been working at home for the past two months. He's been making copper pots and vases and selling them to the shops. People have been raving over them, calling them pieces of artwork. He's making enough to keep us fed.

One morning, early in April, Maeve comes over, carrying Moiré who's seven months old now.

'The top of the morning to you!'

'Come on in! Too late, you're in!' I say jokingly as she steps inside, holding her latest food contribution, hot cross buns. 'They smell lovely.'

'Put the kettle on and have one. You look like you could do with it because you're so pale. You should do a bit more exercise and get the roses back in your face!'

'I must do that, Maeve. I feel grand really. The buns look delicious.' A few minutes later we sit down to hot tea and sticky hot cross buns. James crawls over and pulls himself up by my knees. He has his hand out.

'Ma; me!'

'Here,' I pull off a small piece and hand it to him. 'Niamh, I was passing by St. Vincent de Paul's shop and I saw this outfit. I thought it would suit James.' She produces a bright navy and white sailor top with a navy pants from her crocheted bag.

'It's lovely. You are so kind Maeve.'

'And a pair of shoes and socks to go with it,' she says, holding up a red shiny pair of shoes and white socks.

'They're gorgeous. Thank you, Maeve. Can I give you something for them?'

'Not at all; I know you've been struggling to make ends meet. I thought he needed something new for the party,' she says.

'What party?'

'Seamus's first birthday party. Mary has invited him.' 'Is he one already?'

'He is. Today.'

'So when is the party?' I ask.

'In a couple of hours.'

'I'd better get him ready, and myself.'

'You're not invited Niamh.'

'I'm not?'

'Only James, and Moiré,' she says. 'She likes James. *He's just like his father,* she says to me the other day.'

'But he's like me.'

'Well, she doesn't know Jim's not his father, so I just went along with it.'

'So, are you going to the party?'

'I am! She is very particular who she invites into her place,' Maeve replies.

'Why do you think she didn't tell me herself?' I quiz Maeve.

'If you must know; and don't repeat this to anyone. I heard a few of the women saying you were stuck up since you came back.'

'I'm not stuck up. I just don't trust this lot any more. If they found out about Niall and me, they might take it out on the Connors, or Kathleen!'

'Sure you're full of wild ideas. If I were you I'd let the grass grow again, so try and be a bit civil, for our family's sake!' I just stare at Maeve.

'I'll think about it.'

'Don't just think about it. Do something Niamh,' Maeve suggests. 'Well, I'll take James and I'll be off.'

'Come here James.' James creeps over to us, his face sticky and dirty.

'He's filthy. Give his face a wipe and comb his hair Niamh, before you put those nice clothes on. I'll go and change Moiré's shoes. I think these white shoes are a bit small,' Maeve instructs me as she hurries out the door. Fifteen minutes later she returns with Moiré, who's wearing a bright pink ribbon in her hair and a clean pink baby doll dress, matched with pink socks and tiny black patent shoes. Her face is polished to a fine shine.

'She looks so... clean!' I comment.

'Cleanliness is next to Godliness, you should learn that Niamh,' Maeve says, taking James in her arms.

'Maeve, I'll help with James.' I put him into the stroller Jim found.

'Don't use that ugly thing. I'll put them in the double stroller Paid bought me. I think he was hoping we might have another one!' She laughs. 'God willing!'

'So, are you walking all the way to Mary's place?' I ask, wondering how far away it might be.

'A-no, it's too far. Sure she's in a house now. Going up in the world, you might say.'

'So, how are you getting there?'

'Freda is picking us up. She has a car now!' Maeve informs me.

'Who's Freda?' I ask.

'A friend of Mary's! You wouldn't know her. We met through the craft club. Well, she'll be here in any tick of the clock!' She walks towards the edge of the roadway. I walk with her.

'You go on back Niamh.'

'What's wrong with me?'

'Your hair is dirty and your dress is ripped,' Maeve shudders and shakes her head. 'You look like a tramp.'

'I'll go back then; bye, James; bye, Moiré,' I say, waving as I hurry towards the van, holding the ripped part of my dress, feeling ashamed. I watch from the window as a black car pulls up and Freda helps Maeve with the children. A tear winds its way down my cheek at the same time as the car winds down the road, turning into a small black speck. I take my shawl and put my brogues on. I've decided I'm going on a bit of a walk.

I hurry through the fields, tracing the grassy track to Connor's house. I sit in the long grass behind a blackberry bush and watch the house. Happy memories come flooding back to me, Niall, Finn McCool, Missus Connor, Tom Connor, Toby the dog, Ginger the cat. I sit and bask in the memories of those heavenly days, reliving them. Then my heart gives a big lurch. 'Kathleen!' I stand up to get a better look. I see Missus Connor carrying Kathleen in her arms and chatting to her, then kissing her face. They are so happy together that I feel like crying. They disappear into the rose garden. After a few moments I head off down the track, skipping and humming all the way home. I close the door of the van and lean against it. Thank God Maeve is not back yet! Then I hear someone outside. I quickly pull off my shawl and my brogues, as I don't want her to know what I've been

doing. The door opens. I look up from unlacing my shoes.
'Jim?'

'So, what have you been up to?' He closes the door and stares at me.

'Nothing.'

'Ah-so, your face looks flushed. Where were you?'

'I went for a walk.'

'Where's James then?'

'He's gone to a party with Moiré, Seamus' birthday...'

'Why don't you look after your son?'

'Maeve's looking after him. I wasn't invited!' He throws his head back and laughs sharply. 'Ah! That's a good one!'

'Well it's true. They don't like me!'

'Why don't they like you?'

'I don't know!' He sits down.

'I know. They're afraid!' he says decisively.

'What are they afraid of?'

'They're probably feared you'll take their men away!'

'Don't be an egit Jim!' I exclaim, genuinely serious.

'Don't call me an egit. You're the stupid one, lying to me.' He takes hold of me by the wrists.

'I'm not lying, Jim. And why are you home so early.' I struggle to release myself from his grasp. He tightens his grip.

'I told you on our wedding day, don't ever question me about my private business.'

'You're hurting me.'

'Sorry.' He lets go; I rub my wrists.

'Do you want your dinner now?'

'No. I'm off!' He strides through the door. My heart is thumping so fast I slump into the wooden chair. The room is swaying back and forth. The next thing I know Maeve and James are opening the van door.

'Been sleeping your head off, as usual? Well, we had a great time, didn't we James? He needs a nappy change, so I'll leave that with you.' She shoves James into my arms.

'Thanks Maeve.' That night Jim's voice interrupts my slumber.

'Niamh, I have to talk to you.' I can smell the stale smell of the drink on his breath. I can see his frame in the dim light rocking backward and forward above me. 'What's his name?' He knows I'm awake; my mouth feels dry.

'Whose name?' I whisper.

'You're seeing someone; I know it!' Suddenly his muscular body lands right on top of me. He's too drunk to move. I wriggle from under him, take James in a blanket, still asleep, and head out the door. I'm shaking all over. I bang on Maeve's door.

'It's me,' I call out. The door opens

'Yerra, what's going on?'

'Can I come in?'

'You're shivering. Come on then,' she says, drawing me inside.

'Thanks Maeve.' I lay James down on the sofa and sit next to him.

'I hope you're not stopping long. I've had a bad night with Moiré.'

'Is she sick?' I ask.

'She's just teething. We've had to take her into our bed.' She whispers, 'Try and be quiet, Paid's bunched.' Moiré's whimper rises behind the curtain. Maeve hurries inside and returns a few moments with Moiré in her arms. Moiré is sucking her thumb.

'Don't suck your thumb. Alamax.' Maeve picks up a bottle of milk from a pot of warm water and squeezes a bit on her wrist, then shoves it in Moiré's mouth. Moiré sucks the bottle, staring at me with big blue eyes. Maeve sits down beside me.

'Now, tell me what's wrong?'

'Jim thinks I have another man,' I blurt out.

She pulls her hand away and stares at me. 'And have you?'

'Yerra, no; of course not!'

'Well, you have nothing to worry about, then, if you're telling the truth; I just made myself a cup of tea, would you like one?'

'I would Maeve, please; that'd be grand.'

'Here, take her.' She passes Moiré onto my lap, takes a cup from her shelf and pours out the hot black tea. 'There's no alamax left, Moiré's drank the last of it, so you'll have to drink it black.'

'I don't mind!'

'Paid bought me a lovely Madeira cake on his way home from work. Would you like a piece?'

'Yes please.'

'Ma...' Moiré reaches over for cake.

'No. You have your alamax!' Moiré starts to cry.

'Here, come here. Back to bed then,' she scolds, rocking Moiré and heading inside the curtained doorway. All is quiet. Maeve reappears a few minutes later. I gaze in admiration at my sister.

'How do you do that?'

'You have to be firm with them at this age!' She looks at James sleeping peacefully on the sofa with his head on my lap. 'You're lucky he's an easy child.'

'I am.' Maeve proudly cuts a piece of fine Madeira for me and places it on a saucer; my mouth is watering as I watch her. 'Thanks Maeve. I must be hungry.'

'You were always the greedy one!' She smiles wryly.

'Maybe I can have a small piece myself. I don't want to overdo it!' She cuts herself a piece and we enjoy our tea and cake together. She looks at the clock on the dresser, ticking loudly. 'You realize it's nearly half one?'

'Is it? I'm sorry for disturbing you. I was just afraid...'

'Afraid of what: the boogie man?' She laughs softly.

'Jim.'

'Jim?' she exclaims, shaking her head. 'I'm ashamed to call you my sister. He's your husband, for God's sake. Just talk to him. It works!'

'But he's drunk!'

'When he's sober! Your place is with your husband.'

'You're right, Maeve.'

'Well, what are you waiting for? Go on back, kiss and make up!' she urges, yawning.

'Right, I'll go.' I rise, reluctantly.

'I don't know why you had to disturb James too.'

'I don't know why,' I reply.

'I'll bid you goodnight then,' Maeve says, opening the van door as I take James in my arms. 'Hurry up now, before James gets too cold.' I creep back into our van and step over Jim, who's lying on the floor. I put James in his little cot and throw a coat over Jim. Then I climb into bed, exhausted. The next thing I know it's about ten in the morning. Jim is standing next to the bed.

'Is James my son?' he asks fiercely.

'Keep your voice down, Jim. You'll wake James.'

'So, is he?'

'What do you mean?' He sits on the side of the bed and leans over me. The fumes from his breath are so toxic; I swear if I lit a match we'd all blow to kingdom come. 'I heard that James is not my son!'

'You heard wrong!'

'Then why are they saying things?' He looks me in the eyes. 'I need you Niamh,' he says, rubbing my shoulders, kissing my face and then my lips.

'Not now Jim. We'll wake James.'

'You're my wife; I want you now!' Jim says vehemently. I hear a tearing sound as he pulls my nightie from my shoulders, scratching my arms. 'Prove you are mine,' he says, crawling under the sheets. James cries.

'James...,' I say. Jim sits up and hits me in the face.

'James comes before me. Why is that Niamh?'

'I'm his mother. 'T'was you who told me to look after my son.' I try to get past Jim. He pulls me back by the arm, throwing me back onto the bed.

'You're a whore, like your mother!'

'Don't bring my mother into this Jim,' I retort quickly.

'Someone's been lying to you Jim; about me, and my mother!' Jim's stands up. He pulls his pants on. His face is white with rage; his black eyes are bulging out of their sockets.

'Kieran wouldn't lie to me. Look at you, lying there, wanting him! You're a whore!' Jim is raising his foot. I roll away from the blow of his foot landing on my stomach. His foot collides with my left side. I double up trying to catch my breath.

'Don't Jim!' I cry out as he raises his hand to hit me again.

'Bitch! Bastard!' he mutters as he stumbles out the door. After a few minutes I catch my breath. I pull on my cardigan, take James from his cot and stagger to Maeve's place.

'Maeve...' I call through the open door.

'Not you again! What's up?'

'Take James,' I whisper. I can see her reaching out as I collapse in the doorway. The next voice I hear is Maeve's.

'Get up Niamh!' She helps me up and I lie down on the sofa. 'You're a disgrace! Your nightie is all ripped, and James needs changing,' she says, placing him in Moiré's feeding chair.

'I know; I'll go back in a minute.' I gasp with pain. I must look bad because Maeve immediately leaves James and turns to me.

'Niamh, what's wrong? You look terrible.'

'The baby;' I gasp for breath again.

'We'd better get Nell,' Maeve suggests. Ten minutes later Nell comes hurrying through the door. She takes one look at me and says,

'Death; I see death.'

'Death; Maeve repeats.

'The baby's gone! Slean leat!' Nell says, waddling back out the door.

'She's drunk!' Maeve looks at me, a worried frown crowning her brow. 'I'll get one of the lads to run for the doctor.' She steps out the door and a few minutes later she returns, with Nora on her heels. 'Diarmud's gone running down the hill.' Nora looks at me with pity.

'Will I take Moiré and James for a walk?'

'Do that, Nora,' Maeve says.

'She's a grand girl, our Nora!' She turns to Nora. 'Use the stroller; 'tis outside near the window.'

'I will,' she says. 'Come on, let's go for walkies!' She picks Moiré up and takes James by the hand, then lifts him down the step. Nora turns back from outside the door. 'Will I change James' nappy?'

'Do that Nora! You'll make a lovely mother; not like some people!' Maeve states; frowns at me.

'Thanks Nora,' I call out. 'Jim's not there, so just go on inside. There are clean nappies in the room behind the curtain, on the left side...'

An hour later Maeve comes running in. 'It's the young fellow. The good looking one...' Just then a long thin figure fills the van doorway.

'Hello; you're Niamh?' He holds his hand forward and I touch it. He shakes my hand.

'I'm Doctor Hugh Healy. Let's check baby, shall we?' I nod my head. He puts his stethoscope on my tummy, 'Mmm. Mmm.' He then gets up. His head is touching the ceiling, so he asks

Maeve to go outside with him. A few minutes later he returns bending over as he moves in the small space. 'I'll have to put you in the hospital immediately. You're a very sick young woman.'

'The baby: is she all right, Doctor?'

'She?' He grins. 'You know more than I do, Mam; I'd like to talk to your husband.'

'He's not here,' I say.

'What's wrong, Doctor,' Maeve asks. He lowers his voice.

'There could be a haematoma in the placenta, or incision in the sac.' Maeve's eyes enlarge.

'Oh; is that bad?' she asks.

'Very bad I'm afraid.' He turns to me. 'I want to see your husband as soon as possible. He needs to pay the fees. In the meantime, I'll get you up to the hospital and they can give you a curette.'

'A priest?' I say. Doctor Healy throws back his head and laughs.

'Not a curate; a curette!' Maeve digs me in the shoulders. 'Don't show your ignorance!'

'I'll give you something to calm you down.' The doctor opens his bag, extracting a long thin object.

'It's a needle!'

'It is a needle all right. Steady now. You won't feel a thing.' He gives me a jab in the thigh.

'Oh;' I cry as I feel a small prick. I'm feeling very drowsy immediately afterwards. I don't remember any more until I wake up to the pungent odour of disinfectant. I realize I'm in a hospital. Maeve is standing next to the bed. She looks like she's got a double.

'You're back?' she says, smiling. I attempt to sit up but fail. I flop onto the pillow.

'What happened?'

'They got rid of it!'

'Rid of it?'

'It! We nearly lost you as well!'

'You mean: the baby is gone?'

'Niamh, that's why you came here; it could have poisoned you.'

'But where is she?'

'The nurse?' Maeve asks.

'No, I don't care about the nurse. Where's my baby!'

'She was dead, like Nell said. She's in Limbo now.'

'What about her wake and funeral?'

'You're too late! They've buried her already.'

'Where?'

She stares angrily at me. 'How in God's name do I know? The best you can do is offer up a Mass for her, and say a few *Hail Marys*.'

'I want my baby;' I suddenly scream out.

'Whist now; stop behaving like a baby!' Maeve scolds me. 'Don't disgrace us,' she warns. 'I have to go home now. D'you know Abe McGarry?'

'I've heard of him.'

'He's Paid's boss. He's picking me up in his car in a few minutes. I don't want him to come up here and see you in this state.'

'I'm sorry!' I sniff. 'I just feel upset.'

'Here! Keep this.' Maeve hands me a clean handkerchief.

'Is James all right?' I ask, holding back my tears, wiping my eyes.

'He's grand.'

'What about Jim?' She moves back a step.

'I've got to run like Billy-o now. I'll be back tomorrow, I promise!'

Paid's boss brings the car to pick me up on the Friday. After we get to the campsite, Maeve and Paid insist that I stay with them a while.

'Sit down Niamh. Maeve, can you make her tri a gater?' Paid asks his wife.

'I've just made a pot of tea!'

'Sure that's lovely Maeve. She's a grand wife is Maeve,' Paid says, smiling at her. 'I'll leave you to it then,' Paid says, hurrying out the door to talk with his boss. I watch as Maeve pours the tea.

'I'm going to take your advice Maeve.' She glances up from pouring the milk into the tea.

'My advice; what do you mean?'

'I'm going to talk to Jim, tell him everything...' Maeve shakes her head.

'I think your talking is too late! Now drink your tea,' she orders.

...

It's now six months since I came home from hospital and Jim has not been seen around here. I've had to resort to my old trade again, the one my daddy taught me. I've been hammering out flowers, and making spoons from tin, and if I can get it, copper, and trying to sell these in the village. Sometimes I just sit near a bridge and people drop a coin in my tin pot. Other days I travel around the area, going from door to door, begging. I'm not on me own, there are others begging, so it's getting a bit competitive around here. One evening in the middle of October, I've just come home with James, when Maeve comes over carrying Moiré and a loaf of bread.

'God bless you Maeve,' I say. 'I didn't get a thing all day, so we've got nothing to eat. How did you know?' I ask.

'Begorrah I didn't.' She smiles wryly. 'I always fancied myself as being psychic?' She suddenly laughs. 'Yerra, I'm only joking! Paid was given a whole bag of bread today. I also brought you a few tea bags, and a drop of fresh alamax.' I take the loaf of bread and milk from her gratefully.

'Maeve, that's very kind of you. Don't stay a-standing, come in.'

'Well, I'll only stay five minutes.' She sits down on the stool.

'It's been six months since Jim drowned Maeve!' I say after a few minutes silence while I break off a piece of bread for James, and pour him a cup of milk.

'Why talk about it now?'

'I just wonder if you've heard anything?'

'I have heard some say he didn't drown at all, but found a boat and went to one of the islands.'

'So, why would he do that?'

'Sure if anyone knows you must!'

'No, I don't have a clue why he'd do that!'

'Never mind! Well, whether he's a-dead or alive, I feel he's happier now, far away from all those upsets and things.'

'You mean with myself?'

'You know yourself what went on. But from what I know, I don't blame him.'

'Blame him for what?'

'Running off!'

'He knew I was expecting…'

'If it was his child?' Maeve says curtly.

'It was so!'

'We don't know what goes on behind closed doors, do we?'

'I don't know what you're getting at Maeve?'

'Well, you were always a bit sly!'

'Sly? Is that because I never told him about Niall?'

'Begorrah, it wasn't only your cavorting with Niall that worried us!'

'Cavorting; we were married…'

'If that's what you call it! Did you know that Jim used to come over to our place and ask where you were?'

'I went out for a walks, to catch the air…'

'Catch a man would be more like it!'

'No! I've been going to see Kathleen.'

'Well now, and why are you doing that?'

'I want to see how she is.'

'Niamh, you left her in a better place, you said so yourself. Why go stirring up trouble again?'

'I should never have left her even with Missus Connor I know that now. But I had to see her again.'

'And again... *Laisk my dheel...!*' Frustrated, she stands up. I look at her angry face.

'Don't say that Maeve; what can I do?'

'Settle down and become a family. Rhonan is still waiting for you, and he gets on well with James.'

'Rhonan?'

'Rhonan is a free spirited man. He never wants to settle down in one place, just like yourself. He'd make a great father for James. Then you'll have someone to talk to, a husband! Someone to wander off with...'

'A-Maeve, I don't even like Rhonan! I'd rather die that marry him!'

'You're too good for him then? *Lady Muck*! You get on my gall! Just keep your hands off my Paid!'

'Maeve, that's a horrible thing to say,' I shout at her.

'Don't shout in front of children. I'm going home,' she says, picking Moiré up off the floor. 'Look at the state of her now. Her clean frock is filthy. Why don't you wash the floor, sometimes!'

The fresh autumn winds turn into icy rain as Christmas and nineteen seventy-one approach. James and I have been keeping to ourselves. We go out and beg if the weather is not too bad. Every week or so, we walk to the hill and have our dinner, usually sandwiches, while we watch Kathleen playing, or sometimes just looking through the window of the house. James calls her the *pwetty girl.* The New Year speeds by and almost suddenly it's summer again. Maeve doesn't come over very often, and I rarely go to visit her place, but we are on civil terms with each other.

...

On Wednesday, 4th June, 1971, James and I plan to go to our favourite hill to celebrate Kathleen and James' second birthday. First we're going to the shop to buy green and red jellies with the money I've saved up. James is humming a little tune to himself as we walk across the bridge to the local shop. He is such a happy child. I look down at him and I want to pick him up and give him a hug. He stops and looks up at me; I pick him up and give him a hug.

'I love you James, don't ever forget that.'

'Mammy, lub you,' he says in his tiny voice and then squeezes my neck.

I notice two local country women talking seriously inside the glass door of the shop.

'It's one of those tinkers,' the short woman whispers to the taller, broad woman. The woman adjusts her scarf and turns her head to have a look at me. She puts her finger to her nose as if I'm emitting a bad smell. Maybe we wouldn't smell so much if we had all that running water out of a tap and baths and things like that, instead of an old tin bath and a bucket of water from the stream. I walk straight past them into the shop, clutching James' hand. The short thin woman is talking now.

'The funeral is at three o'clock, I hear.'

'God rest her soul,' the tall broad woman says. 'I didn't know Kathleen that well...'

'...Is she having a high Mass then?' The short woman asks.

'Now I wouldn't know about that...'.

'So, what do you want?' Mrs. Kelly's voice booms at me from behind the counter.

'Jellies,' James replies. Mrs. Kelly turns her attention to the small child pointing to the array of delicious sweets behind the glass.

'Show me your money?' She curls her bottom lip, as

though doubting our sincerity.

'Here,' I say sharply, on his behalf. I place a large shiny coin on the counter. She stares at the money.

'Are we going to spend all that? That's *twenty* sweeties,' she says sweetly to James. She is all smiles now, and very glad to take my coin off me.

'Wenty weeties,' James repeats.

'No,' I say. James looks at me, his face the epitome of disappointment. 'All right then, count out twenty. Can we have red and green please.' That'll give me another few minutes to hear the rest of the conversation of the two women nearby.

'You can, to be sure,' Mrs. Kelly says, delighted to have our custom. This is her lucky day I think, getting all of that money!

'Is there a funeral…?' I ask Missus Kelly as she rolls a piece of newspaper into a cone shape and counts the jellies as they fall in.

'Don't interrupt me now… twenty. There.' She looks into my face. 'Three o'clock I believe. Did you know Missus Connor?'

'Missus Connor!' I almost faint. 'I met her…' I reply.

'I suppose you did. You folk get around.' She looks out the window as though she can see into Missus Connor's. 'Kept to herself a bit… God rest her soul,' Missus Kelly laments.

'Yes, God rest her soul. Thanks very much. I'm off now,' I say, taking James' other hand. The doorbell chimes as we leave.

'Come on James, we're going to see the pretty girl.'

'Pwetty gel,' James says, trudging alongside me. 'Weets,' he cries, holding up the little cone shaped package. 'Don't open it! Not yet James. We have to go up the hill. We'll sing our special song about Missus Kelly?' We sing together, 'Missus Kelly broke her belly sliding down a lump of jelly!' We both laugh, and repeat the ditty until we reach our special spot on the hill.

We sit down on a rock. 'Good boy?' I say as I undo the paper cone. 'Here's a sweetie;' I hand him a green jelly; he chews on it;

I'm chewing on a red one. 'I wish I had a drink James, a nice tri a gater!' James nods his head.

I watch the Connor's house. Half an hour later I see a big black hearse coming up the driveway. Two men in black get out of the front seat. A black car is pulling up behind the hearse. Two men and a woman get out of that and go into the house.

'Oh, God,' I say aloud. A tall blonde haired woman comes out the door of the house carrying a small child.

'It's Kathleen,' I whisper.

'Tatlen,' James whispers back. I smile. One day I'll tell him about his sister.

Kathleen is dressed in a dark coloured dress with white frills. I can see her frilly underskirt. She has black shiny shoes and white stockings. She has a little bonnet with a white ribbon tied over her dark soft curled hair. Mister Connor comes out through the front door, and turns around. He stands beside the blonde women holding Kathleen. The child is lurching towards Mister Connor, but the woman pulls her back, gives her a shake and slaps her on the wrist. Mister Connor ignores the activities around him. The dark shapes of men moving slowly fills the front door, two, four, six men! They are carrying the coffin! Tears fall down my cheeks.

'Mammy, Mammy; not cwy,' James is calling softly to me.

'Missus Connor is dead!' I hug James. A lonely butterfly flutters by. James reaches up to try to catch it.

'Buttafi, buttafi,' he says, pushing away from me and romping through the grass.

I watch as the funeral procession moves slowly along the narrow road, like a tired slug. Tears run freely down my face and along my neck. After a time I feel the cold air blowing on my neck, cooling me. I realize the night is closing in on us. I look around and realise that James is gone. 'James, James,' I'm calling out. I can see the sun sliding away behind the hills. 'Where are you James,' I call as I plod through the high grass. He's gone! 'Oh, God; help!' I wail. Then, I relax as I see a little brogue clad foot behind a grassy rock. There's James, fast asleep. In his tightly closed hand there's a brown and white butterfly. I pick James up and carry him home.

The next day I meet Maeve in the yard around the van. I relate the news to her.

'Missus Connor funeral was yesterday!'

'How do you know that?'

'I saw the coffin.'

'So, you were snooping again. Idle minds are the devil's work Niamh. You should try to keep yourself busy.' I ignore her remark.

'They might send Kathleen away now,' I remark, exposing my thoughts.

'Niamh, it's none of your business. The whole world doesn't rotate around you.'

'You're right Maeve.' I pause before I ask her a favour. 'I was wondering if I could ask you to look after James? He's a bit weary from walking yesterday.'

'You want to see her *ala?*' Maeve says, her hands on her hips.

'Just this once.'

'I've got me own child to take care of, and a husband, and a home.'

'I know that. I just need to...'

'Go on; get it out of your system. Swear it will be the last time? Go on!'

'I swear. This will be the last time.'

Twenty minutes later I'm sitting on the hill, watching the Connors' house. After a long wait I don't see any one, so decide to leave. My bum's stiff! I rise to go, and then I see Tom Connor walking towards the back of the house. I see the woman with the blonde hair coming from the rose garden to greet him. I watch them, shocked by what I see...

I call in to Maeve's.

'I thought I'd give them a bit of food,' she says, mashing up potatoes and carrots for James and Moiré.

'That looks delicious,' I say, my mouth watering.

'Well, there's only enough for these pair. You'll have to cook your own vegetables.'

'I will. Thanks for feeding James.'

'It's what sisters are for! It's a pity you can't do the same for me some time. So, you got to get that girleen out of your system then?' Maeve asks, placing a bib around Moiré's neck. She places a bowl and spoon in front of each of them at the small table.

'No, not exactly. I did see Mister Connor. Maeve, you wouldn't believe it!' Maeve sits down next to me on the sofa.

'What wouldn't I believe?'

'I saw him and his girlfriend cavorting...'

'Niamh, how can you use such vulgar language in front of the children?' She leans closer and whispers. 'Well, maybe he needs *ala* woman.'

'Maeve, he buried his wife yesterday!'

'It's not our business. We shouldn't judge the man. I heard she has been sick for months! You didn't know that did you?'

'No, I didn't.'

'There y'are now. Put the whole thing out of your head now and get back to work.'

'I will, but first I'm going back. Tomorrow.'

'You swore today would be the last time!'

'I didn't see Kathleen!'

'*Awast* with your romancing,' Maeve says, rising up and pouring a cup of milk for the two children. 'I can't bear the sight of you! Go on home; I'll bring James over when he's finished his dinner.'

The next day I take James with me.' Look for butterflies,' I'm

151

telling James; off he goes; after a short while I spot Kathleen. The blonde haired woman plonks her into a playpen in the front yard and disappears inside, leaving Kathleen walking around the playpen. Drops of rain tickle my nose. 'Sit under the rock,' I tell James as the rain falls harder. I quickly do what I came to do, and then return home. I'm just inside when Maeve turns up at the door.

'I wanted to ask you for something...'

'Come in. Close the door!' I literally pull her inside. Her mouth drops open.

'What in God's name...?' She stands with her arms on her hips.

'Kathleen, this is your aunty Maeve.'

'Niamh; what is she doing here?'.

'It's her second birthday! I took her back,' I exclaim.

'Niamh, she doesn't belong here.'

'She does. I love her; Missus Connor's dead; nobody loves her there.'

'How did you get away with it?' Maeve asks in a nasty voice.

'She was stuck in a playpen; out in the rain; I just lifted her in my arms and took her with me,' I explain.

'Niamh, you've kidnapped her; that's a crime! We'll all end up behind bars! Take her back up there! Go on, before they find out what happened.'

'I will not.' I pick Kathleen up and step away from Maeve.

'The garda will be here any minute.'

'Don't be daft, Maeve. They'll think she ran off.'

'Niamh, she's two years old, how can she run away!' She leans over towards me and her face is close to mine: 'If you bring more trouble on our family, you're finished; I'll never forgive you.'

'What else can I do?'

'Get out of here. Leave us alone.'

'Maeve, I thought you wanted me here?'

'Well, I don't any longer! You may as well know what's going on. Paid and I are on a list for a house. We're very close to getting one. We don't need any criminal charges; you have two choices; bring her back to the Connors, or leave!' She is suddenly quiet.

'Maeve, I should never have given her away. I know that I made a mistake.'

'Look, I'm sick of you! You run away, you come back, telling us you were married to some great fellow. All la de da! Then you stupidly give your child away. Then you force your husband to drown himself! After all that you finally decide you made a mistake, and make another one by kidnapping a child! I've had enough of your crazy schemes. Just go, while you can.'

'But now I want to stay.'

'You always want the opposite of what's good for our family. If you don't go I'll tell the garda that you kidnapped the Connors' child.'

'But where can I go?'

'Somewhere! By bus.'

'I never go on the bus. I don't have money.'

'I'll tell you where it goes, and when, and I'll give you money. There's one going this evening, up at the crossroads.'

'So, are you going to look after the children?'

'Not on your nanny; egit; take them with you; they're yours now!'

'All right. If you don't want me here, I'll go; I'll get James' things,' I stammer.

'Put some of James' clothes on Kathleen; say she's a boy.'

'She's too pretty to be a boy.'

'She has to be a boy.'

'Why?'

'Because; they'll be looking for a girl.'

'If she's a boy: why can't we just stay here until it all blows over?'

'It won't blow over in a hurry. I just know that; you'll bring trouble on your whole family if you stay; If you're not here they'll probably not worry us.'

'It took me ages to find out where the Connors' farm is. I don't know anywhere but walking around these parts.'

'We've got some relations near Moycullen. Ballycuirke, I think they said.'

'What relations are they?'

'My aunty Biddy and my uncle Bill McCann; they were at the wedding. They have two caravans and three or four horses; very well to do! They've probably got a house by now! Just say you're my sister and they'll welcome you with open arms.'

'What if they chase me off?'

'They won't; they're your own flesh and blood, on my mother's side. Now, what you have to do is stay with them for a while; and then come back.' I haul out a little pair of trousers and a hat from a cardboard box.

'Will these do for Kathleen?' I ask Maeve.

'They'll do; hurry; don't call her Kathleen; call her, Larry!'

'Larry? She doesn't look like a Larry!'

'Larry is a great name; she looks like a Larry to me; put those things on and you'll see!'

'There!' I say, pulling the trousers up and lifting Kathleen off her little feet with the jerk.

'There, she looks like a Larry now. A real little larrikin!'

'I don't want her to have that name...'

'Bring a bit of food for the night; don't wear your shawl; otherwise you'll look like a Tinceard!'

'But I am...'

'I'm telling you now; comb your hair; put your best clothes on. Go on; quick! I've got to get back to Moiré; Paid's looking after her; he'll be worried. I only came to borrow a cup of sugar to make pancakes; never mind that now.' Maeve leaves and comes back ten minutes later. I have a large canvas bag packed as she instructed, and I'm wearing my best clothes: a light green silk blouse that Maeve gave me on my seventeenth birthday, with a silk ribbon in a band around my hair, and an A-line green and brown coloured tartan skirt that has big pockets on the inside; I make sure I have my savings and rings as well as some bread and milk, and a few other bits and pieces.

'I told him you need company for half an hour; you're depressed *arirt.*'

'I'm not depressed.'

'We'll all be depressed if you don't hurry up!' she says, handing me her old crocheted bag.

'Here're some things to keep you going; come on now: shift yourself; I'll carry James.'

'We're on your heels, aren't we Kathleen?' Maeve turns back with a sour look. 'Call her Larry! Let's use the short cut.' The four of us head off through the fields to where the bus stops. 'All right! You wait here. Now if Aunty Biddy and Uncle Bill aren't there, go on to Cork.'

'I thought you said they'd welcome me with open arms?'

'Oh, they will, if they're still at Ballykuirke. You know how it is; we can't stop in the same place too long. They might have had to move. I'm just giving you a fair warning, that's all. At the wedding they said they were thinking of travelling to Cork. Bill knew someone who had a business there.'

'Cork is such a long way off.'

'They won't find you there!'

'Who?'

'The garda; stupid!'

'Maeve, you and the garda! I don't know anything about Cork. I'll be lost there. It's supposed to be a really big place...'

'Niamh, the bigger the place the harder it will be to find you; you're always talk about going to America; now you won't even go to Cork.'

'But what if I can't find Uncle Bill and Aunty Biddy?'

'God you're a moron! Just go to the priest if you can't find them; someone will help you. Here's ten quid.' She hands me two five-pound notes.

'Thanks Maeve.' I take the notes and stuff them in the bottom of my pocket.

'What'll I do then?'

'Stay in Cork until for a few months, until all this blows over. You can come back and visit us when we're settled in our new house. We're thinking of getting a television as well!'

'Oh Maeve.'

'I've been longing for a television; I don't want anything to go wrong now; do you understand?'

'No; I've never wanted a television.'

'That's not what I mean; Yerra; I think I hear the bus; slean leat! ' Till we meet again.' Maeve gives me a quick hug and runs to hide behind the bushes and high grass.

'Slean,' I say. 'There's sugar in the old brown tea tin on the shelf…' I call out, but I can't see her now.

I climb on the bus with my two toddlers, wondering if it's all a bad dream. I pay the fare with one of Maeve's notes and get my change. I catch a glimpse of Maeve as she heads off home, stopping to watch the bus move on. I wonder if she heard me telling her about the sugar.

Niamh, waiting at Cork Harbour, June, 1971. ©marieseltenrych, 2010

Chapter seven

The bus driver is a withered looking man with a clean shaved look. A few strands of brownish hair are flattened against his polished head. His driver's cap is on the seat next to him. His eyes are alert and bright blue.

'So are them children under four?'

'They surely are. Sean is two and K... Larry is three' I reply sharply.

'They can't sit on the seats. You have to hold them on your lap!' His eyes go even a brighter blue when he says this. 'Them's the rules!' He smiles, showing the gaps in his brown teeth. I notice there are only about half a dozen passengers with plenty of spare seats.

'Right.' I nod and sit down balancing my two children on my lap. My two bags are on the floor near my feet. Nobody wants to sit next to me, so after a short time, when my knee is nearly numb I'm sliding James into the empty part of the seat. He is too small to be seen by the driver anyway. I'm watching the world passing by. I've wanted to leave home but gave up a long time ago; I didn't mean like this; with two toddlers! By the time we reach Moycullen there's nobody left on the bus but myself and the driver.

'This is it then; off you get now. Slean; Dei's Muire dhuit! This is where we stop for the night!' The driver pulls on the brake hard and starts packing up his paperwork.'

'How do I get to Ballykuirke?'

'There's nothing there.'

'My friend's meeting me...' I reply, trying to sound like I know what I'm doing.

'Follow the wiggly woggly road and then you'll come to a lake, if you could call it that.'

'Right'

'When's the bus to Cork?'

'Where do you think y'are? Dublin? They have buses every five minutes there, or so they tell me.' He nods his head and smiles longingly. 'They must make an awful lot of money?'

'They must; what about the bus to Cork?'

'You've got to go to Galway first; tomorrow; around ten o'clock.'

'Dei's Muiré dhuit, agus Padraig,' I mumble. He leans forward.

'The Banshee lives around these parts. If you hear her, cover their ears!' I shiver.

'Gora mait dhuit. I'll remember!' I mumble as I head off down the wiggly-woggly road, with the bus driver watching me as I go. I'm chatting to the children, and glancing back from the corner of my eye. He finally walks off. I'm really wondering what's to become of us. I thought we would be happy together forever in our little caravan. Now I don't know what's going to happen in one night. What can I tell our relatives at Ballycuirke? First I have to find them. After half an hour of a long walk with two little ones, I still can't see any sign of any living creature, just an odd cow, sheep or horse. We cross over a small stone bridge with a stream going under. I notice a stone wall and crumbled remains of a shed.

'There's our house!' I exclaimed to James and Kathleen. I try to sound excited. The three of us run towards the fallen down building. We sit inside the wall on the grass and I open my bag. I have a bottle of milk and two little copper cups that Jim made, and some biscuits.

'Goodies for good children,' I said.

'Dood chlen. Me dood!' James said, clapping his little hands. Kathleen just stares at the food, then reaches out to take a biscuit.

'No', I say crossly.

'Wa, wa,' she screams.

'Shush! Here, have one then!' I shove a biscuit in her hand; she stops crying; 'thank God!'

'Gank Dod!' James repeats.

I am dying for a cup of tea, but I don't dare light a fire and boil my small copper pot, which Jim made for me. I decide to let the children eat and just think about a cup of tea. I cover the children with my tartan shawl-blanket and we sleep very well indeed, sheltered by the firm rocks around us.

'Sure it's just like home,' I whisper into James' ear.

'Mammy…' he mumbles.

…

The next morning the sun is up just before us, hiding its face behind a thick black cloud, which quickly scurries away, leaving the rays of the sun sparkling on my copper pot. I give the children some more biscuits and the rest of the milk. It's a chilly day, so I've decided to light a small fire and make a cup of tea for myself before anyone comes by. While the children are eating their biscuits and milk I head off to an old pump I noticed on the way here last night. It looks like people don't use it much as the pump is stiff as a poker. After a few tries, a trickle of lovely cold water comes out. I'm filling up my little copper pot. I can use some of it to clean the children's faces. Back I go to the pile of rocks and start a small fire with some dry sticks and hay. I have a box of matches in the bottom of my bag. In half an hour or a bit longer, I'm enjoying the best cup of tea I've ever had.

After breakfast we clean up the mess. I get the two children to squat down and go to the toilet near a bush. Kathleen is not properly toilet trained, as she was wearing a nappy when I found her. I put a fresh nappy back on her. Maeve put about six in the bag she gave me, and some baby powder. James has been out of nappies for half a year or more, so that's good news. We head back to where the bus stopped the night before. It takes us nearly an hour to get to the bus stop. I can judge the time from the sun's rising. Well, we wait and not long after, the little green and yellow bus screeches to a halt.

'The top of the morning to ye!' the bus driver yells out in a loud voice.

'Dei is Moiré dhuit!' I reply, lifting the two children up the steps of the bus.

'Did you find your friend?'

'Friend?'

'The one you were meeting?'

'I did.' I reply, not daring to look at the bus driver's face.

'That's a miracle. I never saw a soul over that way for a long time. 'T wasn't a ghost now, was it?'

'It might have been!' I sit in the nearest seat and stare out the window as we fly by the rolling countryside.

'Dwink, Mammy,' James says.

'Here's a sweetie,' I reply.

'Weet, weet!' Kathleen shouts.

'Here,' I hand her a red jelly. A woman in the seat opposite glances over the top of a book she's got her nose into. I look out the window.

'They're grand looking children. God bless them!'

'Thanks very much!' I reply, and I stare out the window again. The woman buries her head in her book. The children are sucking their sweets. We finally arrive in Galway and I help the children off the bus.

'They're lovely children, God bless them,' the woman with the nose in the book says as we climb off the bus.

'Gora mait dhuit' I reply.

'Here,' she says, handing me a pound note; 'you're very young having such a big responsibility. I wish you all the best now with your little boy and girl.'

'Two boys!'

'God, who would believe he's a boy! Such a smashing looking child.'

'Everyone says that!' I say, turning away from her; down the street; 'thank you very much; I think they need to go to the lav,' I add, hurrying towards a public convenience I notice out of the corner of my eye. 'Slean leat!'

'Slean.' She stands staring at us as we enter the toilet building. I give her a friendly wave and off she goes. 'Would you look at this James,' I say, noting the toilet door is shut. 'I need a penny to get this open. I don't have one!' Just then a woman comes out of the last toilet. 'Here, I'll hold the door for you.'

'Gora mait dhuit!' I say, breathing a sigh of relief.

As we come out of the toilets I notice a bus standing at the kerb nearby. 'Is this bus going to Cork?' I ask a bus driver who's boarding it.

'No; we're off to Limerick; in five minutes!'

'All right then; come on, you two, jump up,' I say to James

and Kathleen, giving them a whoosh up.

'Here;' I hand him the five pound note Maeve gave me. He hands me the change. Kathleen falls asleep after a short time. James is still as bright as a button, pointing out cows and sheep as he sees them.   My heart sinks as Kathleen starts sweating and making gurgling noises. The next thing I know she's vomited all over my lap.

'There's a bad smell around here,' a woman in a black coat says from behind me. The woman puckers her face into an ugly contortion.

'She, I mean, he's just sicked up, that's all!' I say in reply to her snide remark.

'Children shouldn't be allowed on public buses, especially when they don't even pay. They should be kept at home with their mothers. That's what I say.'

'I am their mother!' Kathleen's head lurches again and she makes more horrible sounds. 'I need to get off here,' I call to the driver, who's a few seats down the front from me. 'My child is sick.'

'Next stop then!' he calls back. The woman in the black coat nods her head.

'That's a grand idea altogether.' The bus pulls up and we all lurch forward.

'Gort,' he calls out. I stand up, holding Kathleen with one arm, and my bags over my shoulder.

'Come on James. We have to get off here,' I say, holding James by the hand as we wobble down the aisle of the bus.

'When's the next bus to Limerick?' I ask the driver as we embark.

'At half-two.'

'Right!' I'm wondering if I should ask for some of my money back.

'Step down please. You're holding me up.' I don't think I'm getting my fare back.

'Gora mait dhuit.' I step off with my children.

'Slean leat!

'Slean.'

Six hours later, after another fare and bus trip, we finally get to Limerick.

'Limerick! All off,' the driver calls out as we pull up with a jerk. I'm holding a sleepy Kathleen and take James by the hand.

'I'll give you a hand with your bag.' A smiling young man with dark hair and blue eyes says in a lilting Cork accent. I stand up with my burdens.

'I'm all right. Gora mait dhuit, thanks.'

'Here, I'll take the lad,' he says, picking James up and carrying him off the bus.

'Gora mait dhuit,' I repeat, as he places James on the footpath.

'Are you all right then?' he asks. 'Can I buy you a drink?'

'No thanks. I'm just passing through on my way to Cork, to meet my husband!' I lie.

'I see. It's been grand meeting you anyhow!' He salutes me as he heads down the footpath, glancing back once or twice.

'I'm finished with men! I've had enough of them. They only bring trouble, that's all,' I mutter to James as we head off. 'Daddy' he says as he waves to the man.

'No Daddy,' I say, yanking him closer to my leg. 'No Daddy!' he repeats.

'That's right James. Good boy.'

'Dood boy.'

I wondered if we had any relatives in Limerick, so I find the post office and lean over the counter. A thin, grey haired man looks up at me from his work at a small desk. He's wearing very thick glasses. He glares and says:

'What?'

'I was wondering if you know of any Murphys, or

O'Briens, or McCann's living in Limerick.

He turns back to his work. 'Gerroff with you now. You're pulling me leg.'

'How do you mean?' I ask seriously.

'How many fish are in the sea?'

'How should I know?' I reply, still puzzled by his remark.

'How should I know how many Murphys O'Briens or McCann's there are in Limerick?'

...

I find a quiet dry spot near a bridge and camp overnight in Limerick. I decide to head for Cork as Maeve suggested; maybe I can find our relations there. Late the following evening we arrive in Cork. Kathleen doesn't get sick this time, thank God. This is because I've learned the trick of feeding her dry bread while we travel. Well, you never saw such a busy place as Cork. There are shops and buildings everywhere, and well dressed folk rushing about. I feel the excitement of being in a big city. It's like a dream come true. We walk across a bridge to Cobh and sit on a stone wall with the two children beside me. It's a beautiful soft summers evening. I give them milk and biscuits. I find a nice cosy spot near some trees on the side of the bridge and settle the children for the night.

We're not far from the dock, so I go for a stroll in the cool evening air. I walk along the dockside, staring out into the shimmering dark water, which relentlessly surges backwards and forwards, gurgling loudly and then softly. A shiver runs down my spine as I remember the day I almost drowned. Before I can become remorseful the figure of a man pulls up alongside the nearby pylon in a small fishing boat.

'Do you need a boat Miss?'

'Do you go to the islands?'

'I do, every day.'

'What about tomorrow?'

'No. Not tomorrow, there's one ship leaving tomorrow. It's

her!'

'That big ship over there?'

'That's right, Queenstown II; 't'was made right here in Cork; it's off to America. Cargo, and passengers. Now I'd give my right arm to be going on that girl.'

'Me too! I hear the streets are paved with gold in America. It's even bigger than Cork!'

'Aye, and all that.'

'You wouldn't happen to know how much it costs to go on that big ship?'

'It's very dear. Hundreds of pounds, I think! I know someone who's going on her tomorrow. He'll know more about it.'

'Who's that?'

'Mick Brady. Grand lad. Off to make his fortune. Great pal of mine for years. Said I'd have a drink with him before he leaves tomorrow. Did you want to meet him yourself?'

'I'll check on the children first,' I point to the hotel across the road.

'So, you're staying at the Commodore?' I give him a nod as though he's right!

'I'll wait here for ye!' he says politely as I rush off. A few minutes later I join him. 'They're fine.' I see his head nod in the darkness.

'Mick lives over there, next to Flannnery's butcher shop.'

'The name's Maguire, Ted Maguire, fishing entrepreneur,' he says. The lone street light displays his smiling, twinkling eyes.

'Niamh. Niamh Farrell,' I reply, holding my ringed finger for him to see.

'Niamh, Queen of the land.' His lips touch the back of my hand as it collides with his stiff stubble.

'My mother's name was Niamh, and she was queen of Cork, I can tell you that! She never put the cork in the bottle! Too fond of the drink!' He laughs, and then shakes his head. Five minutes later Ted is banging on a stout green door. A thin man with fair hair cut in a fringe across his eyes opens the door.

'Come on in, Ted, who's the young lady?'

'This is Queen Niamh. Niamh, this is Mick Brady.' He looks at Mick. 'She wants to meet a man going to America! I'm out of luck again.'

'She's come to the right place then.' He stares at me. 'Come on in. I've been saying my goodbyes to the lads.' We parade through a hallway and into a room, which is crowded with men of all ages and two older women sitting near a table, drinking shandies, absorbed in their urgent conversation. 'This is Niamh and you all know Ted. They've come to say goodbye.' Several hands reach forward to shake mine. Mick turns towards me, leaning cautiously on a kitchen cupboard.

'So, are you off to America too?' Mick asks me.

'No!'

'She wanted to know how much the fare was?' Ted pipes in from around a corner of the room.

'You couldn't afford it.'

'How do you know that?'

'No offence meant. Nobody could afford it, not the ordinary Irish man or woman. My uncle Brendan is over there. He's sponsoring me. Sure if I lived to be a hundred, I couldn't save enough to get to Dublin, let alone America.'

'Don't believe him, Niamh. He's got the first penny he ever earned.'

'You'd need more than a houseful of pennies to get to America.'

'Sure go on with ye!' Ted mocks. 'He never spends a penny without thinking about it for a month or more!'

'Ted is just jealous of my good luck. Would you like a shandy Niamh?'

'That sounds lovely. Yes please.' Twenty minutes later Mick returns with a large glass of shandy.

'Fit for a queen.' He says handing me the cool glass. I sip. It tastes bitter sweet.

'I've never tasted anything like this before.'

'It's my special brew,' Mick says.

'What time are you off then?'

'To bed?'

'No, to America?'

'Of course, that's where I'm going all right! America the home of the free! Early. Seven sharp.'

'Is Ted seeing you off?' Ted's eyes fill with liquid as he turns towards us.

'I'm seeing Mick off if it's the last thing I do on this earth. I'll be right there on the ship until it sails away!'

'Will they let you on the ship then?'

'Oh, God yes! They usually always do so, however, because of several incidents they may not.'

'Why not,' I venture to ask.

'Because, my dear Queen Niamh,' Ted says in his most eloquent voice, 'they found that some young lads and even lassies were not getting off at all, before the ship set sail, when they hadn't paid their fare.'

'How could they do that?'

'They jump in those little boats on the sides and stay there until she's out at sea, then it's too late to come back. They eventually do, so what's the point.'

'Do what?'

'Come back. But they boast about being to America. They say it's worth it!'

'What's worth it?'

'Yerra girl, gaol! That's where they end up. Mind you,' he suddenly places his hand near his face as if divulging a secret, 'a few have made it!'

'To America?'

'That's correct. Would you like another drop?'

'No thanks. God, what time is it?'

'Nearly ten,' Ted replies, pulling a watch from his breast pocket.

'It's getting late! Ted, Mick, I've had a great evening. Now I've really got to go. Thanks very much for introducing me to Mick. It's been a pleasure!'

'So, you're not staying the night then?' Ted says, jokingly.

'No, not tonight!' I try to sound real casual like.

'Not tonight Josephine!' Ted squeals.

'Stop it Ted,' Mick chides, grinning delightedly at me.

'My husband might be here now,' I lie. 'He's over six feet tall. He's Australian!'

'He's a very lucky man!' Ted's eyebrows rise as he steps back.

'Well, slean leat now,' Mick says, holding his glass of black liquid steady in his hand. I run towards the spot where the children are still sleeping soundly. I sit up all night in case I might be asleep when the boat leaves. I have the privilege of seeing the sun glimmer through the misty morning. It rises slowly, carefully, twinkling all the time. I've brought my old scissors with me, one that Jim made. After breakfast, I take a deep breath and cut Kathleen's curls off, one by one. After that ordeal I've put the children's warm things on them; it's a cold morning for summertime.

...

We're soon on the dock and the Queenstown II is anchored near the dockside, proudly waiting to set sail. It's an amazing sight. I'm sitting near the dock and watching what's going on. James is still half-asleep and Kathleen won't stop eating or drinking. There's hardly any milk left. I'm waiting to see Mick Brady. I'm here a bit too early it seems. Just then he makes his dramatic appearance. His eyes struggle to see from under the long fringe. He's wearing a pink shirt and a pale green suit with fashionable flared trouser legs. He's wearing cream coloured suede shoes and he's carrying two large brown suitcases.

'Mick Brady,' I say excitedly to James. 'He's going on the ship. We're going to talk to him.' Just at that moment he spots us and comes over.

'There y'are now; is the big fella still sleeping?'

'The big fella?'

'Your husband, the Australian.'

'He is, begorrah.' I can feel the lie making my face red.

'It's nice of you to see me off anyhow.'

'It's not often I know someone going to America!'

His chin lifts in mock pride. 'You're privileged then!'

We continue up the ramp to the ship. James is walking and I'm carrying Kathleen.

'So, what part are you going to?'

'Just above the water! C deck.'

'That's nice. But what I mean is, whereabouts in America.'

'Oh that! The Big Apple! That's what my Uncle Brendan calls it. New York, Manhattan, is the place where he lives. He's getting on a bit now, but I can stay a while with him until I get settled.'

'So, do they grow apples there?'

'Well now, I suppose they must with a name like that! They make big money there, for Uncle Brendan paid my fare and all, and I've never met him...'

'So, he doesn't even know who he's paying for! He must have money to burn.'

'He must! He even sent me some American dollars and all. That's how I bought these new clothes.'

'Sure you're looking grand, a real toff.' We move together for a few moments. 'Are there many seeing you off then?'

'Ted and maybe some others. They'll come aboard for a while. We've got nearly an hour yet.' We approach the man checking the tickets.

'They're with me; saying our last goodbyes.' He hardly glances at us.

'That's fine. Just make sure they're disembarked before takeoff. If anyone unauthorised is found on board there are stiff penalties.'

'Well, she won't be staying. Her owld fella is probably coming to get her now,' Mick assures the man. The man grunts and looks at the next couple coming through.

'Begorrah, there's Ted! He's brought Mark and Liam with him too.'

'We'll have to go,' I say to Mick. 'The children need to go to the lav.'

'When nature calls you must attend,' he replies eloquently.

'I must. Well, have a pleasant journey. May the seas rise up to meet you and the wind be always at your back,' I say as eloquently as possible.

'If ever you, and your husband come to America, look me up, now.'

'We will! God, I have to go! James is wandering over there.' I point to where he's heading. 'Before we get into trouble.'

'Slean!' I rush off to get James who has run along the deck. I carry Kathleen with one arm, and two bags in my other. I find James hiding behind some small boats about ten feet away.

'There you are James, I call as I bend down to tie his shoelaces. 'These are the ones people hide in James,' I whisper. 'Good boy James.' I kiss his cheek. He smiles cheekily. 'In this game, everyone has to be really, really quiet,' I whisper. Kathleen stares at me with her big brown eyes, chewing away on a crust. James is listening intently. 'See that little boat, we're going to go inside it and stay there for a long time! This is our secret adventure.' James nods his head enthusiastically. Cautiously, I'm undoing a stiff rope and placing my foot inside the boat.

'Get your foot off me!' A voice calls out from the darkness.

'God Almighty; Sorry. I didn't know you were here.'

'Find your own!' the voice says. I lift my leg back over the side. We move along to the next boat, and ever so carefully I lift the cover. Again, I hear voices. I can see nothing.

'Shush. Get away with you.'

'I'm sorry.' I reply to some unknown person. And I thought I had a bright idea!

'Hello, anyone in there?' I ask as I move on to the fourth boat in the row. No answer. 'This is it!' We climb in and sit still. I give the children sweets, one in each tiny hand. They chew happily. I hear voices outside, and shouting, then footsteps running. My heart is in my mouth wondering if the cover is going to be lifted any minute. Nothing happens. I can hear the engines purring and feel the ship slithering away. I long to scream and shout, 'We're off. Hurray!' but I just swallow and hold my breath for a moment, suddenly feeling sick inside.

'Let's have a little sleep,' I suggest. Kathleen puts her head down on my knee and James leans against my arm. 'Hush little baby, don't say a word...' I sing quietly. It's rather cosy in here. At least we're together, the three of us. I haven't felt this happy since I fell in love with Niall. James and Kathleen are falling asleep and I feel so tired I'm falling asleep myself, even though my stomach is twisting and turning.

...

I don't know how long we've been sleeping, but all of a sudden I'm wide-awake. I'm peeping out from under the covers. There's sea around us! What a sight. We must be miles away from Cork now. I'm feeling very hungry and my tummy is still squeamish. I know the children will be hungry when they wake up. I'm crawling out of the little boat and I feel as stiff as a board. The pins and needles are running through my feet and legs. I'm creeping along the back of the boats next to the rail, breathing in the fresh salty air. Suddenly, two heads pop from another little boat, giving me a terrible fright. At the same moment the boat lurches and my stomach throws its contents upwards. I lean over the rail.

'Don't do that.' the young man says, leaning over nearby and throwing up, making an awful noise. A moment later the girl is doing the same. After a few minutes, I wipe my mouth.

'I feel better now.'

'Me too,' the lad says, 'it's great to spew!'

'Don't say that word,' the girl says, leaning over the rail again.

A few minutes later she joins us.

'I thought you must've got caught?'

'No. They didn't even look for us. That was our friend, Andrew in the other boat. Poor sod,' the girl says.

'We should introduce ourselves!' I suggest.

'Should we?' the girl replies, looking at me under her eyelids.

'I'm not the garda! I'm Niamh Farrell, and my two children; James and..., Larry are in the boat up the back! What're your names?'

'I'm Alice Lennon and this geyser is my brother Peter.'

'I'm not a geyser,' Peter protests. 'And I know my own name!' He pushes Alice.

'Don't you dare push me.' She retaliates, making a fist.

'Stop your fighting or we'll all be caught. Neither of you look old enough to be here on your own anyway!'

'I'm fourteen and he's nearly twelve.'

'Well, act your age, why don't you?' I chide.

'Yeah, why don't you,' Alice says to Peter.

'Na,' he replies, sticking out his tongue.

'That's enough, the pair of you.' I reprimand them, feeling like I'm their big sister already.

Alice is a slim girl, nearly as tall as me. She has dark brown hair, long and straight, parted in the middle, hanging down listlessly around her elfin shaped face. She has the fairest skin I've ever seen. Her eyes are deep grey with a sad look. Peter is shorter, scrawny, with sandy coloured hair, that desperately needs cutting. His freckles cover his cheeks in a mosaic type pattern.

'Where do we get grub?' I ask.

'I'll go,' Peter says. 'My Daddy says I'm a thief at heart.'

'Yes, he could steal your eye and come back for the eyelashes and you wouldn't know,' Alice agrees, giggling happily, covering her mouth. 'But what's the point of eating if we get sick again?'

'If the children don't eat they'll start to cry,' I say wisely, having learned that much in life.

'You'd better get food then, Peter,' Alice suggests.

'Right-o!' Peter scurries off into the shadows.

'I'll go and find where the *lav* is,' Alice says, ducking down and waddling along awkwardly in her mini, tight skirt, close to the rail behind the small boats. 'You stay here. I'll be back.' Ten minutes later she comes crawling back. 'Come on, I found a really great lav. Nobody's there!'

'I wonder if anybody ever comes up here,' I remark as we move in a train, carrying Kathleen and James. We follow Alice along a narrow corridor.

'Here.' She points to a door with a picture of a woman's head with a high hairdo and a cigarette in her mouth. It's a beautiful little lavatory, so clean and sparkling. I place James on the seat and then Kathleen. After that I lift Kathleen on the small bench at the sink.

'I thought she was a boy?' Alice says watching me put powder and a nappy on Kathleen.

'Did you, now?' I reply. She keeps staring at Kathleen.

'I'd keep an eye on her.'

'She's a good child,' I respond.

'People steal children now. They might want money,' she says knowingly.

'Well, we don't have any, so why would anybody steal her?' I ask casually.

'I heard that a baby got stolen in the West of Ireland.'

'Oh, who told you that?'

'Nobody told me. Peter's got a portable radio and we listened to the news this morning. They said the baby got taken a few days ago. Now what was her name? I forget that bit! But they said she was about two, with dark curly hair!'

'Well Loretta doesn't have curly hair.'

'You're right there. It looks like someone's hacked it to pieces.'

'It grows like that!' I reply, red faced now. 'Don't hurt her feelings Alice.'

'Sorry Loretta, that's a lovely name!' Alice says to Kathleen, tickling her bare tummy. Kathleen giggles.

'Can you look after her and James while I go.'

'Of course I will.'

I sit on the toilet and enjoy the peace for a minute, wishing Alice and Peter had stayed in Cork. But then, they're just like me, needing a place to run to. We sneak back to the small tied up boats and can smell the food ten yards away.

'Over here,' a voice whispers. We hurry along and there before us is a feast.

'Peter, you're a wonder!'

'Hot food for all,' he says, his mouth full of chicken.

'I got bread, chicken, chips, cakes and a bottle of drink.'

That was the most wonderful meal. We are all so hungry we forget where we are for a few minutes.

'So, do you have more children?' Alice asks me through eating a plump breast of chicken and passing the bottle of drink.

'I lost a child.'

'So, are you married?'

'I was. My last husband drowned.'

'God that's bloody awful,' Alice exclaims.

'Shh, don't say that word in front of Kathleen and James!' I admonish her sharply.

'Bloody hell, who's Kathleen?'

'I meant Loretta! Sorry, I get mixed up with names.'

'You can say that again. She's your own child, for God's sake!' Alice says, her eyes growing large.

'I'm a bit off colour today. What about your family? Any more sisters and brothers?' I ask, quickly moving the topic.

'Mammy lost a few children. I think she lost twins two years ago.'

'Did she?' Peter asks.

'You wouldn't understand these things. You're a boy!'

'I would so. I brought the grub.'

'You did too. But you don't know about babies and s... e... x (she spells the word) and things.'

'I can spell! I know more than you think. I saw Aunty Joan with her big stomach.'

'She was just fat.'

'She had a baby.'

'No she didn't. She doesn't have any babies.'

'Well, she shouldn't be so fat then!'

'You're rude!'

'Shh, you two.' I whisper. We can hear someone walking towards us. We all keep quiet as a sailor walks by, with binoculars in hand. He peers over the rail and stands there staring out into the ocean. James starts choking on a piece of chicken. I place my hand over his mouth. Peter hops away like a frightened rabbit. Alice takes hold of Kathleen and puts her hand over her mouth. We stare at each other. Our hearts are stopping. We hear someone coughing a few yards away.

'It's Peter!'

'Hey, who goes there?' the sailor asks, heading towards Peter, who is now racing away on the deck. The sailor chases after him.

'Peter!' Alice cries softly. The last sound we hear is,

'Let me go, you big b!'

'He's a goner!' Alice says solemnly, her eyes darting left and right. 'Let's get back in the boats and lie low. He won't snitch on us. I told him I'd kill him if he did!' The four of us climb back into boat number four and stay still. We remain there for several hours. Kathleen and James fall asleep again, out of sheer boredom. 'We might be in America soon!' Alice whispers.

'What are you going to do when you get there?' I ask.

'I'll probably find a job, get some money, and buy lots of nice clothes and shoes; and make-up,' she states categorically.

'What about getting married?'

'Maybe, when I'm old; I'll be a famous film star by then. Actually, you'd make a great film star. You're really gorgeous, you know.'

'I was thinking the same thing about you!'

'Go on!' We both laugh. Suddenly, the covers are pulled back. Two faces peer into ours.

'Who goes there?' A solidly built young male who sports dark hair, rugged features and the whitest teeth I had ever seen accompanies an American accent. He takes Alice out by the arm. 'Get out!'

'You too girl!' The other face, belonging to a more softly spoken American with curly fair hair, says to me. The two are wearing sparkling white uniforms.

'Albert, I think half of Ireland stowed away on this ship.'

'Well, I found myself a little doll.' Albert is holding tightly on to Alice, who is squirming in his arms.

'Let me go; please; I'll do anything you want?'

'Oh yeah!' says Albert.

'I mean it; anything. Just let me get to America, that's all. Please don't send me back to Ireland; father beats me with a strap.'

'Maybe we can help these little darlings? Hey Sam?'

'We have to report them!' Sam replies. He turns his attention to me. 'Your name?'

'Niamh Farrell'

'Niamh. What a quaint name. What else have we got in here?' He stares at Kathleen and James who stare back. Kathleen cries; James sniffs.

'Hush now; don't worry.' I try to comfort them. 'They're my childers.'

'So, come on now; it's fine; we won't hurt you! What's your name little man?' Sam asks James as he lifts him over the side.

'Jaes,' James says.

'James?'

'That's right, Sir,' I confirm.

'Why, hello there James!' Sam salutes James. James stares at Sam.

'Come on you pretty little thing. What's your name?'

'Loretta!' I say quickly before Alice buts in.

'Loretta! Come on; time to go.' Albert is whispering in Alice's ear and then calls Sam over. Sam's face is suddenly a mask of worry.

'Get back in the boat; I'll see y'all later,' Sam whispers to me as they leave.

'What's going on?' I ask, watching them leave, and lifting the two children back into their hiding place.

'I said we'd stay until they give us the word,' Alice explains, getting into the boat next to ours.

'Why don't we hide somewhere else?' I suggest.

'No!' she seems suddenly angry. 'I promised,' she states more quietly, 'and they'd find us, anyway.'

'Probably right,' I remark. We settle down in our small space, and we're all inclined to doze off in the darkness. Sometime later, Alice shakes me.

'It's time; come on; I'll lead the way.'

'Shh; the children are sleeping again.'

'We can go without them!' she says.

'Not on your nanny! Come on James, time for walkies. Kathleen, come on Alanna.' I whisper so that Alice can't hear me saying Kathleen's name. I shake them ever so gently.

'Have it your way; I'll take Loretta.' Alice snaps, reaching down and picking up the sleepy child. I take James and follow Alice down some awkward spiral steps. After four rounds of steps I'm feeling dizzy and nauseous again. The children look white in the face.

'This is it!' Alice declares, walking through a narrow corridor with slim doors on one side; I'm following close behind.

'What are we doing here?'

'We made a deal!'

'What do you mean by: a deal?' I ask. Before Alice can answer, Albert appears in the doorway.

'Hey, come in y'all. Sam, your broad's here.'

'Hi. Please excuse his bad language!' Sam comes through the door at the far end of the room.

'You're with Sam; I'm with Albert!' Alice whispers.

'Come on; I'm in here.' Sam leads James and me through the door into another tiny room with two bunk beds on one side.

'Here, take her.' Alice says, passing Kathleen into Sam's arms.

'Hey there, Loretta,' he whispers. Kathleen jerks backwards. 'Hey there, it's me, Uncle Sam!' Alice closes the door behind her, leaving me with Sam and the two children in the small space.

'What's going on?' I ask Sam.

'Alice offered her services to Albert, in exchange for protection.'

'Services?'

He looks at me with furled brows. 'You know...?' I gasp. 'Do you mean ...s...e...x?' (I spell out the letters).

'Look, it's okay. I owe Albert a favour. We could hand you over.'

'We'd be sent back to Ireland, wouldn't we?' He nods his head.

'What happens if we get to America?' I ask.

'You will probably be exported back to Ireland.'

'It's hopeless then,' I remark. 'I'm an egit.'

'Niamh, you can take your case to the court. You might have the luck of the Irish and be allowed asylum in America.'

'What if I've done something bad?'

'Well, there is still some justice in America. Your voice will be heard. It's a democratic country you know?'

'So, there's hope for me?'

'There sure as hell is!'

'I'm probably going there anyway!'

'What do you mean gal?'

'Hell!'

'Sure!' He grins, thinking I'm joking. Sam looks at James. 'James how would you like to go up in here?' he bounces James off his feet and swings him into the top bunk. James giggles. 'And you Loretta? Up you go.' Kathleen giggles as she is scooped into the air. 'I have some chocolate for you.' He unwraps the foil from a large bar of milk chocolate. He gives them each a piece.

'Mind your manners; say thanks!' I instruct the two happily feeding faces.

'Ganks!' they reply in unison.

'Would you like some?' he asks.

'I would, thanks very much!' I say, 'mm', enjoying the creamy taste, forgetting how ill I've been feeling.

'Sit down, Niamh, relax.' I sit on the bottom bunk next to him.

'Could you get into trouble for this?' I ask. Sam makes a face.

'A lot of trouble, unfortunately. Albert thinks it's worth it...'

'Did you know Alice is only fourteen?'

'No.' He pauses. 'And you didn't tell me, okay?'

'You should tell your friend!' I suggest.

'Niamh, don't worry about Alice; she's not your problem?'

'She's a child.'

'Niamh, let's not talk about them. I want to know more about you.'

'Why?' I ask. 'What if I don't want to tell you anything?' He stretches out on the bed.

'Come on; lay down next to me.'

'No. I'm tired of lying.' He closes his eyes.

'I'm just exhausted. I've been up for twenty-four hours,' he says sleepily. I lie down next to him.

'All right, but just don't touch me.' I say. The sound of low snoring tells me he's sleeping! After lying there, thinking for some time, I doze off too. I wake up to strange noises. I sit up, just in time to see Sam coming out of the small bath room with a towel around him. I gasp in fright.

'Sorry. I didn't mean to frighten you. I'm going on duty,' he explains. 'I have to get dressed!' he adds.

'I won't look,' I reply, turning away. A few minutes later he calls out. 'You can turn around now!' I turn around.

'How do you keep yourself clean,' I ask, noting his smart white uniform.

'White makes it easy to spot the stains.'

'You're very handsome,' I comment.

'Thank you very much.' His white teeth shine as he smiles spontaneously. 'If you want to use the shower please be discrete. It's a communal facility.'

'Others; they'll find us.'

'They already know about you; I just didn't want you to be unduly surprised, that's all.'

'They know about us; they won't snitch?'

'It's just those who live here, me, Albert, and Charlie, who's on duty now.'

'They won't report us?'

'We've made a deal. But there's one snag.'

'Snag?'

'Inspection! We had one before we set sail, so the coast should remain clear for a day or so. They do come unannounced.'

'What'll we do then?'

'I don't know. We can just keep our fingers crossed, maybe we'll reach shore by then. God knows. Well, y'all, I have to leave. I'll bring something home.'

...

I sit and stare at the clock on the wall, watching the hours go by. The porthole is in the room with the shower, so occasionally I get up and stare into the black water behind that. Nothing happens for several hours. I take the children to the toilet and give them a drink of water, and put them back in bed. I lie back on the bed, feeling really sick inside my body. I find that the humming noises of the ship's engines are making me feel drowsy.

'They're coming to get me, gerroff,' I hear myself mumbling as I push the monsters away. 'They're back!' I burst out into a cold sweat.

'What's wrong?' I feel an arm around my shoulders. I open my eyes,

'Sam, Oh, Sam!'

'What happened? You all right? Hey, you're trembling.'

'The monsters... Ugly monsters, with pitch forks!'

'It's okay now!' he soothes me. I take a deep breath and begin to feel better. I stare into Sam's eyes.

'We're going to be caught, I just know it!'

'Hey, you're with me now. Everything's fine.' I jump up and check the top bunk.

'The children: are they all right?'

'They're fine. I gave them a drink of pop at around two when I came off shift; found some baby toys for them too.'

'They'll wet the bed!'

'I took them to the toilet. I changed Kathleen's diaper.'

'Her what? What have you changed on her?'

'She was wet! I just put a fresh diaper on. I found them in one of your bags.'

'Oh, you mean, nappy?'

'Yes, nappy!' He's chuckling with mirth now. I almost fall over with shock.

'But you're a man!'

'I know I'm a man. So what does that imply?'

'Men don't change nappies, I mean diapers!'

'It's just another job!'

'Well, I never heard the like of it before! You're a marvel, that's what!'

'I have never had that title before! Now, you go back to sleep. It's still early.' I notice a blanket and a pillow on the floor.

'Have you been sleeping on the floor?'

'I was afraid I'd upset you.'

'You won't! It is your bed. I can share it!' I suggest surprisingly, even to myself.

'What about your honour?' he asks.

'Well, if you keep your hands to yourself, I'll keep my

honour,' I reply. He sits on the side of the bed and his mouth breaks into a great American smile.

'I hope you don't mind, but I brought you something,' he says, pulling open a bag.

'What?' I ask. He hands me a fresh sandwich.

'I'm not hungry,' I tell him.

'Still feeling nauseous?' I nod my head. I feel worse by the minute.

'By the way, the children have eaten. I also gave them one of these.' He hands me something in a foil packing.

'What is that?' I shy away from the object.

'It's only a seasickness tablet; I thought you could use one.'

'Do you think a little white pill can make me better?' I take the tablet from his fingers. He hands me a bottle.

'Here, have a drink.'

'What sort of drink is that?' I ask as I down a mouthful. 'It's great!'

'Fizzor!'

'That's a strange name for a lovely drink.'

'Glad you approve. I brought you something else.' He takes a garment from the bag. 'Something to wear.' He holds up a pale blue silk nightdress.

'It's gorgeous.' I resist the urge to ask him where he got it, as Jim's angry face comes to mind. 'It's silky!'

'Glad you approve. Now, I must be off, so I'll see y'all soon.' Sam is suddenly gone. About an hour later the twins wake up.

'Come on, we'll all go to the lav, then you can have a drink and breakfast!'

'Lav,' James repeats, holding his wee 'willie'. After that I feel so good I decide we all need a bath! We all take our clothes off and step into the little shower room. 'God this is wonderful; like warm rain!' I laugh. The children sense my excitement and forget their fear. 'Ah, don't touch these taps now!' The children shake their heads. 'Good!' I'm washing Kathleen's hair with some lovely shampoo in a plastic bottle. Next thing I know, she's crying.

'Mammy, Mammy!' She rubs her eyes.

'What's wrong, mo chaileen ban?' I realize it's the shampoo. 'It's all right, Alanna! Mammy will wash it all away.' The shower curtain suddenly flaps against my legs. My skin feels prickly and cool. I peer out from behind the shower curtain and emit a gasp. There's a man! He's wearing a moustache and a towel around his waist. It's not Albert and it's not Sam! It must be Charlie. I crouch down and hold on tightly to Kathleen and James.

'I'm sorry; we won't be a tick,' I call from behind the curtain. 'Please go,' I plead. Suddenly the shower curtain is pulled over and a hand turns the taps off. The man stands in the doorway in a most intimidating manner. I take a deep breath. 'I need the towel.' I point to the three fluffy towels Sam left hanging near the door. He folds his arms and grins.

'Git it yerself Gal!' I reach out between him and the towel. As my fingers grasp the towel, he gets hold of my arm and clenches me tightly. 'You do as I say, or else!' He flexes his muscles, and pulls my face to his. 'What a mighty sight y'all are!'

'Please don't, for the children's sake,' I whisper, moving in front of the two.

'Kiss?' He puckers his lips. Behind me Kathleen and James start to whimper.

'You're Charlie, aren't you?'

'Well, I'll be!' He pulls my face towards his pursed lips. 'We're old friends now darling!'

'Stop it; the children,' I pull my head away from him. He pushes me away, and throws the two other towels at me.

'Here!' he says in a gravel-rich tone. I pin the first towel around myself and quickly wrap the second two towels around the children. My hands are trembling as I try to dry the children off.

'Hurry it up will ya!' he growls at me. 'Let me assist you there Gal,' he says, taking Katheen in her towel and throwing her on the top bunk. He does the same with James. The children screw up their faces and stare at me, shocked. 'Don't ya dare cry!' he says, pointing his finger at them.

'Look at the lovely toys,' I say, handing each one a squeaky animal. They reach out and take their toys.

'Mammy,' Kathleen cries.

'Take your toy under the blanket. They'll get cold,' I say quietly, lifting the blanket up for them. They both snuggle under the warm blanket. I grab my nightie, which is lying on the bottom bunk. I still have the towel around me, which I'm holding onto with one hand, and I'm attempting to pull my nightie over my head with the other hand. Charlie steps close to me. I feel cornered.

'Are you free, Sweetheart?' He takes hold of my nightie and yanks it back off my head. I grasp hold of it until I hear a tearing sound, then I let go. He grabs me around the neck and places his large hand over my mouth. I respond to his move by biting his finger!

'Bitch!' he yelps as he pushes me away. I fall backwards onto Sam's bunk. Charlie's shadow immediately fills the space in front of me. He's sucking his damaged finger and I can feel his anger looming above me. All I can think of is the children. 'Don't, please; the children!' I whisper. He takes a tight grip of my arms and pulls me outwards. His muscles bulge with strength.

'Ouch,' I say, suppressing a scream. Holding my arms, he tries to press his mouth against mine. I twist my head and spit at him.

'Co-operate or: I'll turn you in, Bitch,' he says in his low gravely tone. He tosses me with full force onto the bed like a sack of spuds. I hear a cracking sound as I fall backwards.

'Me back: it's broken,' I whisper as pain sears through my bones and his body lands on top of me.

'Get off her, Charlie, you Son of a Bitch,' Sam's voice rings into my ears and Charlie is pulled off me. I lie still as a fight ensues. I cover my face for a moment, and when I look Sam is pushing Charlie out the door.

'Don't forget your towel!' Sam's angry words give me a strange satisfaction. The door closes. Sam turns the key.

'I'll get you for this,' I can hear as the door is pounded from without.

Sam ignores the noises. 'Are you okay? Did he...?'

'My back; something cracked,' I whisper, clutching the towel, hardly daring to move. Sam places his arm around me.

'Try to sit.' Slowly I move forward into a sitting position.

'I think I'm all right.'

Sam's voice is full of emotion, huskily he asks, 'If he hurt you, I swear I'll kill him!' He's holding me close.

'He was trying to kiss me; he shoved me backwards and I heard a terrible cracking sound,' I tell him. The cracking sound returns right then, throwing us both into the air. The bed has collapsed. Our heads are on floor level, sandwiched to each other; our feet are sticking up in the air on the end of the bed that hasn't fallen down. We're suddenly both laughing. 'Did I mention the cracking noise?' I say, bursting into laughter. Kathleen and James peer over the side of their bunk bed and giggle.

'Get back under the blanket. Now!' I call out. Their faces disappear from view. I'm staring into Sam's face and he's smiling from ear to ear. 'I'm so sorry! I'm so sorry,' I repeat myself.

Sam hugs me. 'It's not your fault. I'm sure you didn't entice him.' I smile into his very close face.

'No, I'm sorry about the bed.' We both laugh. Sam kisses my cheek.

'I glad you're okay! You are okay?' When we wriggle to get out, suddenly I'm aware of pain.

'My back! It does hurt. I can't stand up.' I say, bending forward.

Sam holds me close in his arms. I think he's hugging me again. I gasp as he quickly and strongly jerks my body towards him. He releases me. I'm standing straight. 'The pain's gone!' I say, 'It's a miracle. How did you do that?' I ask, amazed.

'It's an old chiropractic trick of mine,' he replies; he laughs.

'Here, I've been shopping again,' he says, picking up a brown paper bag off the floor. I look inside. There's a green skirt and an apricot coloured finely knitted jumper, plus a really wide belt with a fancy golden buckle on the front.

'They're beautiful. You must know a good shop,' I say. 'Can I try them on?'

'Sure.'

'Turn around!' I instruct him. 'They're on. What do you think?' I ask, swinging my hips.

'Wowee! You look terrific, Niamh.'

'They're exactly my size. It's amazing,' I say smiling happily. I shove my hands into the side pockets of the skirt. 'Lovely deep pockets too, like my other skirt.'

'I'm glad you approve; I brought you this.' He hands me a lovely hairbrush.

'Oh, I really need one of these?' I say, immediately brushing my hair. I'm still wondering from where he's getting these but I daren't ask. As if he's reading my mind, he says,

'Aren't you going to ask where I got these from?' I shake my head. 'Would you like to know?'

'I would love to know, but I don't want to make you mad,' I explain.

'I could never be angry with such an angel as you are.'

'I warn you, I'm no angel.'

'You're very close...'

I smile at Sam, flattered. 'You remind me of Brian Boru,' I exclaim.

'An old boyfriend of yours?' he asks.

'No, he was the first king of Ireland.'

'A king; I like that.' His eyes are suddenly teary.

'What ails you? I ask.

'You; you're such an amazing person; risked so much for your children; the bravest woman I have ever met; braver than my grand-aunt, Elizabeth.' He's not joking? I wonder, staring into his face.

'No one has ever called me brave before.' I reply. I think of Maeve. 'My sister would call me a right egit if she could see me.'

'My great-aunt, Elizabeth, would call you honourable, brave and a beautiful angel.'

'Your aunty?'

'Niamh, sit down.' We sit on the edge of the broken bed. 'She was a fine woman. The Sioux Indians captured her, along with her small sister. She grew up with Indians, and twenty years later she persuaded them to let her go back to her own community with her two small children, after her husband, Big Horn, was killed in a battle. She rode into an American camp, and met my great Uncle Theodore, and;' he pauses here.

'Did they fall in love?' I ask.

'They sure did. They got married and lived happily ever after.'

'Ah, sure you're having me on!' I say shaking my head, smiling. 'I know that's definitely not how my life works.' He opens his top buttons and reveals a leather cord with a gold ring hanging on it. He takes it over his head and holds the glimmering ring.

'Niamh, what I say is the Gospel truth. See this?'

'I do; it's a ring!'

Niamh and Sam, June, 1971: ©Marie Seltenrych, 2010.

'That's correct. Can you see the tiny engraving on the inside?'

'Sure I can't read an ordinary newspaper, let alone a tiny engraving. Can you read it?'

'It says, Elizabeth, love Theo.'

'Sure that's very romantic, but it doesn't prove anything.'

'I know their story is true, and true love can happen.'

'I think that's a very true statement,' I say agreeably, remembering Niall, smiling at my thoughts.

'That's an encouraging statement! Every woman deserves

such love.'

'And every man too!' I say, agreeing, remembering Niall's happiness and mine.

'My Queen Niamh.' His mouth is suddenly on mine. For an instant I respond, with thoughts of Niall flooding my mind. His kiss tastes like chocolate. Oh God, I wish this was Niall, I pray as our lips and mouths become a sweet delight to each other for a single moment.

'No, I can't,' I whisper, faintly resisting him. He hugs me tenderly. I yield myself to his sweet embrace. We do not see the door being unlocked.

Chapter eight

'Arrest him.' A booming voice thunders through the opening, severing us apart as though it was a guillotine. The booming voice is that of Captain Perceval Simms, in decorative array, his shoulders and chest brightly adorned by medals and striped ribbons: a man of distinction, honour and unfortunately for us, power! Charlie, with a sharp expression, steel eyes and trimmed moustache, in full-decorated gleaming white uniform, follows his master, panting like a hound. I get such a fright that I slip off the bed onto the floor. Sam bends down to help me up. We stand up together, holding each other.

'Oh, my goodness; Charlie; why?' Sam exclaims, his face showing amazement. Charlie stares back. His mouth twitches underneath the burnished bronze moustache, which flicks silently up and down in its own intense rhythm. Two more men in uniforms with weapons in their hands fill the tiny room.

'Don't touch her, or the children,' Sam says, shielding me with his outstretched arm. Roughly they rotate him, pull his hands together and clip handcuffs on.

'I hereby arrest you for concealing an unauthorized person. Anything you say can be used against you! They shove him outside the door and they march him off. At that moment I notice something shiny on the floor. I bend down and pick it up. It's Sam's chain and ring.

'Sam,' I call out. Immediately Charlie stands in front of me. 'He's out of bounds, woman!'

'Arrest this woman,' Charlie shouts, 'she's a criminal, a kidnapper!'

'I am not!' I deny his accusation.

'She kidnapped the children,' Charlie advised Captain Simms, who comes through the door immediately.

'God strike me dead; they're mine!' I cry.

'I'm sorry,' Captain Simms says, 'I am Captain of this ship, and it is my duty to arrest all vagrants aboard. Anything you say can be used as evidence against you. You may choose to remain silent. You are hereby arrested for vagrancy and for unlawfully occupying ship's quarters without official consent.'

'Put your hands behind your back,' he says.

'I've got something belonging to Sam,' I reply. 'I need to see him.'

'I bet you do! But you are not going to see that Son of a Bitch!' Charlie says, his moustache twitching horribly.

'Put your hands behind your back. That's an order,' Captain Simms repeats sternly. The second man holds a pair of handcuffs in his hands, and politely waits for me to turn around. I quickly slip the smooth gold bundle into my skirt pocket and then turn with my back to him. My arms are pulled back, and I feel the cold metal handcuffs snapping my wrists together.

'My children,' I cry, beckoning towards the bunk beds.

'We'll take care of them, Sir!' the man who cuffed me, says; swiftly takes Kathleen and James from the bunk bed, wraps them in their towels, and carries them in his arms.

I follow the captain, with Charlie at my rear and the children in the arms of the other man. We parade up two winding stairways. We come to a door and halt. I'm pushed inside and the door is closed. I can hear Kathleen's muffled screams as they move past the doorway. The lock goes 'click'. 'Let me out!' I wail as I bang on the door with my feet. I look around. It's a bigger room than Sam's. There's a small room on the left side of a single porthole, which is being pounded by waves. There's a long cupboard on its right. Two bunk beds are arranged on either side of these two structures. The room is dark, but after a minute, I notice two figures huddled on the floor. 'Alice and Peter? What are you doing here?' I ask as they glare at me.

'You snitched on us,' Alice says cattily.

'How come I've got these on,' I say, showing my handcuffs at my back.

'Oh well, we're all in the same boat!' Alice retorts and then laughs. We all laugh at the joke.

'It's not funny, though,' Alice comments after a minute. We both look at Peter.

'Me? No, I swear I didn't snitch!'

'You said it was Niamh,' Alice shouts at Peter. 'You're always boasting about lying. It was you! There's nobody else?' she screams.

'All right; I did!' he snarls.

'I knew it!' Alice suggests emphatically: 'Tinker!' Peter shrugs his shoulders.

'Don't call me ugly names. Well now they'll probably throw you girls into the freezing water. Boys are more valuable than girls. They can think!'

'Shut your gob.' She looks at me. 'I think they might bring us to America, because we're too far from Ireland now. When I get there I'm going to run off with Albert! He's my boyfriend now!'

'Half your luck,' I say sliding down the wall into a sitting position on the cold floor. There's silence for a few moments. I can feel the fear all around us, like a heavy Irish mist.

'Did you say anything about my childers?' I put the question to Alice.

'No! I said nothing.'

'Yes, you did.' Peter reminds Alice. 'She snitched on you. Alice said the children were kidnapped!' Fear strangles my throat.

'Why did you say that? I never told you that.'

'I heard you call her, Kathleen. Then I remembered what they said on the radio. Her name was Kathleen. I think you hacked her curls off and changed her name.'

'You are so smart Alice! So why did you do that?'

'I thought they'd let me off if I told them.' She shrugs her shoulders. 'I had to look after meself.'

...

'Time to go!' A voice rings in the unlocked door; three officers march into the room; each one takes hold of one of us.

'Are you throwing us overboard?' I ask as we're pulled to our feet.

'Sure are,' the officer replies. 'Come on, single file, up the stairs,' one officer says, pushing me from behind. Alice screams, so they tie a cloth around her face. Peter and I keep quiet after that. All my dreams are vanishing like the stars at daybreak as I trudge down the narrow corridor; we reach an opening and stop.

'Turn around,' one officer with a white hat says to us. We turn around; a cloud of fear falls over me.

'They're going to push us over,' Peter whispers in my ear. Even the thought of the cold sea makes me shiver.

'My childers,' I say, lamenting. I feel someone unlocking my cufflinks.

'Regulation,' he says, strapping a bright yellow lifejacket on each of us. 'Over you go, Mam,' he says to me. I look down and there's a boat alongside the big ship.

'What about my childers?' I ask, trembling.

'Mam, just follow orders and step over. Get your legs around the rope; hold on tight.' I hang onto a rope and I'm lowered into the boat. Alice is followed by Peter. We land in the smaller boat and are greeted by a round, red faced man in a black peaked hat. He smiles, showing a thousand wrinkles on his old weather beaten face.

'Where are we going?' I ask him.

'The smallest town on earth: Cork!' We're told to descend a short stair and find ourselves in a small room with seats in a half-circle.

'James, Kathleen,' I say loudly as I see my two little darlings sitting next to a female officer in two little seats at the end of the room. 'Can I sit with my children?' I ask the woman. Her face buckles into a thin smile.

'Sorry, I have strict orders to care for these children.' A hand is placed on my shoulder. I turn around to see a male officer.

'Mam, please sit down, back here.'

'But these are my children. They need their mother,' I protest.

'I am sorry, Mam. Please put your hands forward.' I automatically put my hands out and he clasps handcuffs on again. I stumble back to where Alice and Peter are seated. They are both handcuffed again and Alice's gob stopper has been removed.

'You'd think we were criminals,' I comment to Alice. An African-American guard sitting next to Peter must have heard me.

'You are!' he remarks, laughing.

...

The remainder of the journey seems long and miserable. Being a smaller boat it lurches much more than the big ship. The engine seems very noisy too, and we have to shout if we want to speak, so we just try to sleep and be quiet for most of the journey. We have been offered food several times, but the three of us feel too sick to eat. I can just see Kathleen and James, who have been lying still most of the way. The conversation is sparse and we're all freezing cold as we return from whence we came: Cork Harbour; 'tis shrouded in a fine mist when we arrive like ghosts on the water. A lone man's voice echoes across the waves as our boat is tied to the dock. A figure stoops to fix the gangplank in the dim night-light.

'Come on out you lot. Get up and be quick about it,' a guard says as we climb up the stairs to the main deck. It's the middle of the night, and all we can see are shadows. The place is so quiet that we can hear the lapping of the waves against the shore. The three of us are paraded down a short ramp and we climb in the back of a black van and are taken to the local gaol, where Peter is subsequently ushered somewhere, flanked by two guards. Alice tries to say goodbye, but he disappears into the misty night in a flash. We are put into a room with bars. It has two hard beds and a sink and a toilet.

'I'll take these off ye,' the warder, says as we enter the cell. 'Give your wrists a good rub to get the circulation right,' she advises us kindly. We both rub our sore wrists.

'At lease we've stopped moving,' I comment as the door of bars is locked.

'My wrists are all red,' Alice says, staring at her hands.

'Maybe you're rubbing them too hard?' I suggest. 'Mine are all right.' I remark, 'Which bed do you want?'

'This one,' Alice says, flopping onto the one next to the wall.

'Why not?' I mutter, as I fall onto the other bed facing the barred door. 'They're all the same,' I say. We must have fallen asleep after that. A loud bell wakes us up.

'Come on you two chaileen, off to the wash house.'

'But I had a one this week!' Alice complains.

'Time for another one; wash all that muck off you,' the female warden says. 'We couldn't wash the muck off your souls, you pair of whores.'

'I'm not one of those, I'm a mother.' I protest.

'And I'm Officer Sheila O'Donaghue. I'm in charge here, so shut up and follow me.' She marches to a room with a bath half full of water. 'Get your clothes off and get in there. Use the soap.'

'I'm not taking my clothes off in front of her,' I protest.

'If you strip for men, you can strip for women,' she says sarcastically.

'I won't look,' Alice whispers, turning around.

'No yabbering you two. Put these on when you come out!' O'Donaghue throws two baggy frocks and two large knickers on the lone chair. 'I'll take these and have them burned. I'm taking your shoes as well.'

'You can take my shoes, but please don't take my new skirt and top. No! They were a present!' I utter, attempting to get out of the bath.

'Rubbish!' The female guard says as she pushes me back in the water. 'You're afraid of water, are you?'

'No!' I reply

'You're very brazen. You need to wash your mouth out with soap! These are rubbish and they're getting burned. Have you anything else to say?' She scowls at me.

'My rings; can I have them?'

'Not on your life! We don't want you doing harm to yourself,' she snarls back.

'How could a ring do me harm? I just wear it on my finger,' I say pleadingly.

'You could use it as a weapon to buy illegal drugs! Don't argue with me. Get in there now!' I sink into the bathtub of cold water, take the soap and I'm washing myself. I get out and Alice gets in.

'It's freezing in here. We may as well have drowned in the cold sea.' Alice whispers. The next day Alice's father arrives to see her.

'Out here, now!' another female warder, Molly O'Toole, says, opening the door with her huge key. She's lucky, I'm thinking, as Alice is marched off; comes back an hour later. After O'Toole locks her in with me, I ask what went on.

Alice says,

'I've got to go to court tomorrow. Me da's going to take me back home.'

'I'm very pleased for you,' I say.

'I don't want to go back to me da; never!' She flops on the bed and stares at the ceiling and I put my behind down on her blank of a bed. I know I'm no priest, but I felt that I had to give her a bit of advice.

'You're lucky your da cares about you.'

'I hate him!' Alice says ferociously.

'Hey, you're getting out of this dump, so don't get your knickers in a knot!' I reply.

'Shut your gob!' she retorts bitterly. The next morning I wake up to a weird moaning noise.

'Alice?' I can barely whisper the words. She is lying half on the bed and on the floor and there's blood everywhere. Her skin has turned as grey as an Irish sky.

'Help, someone help!' I yell, rattling the door as much as I can. I'm screaming as loud as I can. Keys rattle. A male guard follows Margaret O'Halloran, another female warder. They enter the cell.

'What's up?' she bursts out. My shaking finger is pointing towards Alice. 'She's dead, I think she's dead!'

'Call the ambulance, Byrne!' she orders.

'Right; I'll do that!' Byrne says, swiveling on his heels and racing back down the corridor. O'Halloran bends down beside Alice.

'What have you done?' she asks as I shuffle closer.

'Me?'

'Misha, Me, is right! Tell me now, who else could have done this?' Words escape me. I shake my head.

'It could be attempted murder,' O'Halloran says dramatically. She turns towards me. 'If you know anything you may as well spit it out now,' O'Halloran insists. I feel myself going weak in the stomach and at the knees, so I quickly flop onto the bed. Two men in uniforms carrying a pole stretcher come into the small room and take Alice away on the stretcher.

'Come on, out,' O'Halloran says to me. She grasps my wrists and roughly places handcuffs on me. I trail after her.

'In here,' she says, opening a small cell, which has a door with a window of bars. There's one bed and a toilet. She goes to leave, when I call out.

'Are you taking these off?' I raise my handcuffed hands. Her eyes narrow as she stares into mine. She sighs, and whispers as she turns the key,

'We'll find out who did it, you know!'

Two days later a young handsome man, tall, fair, wearing a black full-length surplus and a purple silk scapular, suddenly appears in the doorway.

'The top of the morning to you now; I'm Father Martin O'Reardon, I'm here to help you; may I?' he asks politely. I nod my head. He sits on the bed next to me. I stare at my wrists.

'Is Alice all right?' I ask.

'Now, who's that?' he replies, leaning forward like he's going to hear my confessions.

'They think I killed her,' I say.

'Do you think you did? You can tell me you know,' he says, leaning over so closely a loose strand of his hair is touching my forehead. His voice is soft as melted butter. I move away.

'No!'

'I understand; you're in denial; it's all in your mentality.'

'So; I'm mental now?'

'No; just refusing to face your demons, that's all.' He leans close again and whispers. 'Just confide in me; everything will work itself out; you'll see.'

'I swear I didn't do anything to Alice,' I protest.

'You did kidnap her?'

'No! That was Kathleen!'

'So, who's Loretta?' he asks cunningly.
'Nobody, 'tis really Kathleen.' He pats my hand.
'I see! So, Alice is your third victim?'
'No; she killed herself!'
'Is that right? Was that when you kidnapped her?'
'No! I didn't even know her. She ran away from home. He sighs and smiles.

'You're just confused now. I'll leave you these rosaries, and you can enjoy a time of prayer and penance.' He places a smooth black rosary beads on the bed next to me.

'I'll return tomorrow,' he says and then whispers again; 'Remember I'm on your side!' He calls the guard to open the door.

Over my head, go the rosary beads. I tuck them under my shift neckline. I am definitely getting confused in my thoughts, I concur.

He comes back as promised, and returns every day for two weeks. Each time he encourages me to share something from my past with him. He seems genuinely interested in me. In the last day or two he's been sitting so close to me, holding me, and once he accidentally touched my breasts outside my shift. Around the fifteenth visit he comes in with an extra bounce in his step. He smiles.

'I have good news for you.' I look up. Can there be such a thing?

'What?' I mutter.

'Alice is alive. She's going to be fine.'

'Did she blame me?' I ask nervously. He looks at me with his kind eyes.

'No, she admitted that she tried to harm herself.' He pauses. 'That leaves you in the clear.'

'Will she be sent back to her da?'

'Most likely, but that's not your business, Missus Farrell.' He suddenly stops and stares at me. 'It's enough that your dear husband was drowned.' He suddenly sits down very close to me.

'I am sorry.' He reaches for my hand and holds it a moment. 'May I call you, Niamh?' I nod my head. I slip my hand from under his. He holds his own hands together, like he's praying.

'Now is there anything you want to tell me, today?'

'About what?'

'What's troubling you?' he says quietly.

'My children.'

'Why are they troubling you, today?'

'I don't know where they are,' I reply. 'I've told you that already.'

'I know that.' He suddenly puts his arm around me and holds me tightly. His hand is resting on my right breast again! He whispers in my ear as though he's telling a secret.

'If I tell you they're safe, would you believe me?' I wiggle to move a little away from him.

'I want to see them!'

'Of course you do.' He hugs me again, drawing me right up to his chest, holding me in an unyielding grip.

'You believe they're mine, then?' He stares into my face and brushes a hair away from my eyes, very gently.

'I believe I do.'

'So, can I see them?' I ask, ignoring his bodily contact, concentrating on thoughts of my children.

'Your case has to come to trial first.' He releases his hold on me. I shuffle away six inches. I know priests have unnatural power.

'Can't you do something?' He leans over and places his hand on my shoulder.

'I have connections in high places, you might say.'

'I know! So, you'll help me?' I ask, daring to look into his grey misty eyes.

'I will do everything in my power to help you,' he says in a low croaky voice. He's probably coming down with a cold, I'm thinking.

'I can see my childers?' He looks at me with such compassion that I believe him absolutely.

'I pray to God you will,' he states passionately. There are tears in his eyes and his mouth is set in determination.

...

The next day he returns around the same time. He seems like an old friend already. I'm waiting for him. He sits on the bed and then bends forward with his hands locked together. I think he's praying. He looks up.

'You need evidence,' he says at last.

'Evidence?' I repeat.

'Someone who knows what you say is true.'

'My sister. She knows.'

'How can I find your sister?'

'Her name is Maeve Flynn. She lives near Scriob.' He leans over and takes my hand. He squeezes it; kisses the back of my hand.

'Such rough hands, you need much care! I'll see what I can do.' Just as he goes to rise, he stares at my neckline. He gently moves the neck of my shift and smiles. 'I'm very pleased to see that you're wearing the rosary beads I gave you!'

'They make me feel safer.' He smiles, releasing his hands from my neckline.

'I'm here to help in any way I can.' He leaves; five days go by before Father Martin reappears in the doorway accompanied by the rattling of keys. He looks very powerful in his black priestly garb. I jump up to greet him.

'How are you, Niamh?'

'Grand; what did Maeve say?' I ask excitedly, and then stop because of the seriousness of his expression.

'Niamh. Sit down. I'm afraid I have bad news.' I sit next to him.

'What?' I ask, trembling.

'She wasn't there!'

'But she's lived there for the last five years. Near McCarthy's Barn.' I pause to swallow the lump in my throat. 'Me da lives there too. Did you see anyone?'

'The place is deserted. Nobody has lived there for ages, I was told.' I shake my head, dismayed.

'But I've only been gone about a month!' He places his arm around my shoulders.

'I'm very sorry, Niamh.'

'What am I to do?' I ask sadly.

'Come here, my child,' he says, as he gently leans my head on his shoulder. He kisses my forehead. I suddenly find tears tumbling over my eyelashes. 'Hush,' he croons, tilting my head upwards, toward his. I think he's going to kiss me on the lips when he suddenly gets up and leaves, turning at the door. He has a strange look in his eyes. 'I'll be back soon.' He comes back every day that week, teaching me how to behave in court. On the following Monday he turns up before eight o'clock in the morning.

'Niamh today is your big day at court! I'm coming with you.'

The guards come around a few minutes later and I'm handcuffed and taken along a corridor, out of the building, across the yard and into another building, through a wide corridor and into a dark room. There's a series of seats with desks at the front; up one end there's a huge desk and a big plaque on the wall above that.

'This is the court room for the prisoners.' Father Martin whispers. 'This is Mister Gabriel Curry, your legal representative.' He introduces me to a round looking man in a suit. It's obvious to me he's wearing a wig. He must be bald, I'm thinking.

'Don't worry! Just do as Mister Curry directs you.' He smiles with his compassionate eyes. 'Stand when Judge Declan Moran comes in, remember?'

I sit down next to Father Martin. I notice a couple of men wearing wigs like Mister Curry. A man in a suit, also wearing a wig, comes over to me. He shakes hands with Mister Curry and Father Martin, introducing himself.

'I'm Padraig O'Faoline, legal representative for the Connors.' They shake hands. He tips his head in my direction. 'Missus Farrell,' is all he says. Judge Moran comes in. We all stand up. He's wearing a longer wig. I'm thinking they must all be bald, or cold. I wait while other convicts' cases are dealt with. My name is called out eventually, and I'm told to stand on a small platform. I do that. After I swear to tell the truth with my hand on a fat bible, O'Faoline steps across and catches my eyes with his.

'Did you or did you not take a child from the home of the Connors on the sixth day of June, nineteen hundred and seventy-one?'

'I think so,' I answer; 'I'm not sure about that date.'

'Answer yes or no,' he says coldly.

'Yes...,' I begin.

'Exhibit one.' He holds my shoes in a plastic bag. 'Are these your shoes?'

'They are.'

'And you were wearing them on the day of the crime aforesaid?'

'They're my only pair, except for these new prison ones.'

'Your honour, the footprints found at the Connors matches these shoes exactly.' He takes the shoes and places them on the Judge's bench. 'That is all! You may step down,' he says to me.

Mister Curry comes over. 'Sit down now,' he whispers. I sit down.

'All rise,' a man says. We all get up. The judge goes out. Then he comes back in again. We all stand up to greet him. We all sit down again. It reminds me of what we do at Mass.

'Will the defendant please rise,' he instructs. Mister Curry and Father Martin rise up. They tell me to stand. I stand up.

The judge reads:

'Missus Niamh Farrell, you are hereby charged with one count of kidnapping a baby, which you subsequently smuggled on board a ship, in an attempt to abscond to America with the said child.' He pauses and turns to look at me above his spectacles. 'How do you plead?' he asks.

'What do you mean, your Highness?'

'Your Honour!'

'Sam didn't take away my honour, your Highness, that's the honest truth.' Everyone laughs. The judge purses his lips and scowls at me. I gasp in horror.

'Say: you're guilty, your Honour!' Mister Curry whispers so loudly that others hear. There's a tittering among the small crowd.

'You're guilty, Your Honour!' I repeat. They laugh again.

The judge coughs and his brows are knitting together.

'I will ask you again. How do you plead?' Mister Curry is going red and nodding his head, mouthing 'guilty' to me. I take a deep breath.

'Kathleen is my child. I gave her to the Connors, and then I took her back, that's all. I did get on a ship to America, but that was because I had no money.'

'You are then pleading guilty?' Judge Moran asserts.

'Guilty?' I stutter. 'I....'

'I sentence you to a period of five years' incarceration.'

'In where?' I ask. Some laughter occurs.

'Gaol,' Father Martin whispers.

'Court is adjourned.' *Bang.* Judge Moran hits the bench. I

jump.

'I'm going to appeal your sentence on the grounds of insanity.' Father Martin says as we leave the courtroom.

'Insanity?' I repeat his words. Father Martin holds my shoulders in his firm grasp.

'That means instability of mind...' I interrupt him.

'I know what it means...'

'Okay. I'm going to say that you were deeply disturbed and that is why you kidnapped Kathleen.' I just look at him.

'How will that help?' I ask.

'It might get your sentence deferred. You could have James returned to you.'

'I don't understand,' I say. 'If I'm mad, they'll put me in a madhouse and then I'll really go mad!'

'Niamh, we can only take one step at a time. Trust me.' He looks at me with his kind eyes. Two guards come over and take me back to my little cell. Father Martin visits me every day that week, comforting me, assuring me of his help. A week later when Father Martin comes by I notice that he has his own key to my cell now, so he unlocks the door himself and comes in.

'How are you?' he asks.

'Fine, thanks Father Martin. Sit down.' I indicate the new chair I've just been given.

'Going up in the world!' he smiles.

'Thanks.' He sits. I sit on the bed.

'Niamh,' he says, taking my hand.

'What, Father?'

'I have good news for you. They are going to review your case. I'm going to get you out of this Hell-hole.'

'What about Kathleen?'

'I'm afraid that's out of my league now.' My face drops with dismay. He raises his smooth eyebrows.

'I might be able to get you a visit to see James.'

'Could I?' I stare into his soft grey eyes.

'You certainly shall. I delight in your fresh smile.' He pauses and looks into my eyes. He's my saviour. I adore him. I'm going to see my child, thanks to this saint. He leans forward and with a kiss like a whisper, gently touches my forehead with his lips. Then he gets up, abruptly.

'Leave it to me.' He visits me every other day for a week, assuring me of progress in the arrangements to see the children. A week later he says,

'Niamh, you're going to see James. 'I almost burst into tears.

'Oh thank you! Where is he? When?' He holds my hands in his.

'You are impetuous!' His smile is like a fascinating painting.

I laugh.

'We have to go to Fermoy.'

'Fermoy?'

'It's not far!'

'How will I get there?'

'I'll take you.' I must look surprised.

'I'll have to leave here.'

'I know people in high places, remember,' he says happily.

'When?'

'Wednesday.'

'That's still two days away.' Father Martin places his arm around my shoulders.

'It will go quickly,' he assures me. Wednesday comes and I am up, bathed and ready for anything before breakfast.

'You're bright and early today,' the friendly female guard, Patricia Monaghan says as she unlocks my door. 'Got a date?'

'James!'

'Is he handsome?' she asks with a twinkle in her eye.

'Very. He's my son. He's two.' She suddenly hugs me. 'That's great. I've got something for you.' She hands me a paper bag containing my jumper and skirt.

'They didn't burn them?' She whispers, 'I told them they looked too good to burn, so they agreed to keep them,' she confides in me. 'They wouldn't give me your three rings,' she says. 'They're safe anyway.'

'Thank you.' I give her a friendly smile. 'Sorry, you probably want to put handcuffs on.' I hold out my wrists for her convenience.

'Not today! You're as free as a bird,' she says kindly, not even looking at my wrists. I sigh with delight. Suddenly the world seems bright and cheerful, despite the fact that it's raining outside. Father Martin comes by at ten. He stops when he sees me.

'You look like a picture, Niamh!' I just smile. I'm going to see James. Why wouldn't I be happy! 'Come on. All the paperwork's done.' He walks in front of me and I follow, smiling as I go. I enjoy the cool misty air. I breathe deeply. Father Martin opens the door of a cream coloured sedan.

'Thank you,' I say as I slip into the passenger side seat. An hour later we approach Fermoy.

'We're to meet in a hotel on the main street.' We stop at a public toilet. 'I won't be a minute. Wait here', he says, hurrying off, and heading for the 'Buccal' side. Five minutes later he comes out. He's changed from his official black uniform to a lime green shirt and cream coloured flared leg pants, co-ordinated with bone coloured shoes.

'You look great, normal!'

'I am normal; very normal!'

'I thought you had to wear those funny clothes all the time?'

'We're at liberty to wear casual clothing when we're not on strictly priestly duties,' he says, smiling.

'Oh!' I say. Father Martin whispers.

'People don't know me here, so I'll just say we're together, to save embarrassing questions.'

'I thought it was all official, Father?'

'It is. But tongues wag in these country areas! I don't want any problems, you know, me being a priest and you being a beautiful, young lady.'

'Ah, go on Father!' I laugh. He pulls the car over, stops the engine and turns to face me.

'Niamh, please call me Martin.'

'Right, Martin!' I reply readily. He suddenly leans over and kisses my cheek.

'You're a wonderful, beautiful lady.'

'You're the wonderful one,' I reply. 'What can I do to express my gratitude for getting me out of the Hell hole and seeing my son?'

'You can do something for me.'

'Anything!' I reply sincerely.

'Will you play a little game?'

'I'm not very good at ball games, but I'm a good runner.'

'A pretend game, just to humour me?' he asks with a twinkle in his eye.

'I can do that,' I reply.

'Will you pretend that you're my wife, just for these few hours?'

'Your wife?' I say, astonished. 'No. I can't.' He places his arm around my shoulders.

'Just look at us. Could we be a husband and wife?' I look at him.

'You're too good for me Father,' I say.

'No! And please don't call me Father while we're here. It would give me such a thrill to feel I belonged to a beautiful woman, even for a few hours.' I'm starting to feel nervous about this game.

'I can't. They didn't give me my rings. A wife needs a ring,' I say jokingly.

'You're a smart girl,' he says. 'Of course we need a ring. Why didn't I think of that?' He thinks I'm smart, I reflect smugly! I relax.

'What about this?' he says, holding up his little finger.

'It's got a ring on it!' I exclaim. 'What are you doing?' He's screwing up his face and his finger is turning red as he tries to remove it.

'It's too tight,' he says. He sucks his finger. Suddenly there's a ring in his other hand. 'There y'are! It's off!'

He looks at me. 'You wanted a ring. Show me your finger,' he says. He places it on my finger. 'With this ring I thee wed. Off with your...,'

'Clothes and jump into bed!' I finish the sentence for him. We both laugh heartily at this.

'It nearly fits!' I announce, surprised.

'And I nearly had a fit!' he replies. We laugh again.

'It looks like it was meant for you, not me.'

'It looks like a wedding ring!'

'My father gave it to me when I was ordained. 'Married to God,' were his very words. It fitted my ring finger then. I was a skinny lad.' He turns to me and with his misty grey eyes, and stares into mine.

'Niamh, you're great company. I'm really enjoying myself. Let's pretend we're on our honeymoon, just for fun.'

'Go on! I'm only coming to see James. Shouldn't he be here now?'

'He should be. This is the hotel.' The place is deserted. We sit in the lounge. 'I'll see if I can get you a drink.'

'That'll be nice.' A few minutes later he returns from the bar.

'Irish coffee! I recommend it.' He sits down in the armchair next to mine. I'm beginning to feel anxious about

James' arrival.

'What's going on; where's James?'

'I have a bit of bad news.'

'Jesus, Mary and Joseph, what's happened to James?' I say, jumping up.

'Sit down Niamh; it's nothing like that. The river burst its banks and they can't get through right away. We'll just have to wait a bit. At least you're out of that hell hole!'

'But; what about James? I'm so longing to see his little face again,' I whisper. He leans over and puts his arm around me.

'I know. I feel the same. Such a lovely child,' he says.

'So, you've met him?' I ask.

'I have met him, and Kathleen, and their guardians.' 'They should be with me, not some guardians. I'm their mother.' I say lamely.

'I know you are. Niamh, I don't want you to get upset just waiting here. Let's kill a bit of time and have a walk around the town?'

'You're right. I just wish he was here now.' I finish drinking my Irish coffee. We sit under a shady oak tree near a pond and enjoy fish, chips and lemonade for lunch.

'Let's feed the ducks,' Martin suggests as two little greenish ducks come quacking along and we throw bits of our food towards them. I slip on the edge of the bank,

'Mammy,' I cry out. Martin quickly hooks his arm around my waist and retrieves me. For a moment I think he's going to plant a kiss on my lips, but then he lets go. At four o'clock we return to the hotel and he goes off to make a telephone call. I'm waiting in the lounge, anxiously sipping an orange juice. Martin looks worried when he returns.

'Niamh, they're not going to get here today. The roads are blocked. They're going back to Dungarvan and they'll try again tomorrow.'

'Oh no! We'll have to go back to Cork then.'

'I've rung the *Gates of Hell* and told them what's happened. They understand, surprisingly.' He laughs at this. 'We'll have to stay the night.'

'Where?'

'I'll book two rooms.'

'All right.'

'Wait here.' Ten minutes later he returns. 'Niamh, they only had one double room available tonight. I said we'd take it!'

'You didn't say that we're married!'

'It's none of their business! Don't worry, I won't touch you.'

'Maybe there's a tinceard's camp around here?' I say my thoughts aloud. 'We could stay with them.'

'I won't let you go back to that way of life! Anyway, I'm obliged to take care of you myself. That's the agreement I have with the warders.'

'I think we should go back to Cork,' I suggest. Martin seems slightly perturbed by that suggestion, pauses and says,

'It's too late. I've paid for it now.' I don't want to upset him after all he's done for me. I try to smile and say,

'All right.'

'Don't look so downcast, fair maiden. I shall sleep on the floor and you shall sleep on the feather bed. What I propose is this: I dine you and wine you and then we return here for the night!' Martin looks so happy. It's only a game I suppose. It's only one night!

'At least I'll see James tomorrow.'

'That's the spirit.' He offers me the crook of his arm. 'Come, I shall show you to your boudoir.' I still feel worried, even as I tuck my arm in his and we stroll through the corridor, walking on soft carpet, ending up at a door with a shining brass number eleven. We go in. The room is lovely, with a double bed and bathroom next to it. It's now I realize something.

'Martin, I've got nothing to wear in bed!'

'That's not a problem for me,' he says grinning. I feel pink in the face. 'It is for me, Martin, seriously!' He sits on the bed staring at me with a sheepish look of repentance.

'I don't want you to have any problems Niamh. I'll get you something suitable to wear.'

'Where?' I ask, looking around.

'In the shops!' he replies whimsically. I shrug my shoulders. I never thought of that! Off we go down the streets, gazing into a women's dress shop. There's two, one either end of the town. We traipse to the second one.

'Do you like these, darling?' he asks me as he picks out this lovely light blue coloured satin nightdress and a robe to match, and underpants in blue satin. I just let my eyeballs fall out. I nod.

'My wife would love these, please!'

Liar, liar, I'm saying inside. 'They're lovely,' I say politely but meaning it. They're glorious!

The shop assistant, a woman with slicked-back dark hair, deep-set eyes, a long bony nose, high cheekbones and bright red cupid lips, smiles by pursing up her lips!

'Will I gift wrap them for you Sir?' Martin winks at me and replies,

'Yes please. We're on our honeymoon.'

'That's lovely! You won't need these for long then!' She takes a piece of floral wrapping paper from under the counter and begins the wrapping process, glancing at us in between moves, smiling cupidly. 'This is your lucky day!' she says warmly.

'How's that?' Martin asks.

'It's ten past five! We should have closed ten minutes ago.'

'Is that right?' Martin replies. 'This is our lucky day then.' He hands over his cash. 'Thank you kindly, Mam,' he says. She watches us with amusement as we leave.

I shake my head as the doorbell of the shop rings to signal our exit. He glances back into the shop. The woman is watching attentively. Martin suddenly spins me around to face him. 'Kiss me!' he commands. 'She's watching!' Somehow our lips meet, and we kiss. Martin holds me under the armpit and smoothly moves me few steps away from the shop as he's kissing me, almost roughly. He looks into my eyes and then he releases me from the suction power of his lips.

'You shouldn't have done that!' My lips are tingling. I give them a rub.

'Why not? We're on our honeymoon!' I recollect my wits.

'Martin! It's a big fat lie.' He sighs.

'I wish it was true Niamh. That kiss was tremendous!' He nods his head agreeably. The kiss was more of a shock than a nice surprise. I wouldn't want to say that. I just smile.

After finishing a bottle of wine with our dinner we make our way up the stairs to the bedroom. I collapse on the bed. My mind feels fuzzy.

'Shall I run Madame's bath?'

'Mm,' I reply hazily. After having a bath my head feels clearer.

'How about giving me a fashion show,' Martin says, lying on the bed in a very relaxed pose as I emerge from the bathroom. I twirl around in the blue robe.

'That's lovely. What about the other gear I bought you?' he asks. I remove the robe and flaunt the nightie.

'You're like a queen,' he says. 'What about the knickers?' He comes over and puts his arms around me now.

'You saw it in the shop!' I say, removing his arms and climbing between the sheets. I sigh. 'This is like Heaven.'

'It is,' Martin agrees with me. He grins from ear to ear as he heads for the bathroom. 'I'll get some of the muck off me.'

I close my eyes and drift into sleep.

'I shall camp here, like a Tinceard!' Martin says, coming from the bathroom with nothing but a towel on. He flops down on the floor, pummeling his trousers into a pillow, using the towel as a blanket. I feel myself being pulled from my sleepiness by his voice.

'You're in the nip!' I say, alarmed, blinking as I stare at his silhouette through the towel. He forgot to get himself pyjamas, I'm thinking. Maybe all his money was gone on my expensive nightwear? I stare at the wall.

'I always sleep like this,' is his response, 'This floor is as hard as a rock,' he grumbles momentarily. 'The towel is damp too...' I feel bad about his discomfort. I close my eyes tightly.

'Goodnight Martin!'

'Niamh,' Martin whispers after he puts the light out. '

'What?' I say, responding to his voice.

'The floor must be concrete. It's terribly cold. Can I sleep with you? I promise I won't touch you, not even with my breath.'

'Ask for another blanket,' I suggest.

'I did that. They said some of the blankets are at the dry cleaners. They suggested we keep each other warm.' His reply shocks me.

'They're rude,' I say. He sighs and lies back down. I can hear him groaning pitifully, rolling around. He'll never get to sleep on that hard floor, without a blanket.

'All right. You can sleep under the blanket, just to keep warm. Remember, no touching.' He creeps under the blankets. I fall into a deep sleep until I hear this terrible noise. I wake up, alarmed.

'You're snoring.' I give Martin a dig in the ribs.

'I am still freezing,' Martin says, curling up. I can feel him shaking with the cold. I hate that feeling myself.

'Snuggle up to me then, and stop snoring,' I suggest, sighing.

'Thanks, Niamh. You are a real angel of the night!' He puts his arm around me and I can feel his body warming up next to me. The only barrier between us now is the silk nightwear! We both wake up early, before six. His face is next to mine. He's got a scapula around his neck.

'What's that for?' I ask. He smiles.

'I'm going to confess something.'

'I thought you wore that to hear confessions, not to confess,' I say.

'You are so smart. Here I'll put it around your neck.' He takes the purple scarf with fringes and places it around my neck, holding each end close to my breast. 'There! I confess this a dream come true for me Niamh; waking up next to a beautiful wife.'

I stare into his misty eyes, replying sleepily;

'And, hearing your confessions.'

'What's my penance?' he says, grinning with his beautiful smile. I shake my head. He's mad! 'How about I have to kiss you a hundred times?' he says, laughing.

'You've been kissing the Blarney stone,' I say, sighing. I move my face close to his.

'You're my blarney stone.' He kisses me on the lips.

'Definitely softer.' We kiss for a few moments. He suddenly sits up. 'Sorry Niamh, I forgot myself. I'd better go and ring this chaperone and see what's happening?'

Niamh and Fr. Martin, July, 1971. ©marieseltenrych, 2010.

'It's quarter to six. It might be a bit early.'

'You're right, Niamh. I am still jaded,' he says, snuggling under the blankets.

'It's too cold out here,' I say pulling the warm blanket over my shoulder and closing my eyes.

'You look like an angel now,' Martin says, running his finger down my cheek. I turn around. His eyes are full of love. He kisses me all over my face, then on the mouth.

'Twenty, twenty one,' he says, between kisses. I close my eyes and think of Niall. I find myself responding to Martin. Before I know it we are going 'all the way'. Afterwards, we're together, quiet.

'I'm sorry Niamh. I didn't mean for that to happen, please forgive me?'

'I forgive you!' I reply. He props himself up on his elbow and looks at me lovingly. 'But it was wonderful! Niamh. I've been thinking.'

'Thinking of what?' I ask.

'You, James and Kathleen.' The faces of my children leap into my mind.

'What about us?'

'I'm thinking of leaving the priesthood.' I sit up at that remark and look into his disturbed face. 'Why?'

'I don't think I can live as a priest any longer. I think I'm in love. With you, James and Kathleen!'

'You can't be in love with three people!'

'All three!'

'You must be joking! He shakes his head.

'I'm deadly serious.' He looks at me so seriously I laugh. 'Sorry, I shouldn't laugh! You can't do that. You made a vow!'

'Nobody can tell the future, Niamh. My dream now is to vow to marry you and go to Australia with you James and Kathleen.'

'We can't do that. Remember, I'm a convict. I still have nearly five years to do. I probably shouldn't even be here.'

'I nearly forgot about that. You are so beautiful any man would forget himself with you.' He kisses me passionately again, and then stops suddenly. 'I'm sure I can get you out of that prison. I'm bloody well going to try, if it's the last thing I do on this earth.'

Finally, that afternoon, a woman who's wearing a navy business suit and white tailored shirt arrives on the bus with James. Just before we greet them, Martin whispers, 'They think we went back to Cork, so don't say anything about staying here overnight, will you? And they were not told I'm a priest, for political purposes, so mum's the word!' James is here, that's what matters to me right now.

'All right,' I reply lightly.

'Mammy, Mammy,' he yells when he sees me coming towards him. I hug him and give him a big swing.

'James! Mammy loves you.'

'Lub you,' he whispers back.

'Martin O'Reardon - Niamh's chaperone.' He extends his manly hand to Jane.

'Jane Priest.' She holds her slim hand out, looking down her large nose at Martin. The largeness of her nose contrasts with her pale elfin shaped face. Her brown hair is tied in a bun at the back of her head. Her eyes are hazel and sharp. Her lips are pale and uncoloured.

'That's an interesting name!' he states, his face remaining blank.

'Thank you Mister O'Reardon,' Jane states politely, lamely dropping her hand into his.

'Call me, Martin, please!'

'If you wish.' Her French manicured fingers move to her face decorously. Her index finger rests for a moment under her jaw line. He returns her smile, catching her eyes in his for a moment. Under her watchful eyes we play games, feed the ducks and have lots of hugs for around an hour and a half. We're sitting on a bench seat watching James running back and forth in a lush grassy patch.

'The bus is due to arrive at half four,' Miss Priest announces, glancing at her watch. James falls over at that moment, so I rise up and rush towards him. Martin follows me. I pick James up and examine his knee.

'Mammy will kiss it better.' I kiss his knee and brush a piece of grass away. James giggles. A feeling of anxiety suddenly grasps my heart. 'Martin, how can I say goodbye. He's going to be so upset; I haven't prepared for this.' Martin kneels down next to me and speaks quietly.

'I'll handle it. Watch me.' He turns to James who's just about to run off again. 'James, why don't we get you an ice cream, then you can get on the bus for a drive.' James stops and revolves himself.

'Ice keam!'

'You wait here with Mammy.' Martin says, going to nearby shop with an ice cream sign hanging outside. A few minutes later he comes back with four soft ice cream cones, two in each hand.

'Very good value, much better than Cork!' he exclaims as he gives Jane Priest and me an ice cream.

'Serviette!' he adds, pulling some paper napkins from his back trouser pocket.

'Thank you kindly,' Jane Priest says demurely, and then notices the bus coming around the corner.

'The bus, it's early!' My heart drops at her words. I try to lick my ice cream cone. The bus pulls up. James is sitting in the grass, hand outstretched for his ice cream.

'Now before you get this you have to go on the bus,' Martin says.

'Bus.' He pushes himself off the ground and immediately marches towards Martin. Martin lifts him as though he's a feather and puts him on the bus. Miss Priest sits next to him. I stand near the doorway of the bus.

'Here's your ice cream,' Martin says, placing a serviette under the neck of his shirt and putting the cone in his hand.

'Wave to Mammy,' Martin states authoritatively. James waves momentarily. His eyes are on his ice cream. He licks it greedily.

'Quick, let's get out of sight,' Martin says, leaping off the bus and hurrying me along the footpath in the opposite direction.

'I can't,' I whisper, stopping in my tracks. Martin puts

his arm around me.

'You can. Don't look back. You've had a good time. Remember that!'

'I will.' The tears drop onto my ice cream. 'You're always right!'
The bus disappears out of sight. My last picture of James is him with a blob of ice cream on his sweet nose. Shortly after that we head back to Cork. On our way out of town we stop at the public toilets. I go to the *Chaileen* side. Martin goes in with a bag and comes out dressed in black.

'Right! I'm a priest again. Remember Niamh, if you want someone to marry you, always call a priest.' I laugh. Martin has been good to me, I reflect, even if we did do the wrong thing last night, and I wonder if God will forgive us! I know now that he's just another human being trying to help others.

'You're funny! Thanks for a special day, Martin.'

'My pleasure, all my pleasure,' he says, pressing his foot down hard on the accelerator. In less than two hours we're back in Cork.

'So, you look refreshed. Had a good time in Dublin then?'

'Dublin? We didn't go to Dublin, just Fermoy,' I reply to Patricia Monaghan, as I check in; while Martin is talking to the supervisor. She runs her hands over my body. It makes me think of someone creeping over my grave.

'I won't ask you to take off all your clothes. It's too cold.'

'Thanks!' I suddenly notice I'm still wearing Martin's ring. I slip it into my mouth while she's writing something in a book.

'So what did you do there, in Fermoy?' I can feel the blood rushing up my neck. It's hard to talk with a ring next to my teeth.

'We had to wait for James because of the river bursting its banks.'

'What river?'

'Blackwater,' I mumble.

'That's the first I've heard of it! God we hear nothing in this place! You'd think we were in prison!' she exclaims. 'Here, put this on.' She hands me a clean prison dress. 'Put your things back in the bag. I'll make sure they're safe. Oh, and spit that thing out,' she says coolly. I nearly swallow the ring with fright. I spit the ring into my hand, wipe it in my prison shift, and hand it over.

'How did you know?'

She looks at me with amusement. 'I didn't come down with the last shower!' She looks at me. 'You didn't nick it by any chance?'

'No, somebody gave it to me.' My face feels red even as I speak.

'I have a mind to report O'Halloran.'

'Why, what did she do?' I ask, mystified.

'It's what she didn't do. She should have seen that ring when you first came here.'

'Please don't say anything. I don't want trouble,' I beg. She folds her arms and stares at me, then unfolds them.

'All right, I'll do that this one time! At least it'll be safe if I put it away.'

'You're very kind.'

'On this occasion.'

'Thanks, Miss Monaghan,' I say as she hurries me into my cell.

'Call me Patricia,' she says quietly.

As the days drag on I am beginning to doubt I will see Martin again. It's the fifteenth of August, thirty five days since we were together. The next day he marches into my cell and sits on the edge of the bed as though it was yesterday we were together.

'How are you Niamh?' he asks casually. He's got his hands together, praying, I suppose.

'Fine! I thought you might not come back!'

'I had things to sort out.'

'They took your ring. I'm sorry,' I say.

'I could say you stole it?' He laughs heartily immediately. 'Sure no, I'm only joking!' He sits beside me on the bed. 'Keep it for now. It's only rolled gold, so it's not worth much! The important question is us! I need you Niamh, like a duck needs water.' He puts his arm around my shoulders and hugs me tightly. 'And I've got great news for you.'

'I can see Kathleen?'

'Sorry! No! She's gone back to be with her parents, the Connors. Guess again?'

'Something about James?' He pats my hand.

'You're dead right! You can pay him a visit once a month.'

'How did you manage that?'

'I pulled a few strings in high places.'

'Next Wednesday, be ready. We can have a grand time together again.' His hand grasps my breast through my coarse cotton frock. I ignore his hand and stare into his face.

'I've been sick!' He removes his hand. 'Oh, my poor darling. The warder didn't say anything.'

'I'm expecting!'

'You're joking!'

'No, I'm not; honest to God. I always get sick in the mornings when I'm expecting, or when I'm on a ship.' He comes so close I see tiny lines under his misty eyes.

'Niamh, that's terrible! You need to see a doctor, quick!'

'You mean to check and see if I am?'

'If you are he'll get rid of it.' I feel startled at his reply.

'Get rid of it?'

'It's best to do it quickly, while it's still an embryo.'

'What are you talking about, Martin?'

'It's not really a human at this stage! It's just cells joined together, like a bag of marbles.'

'Marbles?'

'I've seen pictures.' He sits a bit closer again. 'I'll explain... You see it doesn't become a real human until around twenty weeks! We can go to Dublin and visit a doctor, discretely. I'd work that out, and pay the cost. If you're quick you can get it done there, otherwise you'll have to go to England.' He stops and reflects for a moment. 'That might be a problem.'

'What about God? What about your religion?'

'Niamh, we're not in the dark ages now, we've..., well some people have, advanced. These things have been going on for millions of years.'

'This has only been going on for five weeks! It's my child, and I'm keeping it!'

'Niamh, you're too ignorant. Don't be an egit.' He's grinning at me. I can feel the colour fading from my face. I shiver. He sees how upset I am, so calms down. 'I'm sorry, I shouldn't have said that. Listen now. I have taken care of you up to now, haven't I?' I'll continue to do so!'

'Please, don't murder the baby!' He looks at me with utter contempt 'How dare you accuse me of murder, Niamh, when all I'm trying to do is help you. I have compromised myself for you!' I take a deep breath.

'What about what you said about us being a family, going to Australia. Now we can have our own child as well?'

'Keep your voice down.' He's holding both my wrists tightly. 'I thought I loved you, but you might have planned this pregnancy, even seduced me!' I begin to cry. Tears cascade down my cheeks. His demeanour softens.

'Don't cry. I really want to help you, Niamh. Please say 'yes' to my generous offer?'

'Offer?' I reply, 'to have an abortion? No thanks!'

'If it's gone we can continue to have good times together.'

'And what if it's not gone?'

'Niamh, my reputation is at stake! I just can't have this happen; It's your choice. I won't force you to do anything!' I just shake my head. I don't trust myself to speak. He turns away.

'All right. Have it your way!' he says gruffly. He turns on his heels and storms out the door. The next day Patricia Monaghan makes a comment as we head down the corridor to the bathroom.

'What was that all about, yesterday?' she asks.

'What?'

'Your man.'

'What do you mean, 'your man'?'

'You know very well: Father O'Reardon! Walls have ears.'

'What did you hear then?'

'Just urgent murmuring! We were close to barging in! He's not done you harm, has he?'

'No!' I assure her. 'It's James,' I say, licking my lying lips. 'Patricia, I don't think I'm ever going to see him again. He'll be nearly eight before I get out of here.' We stop at the door of the bathroom.

'I'll tell you a little secret, Missus Farrell - Niamh.' She leans towards me and whispers, 'If you're a good girl you can be out of here in less than two years!'

'Two years? '

'That's right. I've seen it with my own eyes.'

'But even within two years time James will have forgotten me altogether.'

'Children don't forget a good mother, remember that!' she says as she holds the door of the bathroom open and I enter. 'I think you're probably a good mother!' she concludes as she sits on the chair near the doorway. I turn on the tap. A gentle trickle pours over my hands. I cup my hands and bring the cold water to my face. My tears are mingling with the water.

...

A fortnight later a different priest visits me.

'Father John Hurley wants to talk to you,' Patricia Monaghan announces as I sit in my cell staring at the wall. A tall, grey haired man in a black suit and white back the front shirt collar calls out,

'Hello, you're Niamh Farrell?'

'I am.' I look up at him.

'May I come in?' He smiles at me. His face crinkles and his eyes twinkle.

'Come in.' He sits on the bed and leans over to me. 'Niamh, you're to be reunited with your son James.'

'When?'

'In a few days time. I have received this from the Minister.' He hands me a piece of crisp paper. I stare at the black words on the cream coloured parchment, then hand it back. 'I don't, I mean, I can't read.'

'I understand. It's an emotional moment for yourself. I'll read it aloud if you like?' I simply nod my head. Father Hurley reads, *'In response to a request by Father Martin O'Reardon, Missus Niamh Farrell is hereby deemed to have been mentally unstable during her previous misadventures due to an emotional occurrence, from which she has since recovered. This has prompted the Judge and the Minster to accept the appeal against Missus Farrell's incarceration. Forthwith Missus Farrell is be exonerated and is placed on a good behaviour bond for a period of five years, commencing from the first day of September, nineteen hundred and seventy one...* 'He puts the paper down and stares at me. I'm not sure whether to shout or laugh.

'What does all that mean?'

'You are free!'

'I am?' I say in astonishment. 'I can go to Scriob?'

'No! To Australia!'

'I don't know anyone in Australia,' I say, blankly.

'I will escort you.'

'But I don't know you.'

'We shall become acquainted on the voyage.' He is pretty ancient, so he can't do me much harm. I find myself smiling at my thoughts.

'Why you?'

'I will answer your question, although I am not bound to! I am retired, and I have a brother in Australia. I was going to travel there shortly anyway.'

'What about Martin, I mean, Father O'Reardon?'

'Father O'Reardon has been transferred to a parish in northern Spain.'

'Oh'. There's a pause.

'Spain?' I exclaim.

'Yes. Permanently. God has called him.' He looks at the floor, and then looks up at me. 'Well, I'll return in a few days with some official papers. You can start packing.'

'And James?'

'James? All in good time.'

'I'll see him soon?'

'You will. Just one other thing.' He stops on his way out.

'What?'

'You need a full medical examination.'

'With a doctor?' I ask.

'Yes, of course. That will be arranged immediately.' He pauses and stares at me with compassion in his eyes. His mouth opens again. 'It was grand meeting you. I'll say good day to you now.'

A week later, he returns. 'I have a message for you, from Father O'Reardon.'

'What message?'

'He gave, I mean, he sent you this.' He hands me a sealed envelope. I open it; the sea of words mean nothing to me as I still can't read properly.

'Thank you,' I say, folding it and replacing it in the envelope.

'He also sent you these.' The priest hands me a brown paper bag, sealed with tape. 'He said they were personal.' I accept the bag.

'Thanks.'

'You just need to sign these papers.'

'What are they?'

He places them on the seat of the chair, 'Emigration papers, saying you're willing to travel to Australia.'

'What about the doctor's examination?' I ask.

'He stated you are in good health.' He pauses and looks up at me. 'Here's his report. His eye scans the document. 'Doctors are terrible writers, and me eyes aren't that good either! Now let's see, Heart, that's ticked as good; blood Pressure: good.' He looks at me. 'You've had all your vaccinations, I see.'

'What would happen if I was expecting?' I ask. He coughs and looks at me.

'That would be a rather serious matter, which would jeopardize your future.'

'Why would that be?'

'That's the law. If you became pregnant whilst under the jurisdiction of the crown, the child would become a ward of the state.'

'I'd have to stay here?'

'You certainly could not travel to Australia.'

'Could I still see James?' He leans closer to me.

'Probably not; I hope you aren't considering having a child?'

'No, I wasn't!'

'Well, there's no problem then.' He takes off his glasses and rubs them with a large white handkerchief. 'Missus

Farrell, this is a great opportunity for you and James. I trust you can see that?'

'I can, Father; at least I can be with my son.'

'That's the spirit! I shall make a final report that you are stable both in mind and body. If you desire confessions, I shall oblige on another occasion.'

'No. I received confessions a few weeks ago.' A distracting picture of Martin, in the nip, with the scapular on in bed flashes through my mind. 'Where do I sign?' He points to a dotted line and hands me his ballpoint pen. I sit on the edge of the bed and begin to write.

'Here.' Slowly I write Niamh Far..., and stop.

'Sorry, I forget how to do the rest.' He looks down at it.

'That'll do; I'll witness it.' I move over along the edge of the bed. He sits awkwardly beside me and takes the pen. After a quick scribble he turns his face towards me. His eyes sparkle as he smiles at me. He suddenly looks familiar. 'Start packing your bags. God willing I shall return in a few days.'

Ten days later I'm saying goodbye to Patricia Monaghan. She hands me my two bags, with everything still inside, including Kathleen's nappies. 'I think you'll find everything there, including four rings!' she remarks, making her eyebrows rise and fall. 'I hope you get to meet your son. I'll miss you, Niamh.' She puts her hand out and I hold it for a moment. Her eyes look like an Irish mist.

'Thanks very much for the rings and, everything, Patricia.'

...

With Father John Hurley by my side I'm having my first aeroplane flight from Cork to Southampton in England. I'm enjoying the experience and the strange shapes of the clouds beneath us when I suddenly get this retching feeling in the pit of my stomach.

'Niamh, you're turned as white as a ghost. Here,' Father John points to a paper bag. For the remainder of the journey, my view is focused on the serrated edges of its rustic perimeters.

...

Two days later we board the *Australis* and leave for Australia's shores. As we head down several flights of steps towards our cabins, a peculiar fear comes over me. I haven't seen my son yet. 'What about James, Father John?' I ask, as he sits with me in a small cabin on 'D' deck. I look around the room. The porthole is covered by a view of a deep green sea, which means we're right under the water. I quickly pull a small blind across the round window. There are two bunk beds along one wall and a small bathroom and a cupboard along the other side. I'm looking around as though his little face might suddenly appear from under the furniture. 'Where is he?'

'You'll meet each other in good time; patience is a virtue, remember that. Now do stop biting your nails Niamh. It won't help. If you need to leave the cabin, knock on this wall,' he informs me. 'I'll be right next door.' He turns to leave, smiling apologetically. 'Sorry, but I'm obliged to lock this, for your own good.'

A whole week goes by. I'm lying on the little bed in the tiny room, which is around the same size as my cell in prison. There's a knock on the door.

'Come on in,' I call out.

'How are you feeling now, Niamh?' Father John asks, still standing in the doorway.

'Still sick,' I reply feebly, trying to sit up.

'You are very pale. But, if it's any comfort, there are several cases of sickness on board. It's quite normal. 'Are you quite sure you don't want to take something for it?'

'No. Sure I'll be all right.' He sits on the bed beside me.

'Fine; I know how anxious you have been about your son, so I have arranged a meeting with James at noon today. Do you think you will be up to it?' I sit up when he says that.

'That's the best medicine I've had today.'

'That's the spirit!' he says, patting my hand. 'I'll escort you.'

At twelve noon exactly I enter the port side lounge with Father John. Everything is decorated with a pink textile fabric. The tables are veneered in a dappled pink colour. The walls of the counter, which is also a bar, are in pink. I immediately spot James, seated with a female a bit older than me. They're in a corner seat at the window, looking out into the ocean. As I come closer, James' cry echoes through the room,

'Mammy... Mammy!'

'James.' I thank God he hasn't forgotten me! I hold him for a long time. Then I realize the woman is waiting. Father John introduces me.

'This is Niamh Farrell, James' mother.' The sandy haired heavy-set young woman, with round eyes and a round face to match, smiles to display straight white dentures. She tosses her petit nose in the air as she lunges forward.

'Pleased to meet you; I'm Colette Dunn. I'll be taking care of James as far as Melbourne.' We enjoy our time together.

...

As we leave I ask Father John: 'Are we staying in Melbourne?'

'No, we're travelling to Sydney and then to Queensland.'

'That's interesting,' I comment.

'Why, Niamh?' Father John asks, peering at me inquisitively.

'My name means Queen of the land?' His eyes veer upwards.

'It's providence!' Every few days I have half an hour with James. It seems to take weeks before we reach Melbourne. One morning, bright and early, Father John knocks on the cabin door.

'Come in,' I call from underneath the blanket. He unlocks

the door and enters.

'Are you all right?' he asks anxiously.

'I do feel a lot better today. I wonder why?' I say, relieved.

'Perhaps it's because we've stopped! We're in Melbourne!' he informs me.

'Are we now? Can we get off?' He shakes his head.

'I'm very sorry! No, not until we reach Sydney.' Father John explains to me. 'Are you well enough to say farewell to Miss Dunn?'

'I'm well enough! I'll get dressed,' I reply.

'I'll wait outside.' Father John steps outside and pulls the door shut. 'Don't be too long,' he calls out after five minutes.

I wave goodbye to Colette Dunn. There she goes, walking off down the street with a couple of people, stepping jauntily. She glances back, and gives me such a wave you'd think we'd been friends forever! I move away from the rail to where Father John is standing, holding James' hand.

'He's your responsibility now Niamh,' Father John says, as he nudges James towards me. James suddenly tears across the space into my outstretched arms. I grasp him tightly and swing him around for joy.

'That's enough of that!' I hear Father John's voice as it intrudes on our delightful play. 'Let me buy you both a nice cool drink.' We walk happily along the deck, down the steps to the starboard side of the ship and through the door marked 'Blue Lounge'. James and I just sit and smile at each other, like two children discovering friendship for the first time.

'Lemonade,' Father John's voice penetrates our happiness. The sparkling drinks in shiny glasses reflect our mood.

'Say: yes please!' I remind James. Father John sits down next to James, facing me. 'Now that I've got my wits about me, can you tell me whereabouts we'll be stopping in

Queensland?' I ask.

'You're bound to find out anyway; sure they're sugar-cane farmers.'

'I don't know anything about sugar-cane farming.'

'Don't worry your head about that. They need someone to help with the children.' I help James hold his drink with two hands, then turn towards Father John.

'Will I be a governess, Father John?'

'You will, and more! I believe they have twins. They'll need help in the kitchen too!'

'What in God's name are children doing working in the kitchen?'

'No Niamh, you will be working in the kitchen, not the children,' he explains.

'I can do that; what are these twins like? Maybe I won't be able to handle them!'

'I hear they are a wild pair, but I have a hunch you'll be on top of it all in no time.'

'I'm very glad someone has confidence in me, Father,' I comment wryly. We wait for James to finish his drink, and then Father announces,

'If you're feeling up to it, James can stop with you for the remainder of the journey!'

'I am. I do. I never felt better in my life,' I laugh happily, hugging James.

Somehow my sickness has almost gone completely since Melbourne. During the last couple of days, Father John takes me to see a film about Australia, its climate, schools and some amazing creatures, such as the kangaroo, koala, funnel web and red-back spiders, and a variety of slithering snakes. They show enlarged pictures of mosquitoes, which seem prolific in the area we're going to. That night I wake up covered in perspiration, from a nightmare in which I'm surrounded by giant mosquitoes! A few days later we sail into Sydney

Harbour. The opera house looks like a big white sailing ship surrounded by a rainbow made of intrigued steel, which flashes hues of colour from the slowly rising sun. 'I've never seen the like in my life. It's spectacular!' I exclaim as we sail into her inviting arms.

'It is indeed,' Father John states agreeably. 'Time to disembark!' he announces brightly. He seems as relieved as I am to be going on shore.

'James, we're here!' I hug James and we both laugh. Father John looks on with a reserved smile on his face.

'We'll be staying in a hostel for a few nights, and then we fly up to Queensland.'

"Is that the place where they have really big bananas?"

"So I hear."

"Well now, James, we thought we'd go to the Big Apple but now we're having a change of fruit. Is that right Father?"

"'Tis surely." He turned to face me, his eyes were like a leaking tap. "Now Niamh; this is your new life and I'm hoping that you will make the best of your new opportunities. 'Tis a great land, full of convicts and poets, and I'm sure you'll find a new life here; that's what I'm hoping anyway." He turned away and I saw him brushing his face. I think his eyes were sore.

"I'm sure I'll find a new life here among the convicts and poets. I promise I'll do me best to start a new page in my life, me and James."

James can't keep his eyes off the people waving and shouting on the shore. Father John turned slightly, "'T'will be a new more than a page in your life. More like a new chapter."

"A new chapter," I said, savouring the moment. I can already feel the fresh breeze of a new life swirling around me and my hopes and dreams of a grand life are returning quickly. I have to make the best of my new opportunities for the sake of James and my unborn little one. "You know, Father, life is really an adventure, and the more I have the more I think I like it."

"That's the girl," Father John said. He put his arm around me and gave me something I could describe as a 'hug'.

Now I've got a leaking tap in my eyes, but it feels like everything will work out after all. I always wanted to get away from the cold and damp Irish winters, the bigotry and the hardness of my own life and now, here I am, in the lucky country, Australia. Could I ever dream of a better place; but what about the snakes and the dust and the kangaroos? I suppose I'll just have to get used to it now!

End of first part of Five Golden Rings and a Diamond.

Acknowledgements and thanks:

Thanks to the work of R.A. Steward Macalister's *The Secret Languages of Ireland*; Cambridge University Press, 1937 Ch V1pp 174 – 224;
Thanks to John Bear of Canberra for his kindness is

giving me details and in helping to sustain the Shelta languages of the Tinceards of Ireland for another generation.

Thanks to Anita Mathias for information regarding quote from Somerset Maugham's apt quote at front of book. Thanks to everyone who read my original Five Golden Rings and a Diamond and gave me a good review, including Rod, Keith, Nina.

A big thanks also to my husband Henry, who loves to promote my books and who proudly has my website on his car: http://www.aussieoibooks.com.au
Thanks also are due to my children, Kathy, who takes every opportunity to promote my books and who has done wonders for my ego; thanks to Steve, who has been supportive for many years.

Thanks also to staff at the Commodore hotel in Cork for information about their fine hotel.
Also thanks for inspirational picture on their website, which inspired my picture of Niamh at Cobh. Visit their website at:
http://www.commodorehotel.ie/history and even better, visit the hotel for a great time in Ireland altogether.